BLOOD DAHLIA

VICTOR METHOS

And God saw that the wickedness of man was great in the earth, and that every imagination of the thoughts of his heart was only evil continually.

-Genesis 6:5

<u>Ten Years Ago</u>

1

Deputy Will Lowe walked around the tree in the midmorning sun and nearly gagged. The blood coated the base of the tree and ran down into the grass. It was a frosty Lancaster, Pennsylvania, morning, and Lowe could see his breath rolling like fog in front of his face. He tried to focus on it for a second, turning his eyes away from the horror in front of him.

The body was just a little way off from the tree. A woman—he guessed but couldn't quite tell. She was nude, and he thought she was covered in dirt because her skin was nearly black, but only after observing it from up close did he realize those were bruises. They went from her neck all the way down to her feet. Her face was buried in the dirt, and he couldn't see it, but he didn't want to see it anyway. That was something he could live without.

The woman was cut in half at the waist.

Lowe turned away and trudged back up the hill to his patrol car. He leaned against the car and tipped his hat up. Two boys out ice fishing at a nearby stream had come across the body. One of them was no older than twelve. He wondered what seeing something like that would do to a young boy.

Another patrol car came to a stop behind his. Sheriff Mitchell Bullock stepped out, his heavy frame making the car lift as he removed himself and shut the door behind him. He ambled over, pulling his scarf tighter.

"What do you have, Will?"

"Same thing, Sheriff. Young lady."

The sheriff looked down into the gulley. "Did you check?"

"No, Sheriff."

"Well, you can't be sure until you check."

Lowe swallowed. "All right. Lemme get some gloves." He reached into the backseat of his car for a box of latex gloves. He snapped them on. He wasn't by any means a forensics guy, and in fact, a lot of the science behind crime scene investigation confused him. He became a cop because he liked helping people. He didn't care about anything else. He wished like hell the county could afford their own forensic people instead of calling over to Philadelphia PD when they needed it. This wasn't what he'd signed up for.

Lowe hiked back down the hill to the tree. The body was still there. He didn't know why he hoped it wouldn't be, but he had and now felt stupid for doing it. He bent down near the head and lightly lifted it with both hands. The face was missing. In its place was a slick red surface and jagged tears where the flesh had been cut. He placed the head back down and immediately snapped off his gloves. He strode back up, got a plastic bag out of his car, and put the gloves inside.

"Well?" the sheriff said.

"It ain't there, Sheriff."

Sheriff Bullock exhaled and leaned against the patrol car. Neither one of them spoke for a long time.

"That's three bodies, Sheriff."

"Hell, I know that. Don't you think I know that?"

"Well, what we gonna do?"

He shook his head. "We need help. Medical examiner said this sumbitch burns the bodies with acid after to take off any prints and DNA."

Lowe spit onto the frozen ground. "I ain't… I ain't trained to deal with this, Sheriff."

"I know… I know. I'm sorry you had to see it, Will. But sometimes the Lord does things we ain't meant to understand."

"Yeah, suppose so. So who we gonna get to come help us? I saw this show where the local police called out the FBI and they can come in and help."

"I ain't havin' no fed come up in here and boss me 'round in my own county. I had them out once on account of 'em bank robberies 'bout two years before you joined up. Didn't much care for how they treated us."

"Yeah, but we ain't got no one else."

The sheriff thought a moment. "I wanna go talk to someone."

"Who?"

"Little girl. 'Bout ten years old."

Lowe drove with the sheriff as they entered the small Amish community in Lancaster. Lowe had grown up seeing their horses and buggies, the men with long beards and plain clothes, and the women with dresses that came down to their ankles. He knew about them and knew about their *rumspringa*, their "running around" that the teenagers did before settling down with a spouse. But he never ventured into their community, except once to eat at a restaurant they had set up for tourists.

They stopped at a plain-looking house with a barn behind it and got out. The sheriff knocked on the front door several times. Finally, a man in slacks and suspenders answered the door. His beard was long and scruffy, and he was wearing thin glasses that appeared like they could fall apart at any moment.

"How are ya, Isaac?" the sheriff said.

"Good, Sheriff," the man said in a thick Pennsylvania Dutch accent.

"I was wondering if I might have a word."

The man looked from the sheriff to Lowe and then back again. "Not sure I can be much help."

"You haven't even heard what I'm gonna say. Let us come in and talk about it for a bit."

He sighed. "Suppose so," he said, stepping aside so they could come into his home.

The interior was simple: wood furniture, a few handmade rugs, and windows that overlooked the white field of snow that was lush green in the spring and summer. Lowe thought the home was nice enough that he would like something similar when he got the money.

The sheriff sat on an old blue couch that looked handmade, and Lowe sat next to him. Isaac sat across from them and offered them some hot tea, which they declined.

"So what can I do for ye, Sheriff?"

"I was hoping we might have a word with your daughter, too. Maybe just take her and you out on a drive somewhere to see something."

"Why would I possibly let my little girl out with two grown men?"

"Because I'm stuck, Isaac. I feel like this man, the one I'm looking for, might not be a man. And I need help finding him."

Isaac gently rocked back and forth, and Lowe wondered if he knew he was doing it.

"You came here once before, and I told ye I didn't want her goin' out again."

"I know. And I'm sorry I have to ask this."

He inhaled deeply. "I think I'm gonna have to refuse, Sheriff."

The sheriff opened his hands placatingly, as if showing him he had nothing else. "Isaac, I am stuck. This sumbitch cuts these girls up so much I can't even imagine what they go through. And he's gonna keep doin' it 'less we catch him. This is God's work, Isaac. Your little girl is his instrument."

"I don't know nothin' about instruments of the Lord, Sheriff. I just know it ain't good for my little girl."

"The young woman we found was eighteen. Sarah's gonna be that age in a handful of years, ain't she?"

Isaac stared at both men a long time, gently rocking without saying a word for a moment. "She's at school right now."

"It won't take more than an hour."

He nodded. "We'll have to follow ye."

2

The patrol car Lowe drove could go no more than twenty miles an hour or they'd lose the buggy rolling behind them. It would have taken a fraction of the time if they'd just rode along with the sheriff and him, but Isaac had refused.

The patrol car crawled back to the crime scene, and Lowe parked on the side of the road. He waited for the buggy to catch up. Lowe glanced at the sheriff, who was staring out the window at the collection of aspen trees blocking the view of the gulley. Neither of them spoke until the buggy arrived.

Lowe followed the sheriff out. Isaac hopped out of the buggy then went to the back and reached in, helping a young girl out.

The girl had black hair. A long streak of pure white hair ran along one side as though a paintbrush had streaked that side of her head. Her dress was blue and looked thick and sturdy. *Handmade*, Lowe thought.

She appeared weak and pale, with dark circles under her eyes. Her father took her hand and led her around the buggy to meet the sheriff and Lowe.

"I don't want her seeing no dead bodies," Isaac said.

"No, of course not. Maybe if she can just look down there… or something. I don't know. I don't know how this works."

Isaac exhaled loudly and bent down to look the girl in the eyes. "Sarah, be a good girl and look where the sheriff wants you to look. Tell them what you see."

"Okay, Daddy."

Sarah took the sheriff's hand, and he led her to the edge of the gulley. Lowe stood next to them; he wanted to see what this was all about.

They had a view of the tree and, just visible past it, a hand and some hair from the body. The sheriff turned to Lowe and whispered, "We'll call it in after this, but this stays between me and you. All right, Will?"

"All right, Sheriff."

The sheriff bent down to eye level with the girl and said, "Sarah, do you see anything, sweetheart?"

The girl was quiet a long time. So long that Lowe began to feel the biting cold on his exposed face. He rubbed his ears with his gloved hands to warm them up and glanced back at Isaac, who was feeding his horses some treats.

"No," the girl said.

Lowe and the sheriff both looked at her. Her face had changed—she looked frightened.

"I don't care," she said, looking down at the gulley. "No, I don't want to. I don't want to! Daddy!"

The girl was crying and ran to her father, who threw his arms around her.

"It's okay, Sarah. It's over. It's over."

The sheriff looked at Lowe and then back to the girl. "What did you see, Sarah?"

Isaac said, "That's enough, Sheriff. You wanted her to come look, and she did."

"Don't mean anything if she doesn't tell me what she saw."

Sarah looked up at the sheriff, her eyes glistening. "She was hurt really bad, and she was crying. She was telling me to help her, and she started running to me."

"It's okay," Isaac said, lifting her up into his arms. "It's time to go."

The sheriff strode up to the buggy and peered in through the opening as Sarah was placed inside. "Did you see anything else, Sarah? Did you see a man?"

She nodded.

"What did he look like?"

Isaac, his face contorted with anger now, shouted, "That's enough, Sheriff! We helped all we could. Now please move aside."

The sheriff ignored him. "What did he look like, Sarah?"

"He was at a big place with sick people. That's where he saw her. He really liked her, and she really liked him. She said he likes lots of girls. He sees them there. He walked with her at night to her car."

Isaac had already gotten in and got his horses moving. The sheriff followed the buggy.

"What else, Sarah? What else did you see?"

"She said she scratched him."

The buggy turned around and headed back toward the Amish settlement. The sheriff stood in the road, his breath like smoke in the cold. He had his hands on his hips and stood there awhile before walking back to Lowe.

"Sheriff, what the hell was that about?"

The sheriff didn't answer as he ambled back to his cruiser. "Call in the body, Will. Stay here until the forensic people are done, and then get the medical examiner's people out here to haul it outta my woods."

With that, the sheriff drove off, leaving Lowe alone with the trees. He glanced down to the body and then decided to sit in his car and make the call from there.

3

Lancaster General Hospital was the largest hospital in the county. Sheriff Bullock drove his patrol car into the lot and parked up front. This would be considered crazy, what he was doing. But it didn't seem so crazy to him.

He stepped out of the car and strolled into the hospital. If there was any place in the county that had a lot of sick people, this was it.

There were at least forty doctors here at any given time, and he'd have to meet all of them. That wasn't even counting the nurses and front desk staff. And there was the fact that some people would have today off.

Hell with it. I don't have anything else to go on.

The hospital was circular and modern. The sheriff remembered his grandfather talking about when it was founded and how it had started in just a small home. His grandfather wouldn't have believed what it had become in such a short time.

The sheriff walked around the front entrance to a little cart selling drinks and pastries and ordered a coffee with skim milk. He had detectives for this. An entire homicide unit... that couldn't give him anything on the first two girls. He could've had this place swarming with deputies and detectives if he wanted to. The sheriff's office, once a small operation of two people, had also grown into a modern organization. They weren't a Las Vegas Metro or an LAPD, they didn't even have their own crime scene forensics unit, but they were capable and growing. But something like this... this wasn't like anything he had ever seen before. And the last thing he needed was everyone saying the sheriff had lost it because he was talking to little girls he brought to crime scenes.

He sipped his coffee and paced around the entrance and the small gift shop that sold snacks and little toys. He didn't even really know what he was looking for. The emergency room was just off to the side, and he walked in. He nodded to the front desk receptionist who didn't say anything.

The sheriff mulled around for a bit and then came over to her. "How ya doin'?" he said.

"Good."

"Um, I'm Sheriff Bullock. I was wondering if you'd mind letting me back into the rooms there."

"Are you a visitor?"

"Yes, that's right."

"Who are you visiting?"

"Well, no one. I just want to have a look around."

She thought a moment, her face crinkled up. "I don't know if I can do that."

"Listen, darlin'. I'm the sheriff of this county. I ain't goin' back there to steal nothin'. I just want to look around and meet your staff is all. Look me up online. Go ahead, do it now. Just type in 'Lancaster County Sheriff'."

Hesitantly, the girl did it. His photo came up, along with a breakdown of the different divisions of the Sheriff's Office and various phone numbers and addresses.

"Oh," she said.

"Yeah, so how 'bout you just open up that door there and let me just walk around a minute? I won't touch nothin', I promise."

"Well, I guess it would be okay. But can I have our security guard go with you? I just don't want to get in trouble."

The sheriff exhaled. He was the top law enforcement officer in the county. The hell did she think he was gonna do, steal Q-tips?

"Fine, bring out the security guard, and I'll walk around with him."

Relieved, the girl picked up the phone, spoke into it a moment, and then said, "He'll be right down."

"Thanks."

A few magazines were spread out on a side table, and the sheriff sat down and flipped through a few of them. A two-month-old *Sports Illustrated* had an article about steroids in college football, and he'd started reading that when the security guard walked in.

"Hi, you the officer that needed me to take you around?"

The sheriff looked up, about to respond, and froze. The man was young, maybe thirty or thirty-five, and had hair that came down over his ears. He had some scruff on his face and bright blue eyes, but what stopped the sheriff cold was his neck. On the right side, just underneath the jawline, he had three scratches. They ran down to the base of his neck and were bright and red, recent.

"Yeah," the sheriff said, slowly getting up. "Yeah, just wanted to take a look-see around if that's okay."

"Anything to help the police," he said with a wide smile.

The security guard walked in front of him. He swiped an ID badge at a scanner near the double doors, and they clicked open. He led the sheriff through.

"So what are you looking for exactly?" the security guard said.

"Oh, nothin' too important. Just wanted to have a look at the ER. Need to know my way around 'cause we sometimes have to drag people outta here. Had a few extra minutes, and I was in the neighborhood."

"Well, not much to look at really. Just a normal emergency room like anywhere else."

"Yeah, still wanted to have a look." The sheriff hesitated. "Those are some pretty nasty scratches you got there."

The guard glanced back at him. "Yeah, it's my cat. But what can I do? My dad left me the cat, and it reminds me of him."

"Your father passed, has he?"

"Yep. About two years ago."

"Sorry to hear that."

"Well, like I said, what can you do?"

They circled around the emergency room. Not many of the rooms were filled, but the sheriff didn't really look inside them anyway. He had his eyes fixed on the security guard.

"So what'd you say your name was?" the sheriff asked.

"Nate. And you're Sheriff Bullock, right?"

"Right. You've seen me, huh?"

"Just on the news a few times."

The sheriff was quiet a beat as they walked. "So how long you work here, Nate?"

"Oh, five years or so. I tried to become a police officer, actually."

"Really? What happened?"

"Just didn't work out, I guess. My brother was an officer for a little while, though."

They'd circled the entire emergency room and were back to the double doors that led in. Nate stopped and looked at the sheriff. "You know, it'd go a lot quicker if you just told me what you were actually looking for," Nate said with a toothy grin.

The sheriff thought about taking him down to the precinct to talk, but he seemed smart and articulate. He probably prepared himself for interrogation. What he wouldn't be prepared for was honesty.

"Sure, I guess it would. I'm looking for a young man, Caucasian, that works here. He'd be handsome, quite the ladies man, and he'd have fresh scratches on his face from a young woman of about eighteen that worked here. He probably helped her out to her car at some point and got her license plate. Then found out where she lives from that. Or he mighta just followed her home one night."

Nate was still as glass. He didn't blink, move, or say anything. He swallowed, and the sheriff got the impression that he wanted to speak but couldn't.

"Nate, why don't you and I go down to the precinct and talk? Just talk, me and you. What'dya say?"

Before the sheriff could speak another word, the blade was exposed. Nate held it in his right hand and swung wildly, as though he were swinging a tennis racquet. The blade cut across the sheriff's cheek, blood spattering over the wall near him. The pain was instant and burning. The sheriff shrieked, and his hand went up to the gaping hole in his cheek.

Nate came at him again, but the sheriff ripped his pistol out of the holster. Just as the blade came down, he fired. Nate was thrown off-balance, and the blade cut down the sheriff's arm rather than his neck or chest.

The round had entered Nate's head, just under his jaw. The young man fell and was bleeding to death on the floor as some nurses ran out to try to help. But the sheriff had seen wounds like that before. The boy wasn't going to make it.

Present Day

4

Kyle Vidal had been with the FBI for eleven years now, and the one thing he'd learned above all else was that you covered your ass. Any move you made had to be documented and approved by a higher-up. If it wasn't and something went wrong, then everything fell onto the lowest man on the totem pole who hadn't covered his ass.

His direct boss, the unit chief of Behavioral Science, Gillian Hanks, left him alone to do his job. Any higher than that, and everybody was looking to blame him for something.

And with this case, he definitely had to make sure he was protected. There'd been a lot of media coverage and six victims. Everything told him there were going to be a lot more before this guy screwed up enough to get caught—if he ever did.

Kyle's official position was special agent in charge of the DC office. As the SAC, it was his responsibility to oversee the entire office. That included special agents in every field, from forensic accounting to terrorism. But Behavioral Science had always been his baby.

Violent crime had been his area of focus in the sociology program at Harvard. It fascinated him with an allure that no other field had, so he personally oversaw both Behavioral Science—the theoretical, research, and training arm—and the Violent Criminal Apprehension Unit, the practical fieldwork arm.

This case fell in both areas: it was as interesting as they came.

He heard a knock at his door and looked up to see Agent Giovanni Adami. The special agent was dressed in a black suit, white shirt, and dark tie, the look J. Edgar Hoover had established over seventy years ago. It would have made more sense for agents to wear street clothes, but tradition was a tough thing to change in the Bureau.

"Special Agent Adami."

"Sir. You wanted to see me, sir?"

"You're not in the military anymore, Gio. You don't have to do that. Just call me Kyle. Have a seat, please."

Giovanni sat across from him. "Sorry. It's ingrained."

"You were in the army, right?"

"Yes, si—Yes, Kyle. I was in the Rangers."

"Did you see some action?"

He shifted in his seat. "Two tours in Iraq."

"Well, thank you for your service." When Giovanni didn't say anything, he continued. "You haven't actually been assigned to a unit yet, have you?"

"No. I've been helping out in screening and with a little fieldwork on some bank robberies."

He nodded. "How would you like an assignment to Behavioral Science?"

He was quiet a moment. "I would like that, sir. Sorry. I would like that."

"You said like, not love. Most people I offer this to say they would love the position."

"I was hoping for the paramilitary unit, sir."

"I'm glad you're being honest. That's what I need. We need some real cops on the front line. Despite everything you hear and the image that's portrayed in the news, that's all we are at the end of the day—cops."

"I know, sir. I was a police officer for five years before joining the Bureau. After the army, it seemed like the right choice."

"They're similar in a lot of respects. The sense of brotherhood and belonging. Don't lose that. It's not as prominent in the Bureau, but it's here if you look for it. But we can talk about what being assigned to BSU means later. I have something for you right now."

"Of course. I'll get right on it."

"It's in your in-box. There's a request there, too. A place to start. You ever heard of the Black Dahlia murder?"

"Yes. Instructor Parsons had it as required reading at the academy."

"Yeah, that sounds like something Mickey would do. Pick it apart to the microscopic level. This is a copycat the media dubbed the Blood Dahlia. Agent Rosen is going to be the lead on this. I've informed him that you've been assigned to assist him."

"Thank you, sir. I appreciate this opportunity. I won't let you down."

"I know you won't. Go ahead and get prepared. I think Agent Rosen has a drive up to Pennsylvania planned for you two."

5

Sarah Helena King woke up and didn't know where she was for a moment. She sat up and saw her clothes crumpled on the floor. A man was next to her, snoring, handsome, and young. She deduced that she was in his apartment, and certain images from last night came to her. Drunken sex, some pot, and massive amounts of tequila.

She slipped her clothes on and then had to crawl around until she found her shoes. The man, whose name she couldn't remember, stirred and looked up at her.

"Hey," he said. "You leaving already? I was hoping we could grab some breakfast."

"Maybe later," she said as she slipped her shoes on. "See ya around."

A bottle of tequila and two shot glasses were on the windowsill. Sarah filled a shot glass to the brim and drank it down in two gulps.

She walked to the door and shut it behind her. Catching a glimpse of the man as the door closed, she'd seen that look of surprise many times. Somehow, it was okay for a man to not want an emotional attachment to someone after sex, but it was frowned on in a woman. She had never been one for convention.

She adjusted her shoes as she walked down the hall and took the four flights of stairs to the bottom level. As she was walking to the front door, she saw a boy staring out onto the street. The door was made of glass. He had his nose pressed up to it and was leaving a perfect little imprint of a child's face. A teddy bear was tucked under one arm, and he was still wearing his pajamas.

"Hey, what're you doing up?" she said.

"I'm waiting for my mommy. She said she was going to bring me a treat."

"You live in these apartments with your mommy?"

He nodded. "My daddy's in the navy, and he's protecting us right now."

Sarah's head suddenly pounded with an acute pain that hit her between the eyes. She could feel it in her bones. The pain had caught her completely off guard.

She saw a broken image. A man inside a cell, writing a letter. The man bore a strong resemblance to the boy. His father. The letter was given to a guard who walked the halls of a random prison.

"Well," she said, pushing the pain away and closing off her mind, "you must be so proud of your daddy helping to protect us all."

"I am."

She watched him a moment, tousled his hair, and then left. Up the street on the corner was a convenience store. She purchased ibuprofen, a diet soda, and a chocolate candy bar. She walked back to the apartments. The boy was still there, waiting for his mother to come home. Sarah motioned for him to open the apartment complex door, which was key-code locked, and he did.

"I got this for you," she said, handing him the candy bar.

"Wow! Thanks."

"You're welcome. Who's watching you right now?"

"My sister."

"You should go back to her. Okay?"

"Okay."

Sarah waited until she saw him mosey back to his apartment and shut the door. Then she turned and tried to find her car.

Another image was breaking itself into her mind, but she pushed it back. The sensation was similar to trying to close a door when someone was attempting to push their way through from the other side.

Sarah had to close her eyes. "Stop," she mumbled, "stop, stop, stop."

The sensation of pressure in her head eased and then went away. She breathed the warm summer air deeply and exhaled through her nose. Her car, a black '77 Mustang, was parked with one wheel up on the curb. She checked the clock on her phone. As a bartender, she only worked nights, and so she realized she had ten hours to kill before her next shift.

She decided she would go home, drink some water, and hit the gym. And she began making plans for what she would do for the rest of the day. She had to keep her mind occupied... or else she would be fighting herself all day.

The car was warm as she climbed in and turned the ignition. As she pulled away, she looked in the rearview and saw the boy standing behind the glass again, his face pressed against it.

6

The condominiums were someplace grandparents went to retire. This was the impression Giovanni got when he parked in front of Arnold Rosen's condo and sent him a text message that he was here. He waited a solid fifteen minutes, and Rosen didn't come out and didn't text back.

Giovanni stepped out of the car and glanced around. One thing the condos did have going for them was how quiet they were. No children, no cars racing up and down the road. In fact, the street leading up to here was a side street in the industrial section of DC, away from the politics, the glitz, and the glamour.

Rosen's condo was on the second floor, and Giovanni hopped up two steps at a time. He found unit 2F and knocked. Rosen answered a short while later.

Rosen was older with white hair and the weathered face that said he'd seen a lot in his years. He was wearing almost the same outfit Giovanni was—black suit and dark tie—but he somehow wore it better. *More naturally*, Giovanni thought.

"Agent Rosen? I'm Giovanni Adami."

"You're late."

"Um, no, sir. I've been waiting outside fifteen minutes. I texted you."

"I don't text, son. Let me get my sidearm."

Rosen took off his jacket, put the holster on with his Bureau-issued sidearm, and then walked out of the condo and locked the door behind him.

"Agent Vidal said we're going to Philly."

"We are indeed," he said, putting his jacket back on. "You drive."

Giovanni unlocked the doors and waited until Rosen climbed in and put on his seat belt before he started the car. He pulled away from the condominiums and headed toward the freeway entrance.

"I read the reports," Giovanni said. "A copycat of the Black Dahlia. That's pretty crazy."

"I'm not exactly sure what it is. And I'm not convinced it is a copycat of that exactly."

"Looked like it to me. The victims are cut in half, raped, and sodomized before death. Fecal matter is found on or near the victims. Tattoos are cut out and shoved in the throat. It's nearly identical."

"Nearly, but not quite."

"The faces?" Giovanni asked.

"Yeah. The subject removes the victim's faces. Six victims and we haven't recovered a single face. So that begs the question, what's he doing with them? And why is that the one thing he does differently from the Black Dahlia?"

"I was thinking maybe because it makes it harder for us to identify the bodies."

"Maybe. But if he's even done an internet search on forensics, he'll know that the teeth are how we identify ninety-five percent of victims in homicides. And he didn't remove any teeth. So I'm not sure that's it."

Giovanni noticed a wedding ring on Rosen's hand, but he hadn't said goodbye to anyone in the condo.

"So who we going to see?" Giovanni asked.

"A retired sheriff."

"Yeah? For what?"

"There was another series of murders before your time. About ten years back. Similar to the Black Dahlia, except that the Sheriff's Office and the forensics units didn't know what the Black Dahlia was, and they never contacted us about it. They were nearly identical… except that the subject removed the victim's faces."

Giovanni didn't know how he felt about Rosen calling these sick bastards "subjects." It made them sound less monstrous—as if they were part of some clinical study or something.

"Did they catch the killer?" he said.

"Yeah. This sheriff put a bullet into his throat that blew out the back of his head."

Giovanni thought about this. If the case in Pennsylvania was a copycat, then the case they were dealing with now was a copycat of a copycat. He'd never seen or even heard of such a thing. He wondered why Kyle would assign this to him as his first case in Behavioral Science.

The drive was long but pleasant. In the summer months, Pennsylvania was about as pretty as any place Giovanni had ever seen. During winter, there was almost nowhere he had been to that was more bleak. Then again, he'd grown up in Arizona, and the heat of the desert had always appealed to him. During the summer, growing up in the small town of Hyrum, you couldn't even sit down in your car while wearing shorts because the leather seats would fry your skin.

Once they hit I-83, they'd already been in the car nearly an hour and a half. And in that time, they had hardly spoken fifty words. Giovanni would ask about Rosen or the Bureau, and the old man would answer him with a "yes" or a "no" but wouldn't engage. He wasn't a man used to talking about himself, Giovanni thought. Which was just fine by him—he preferred silence, too.

"Take the Harrisburg Pike exit," Rosen said.

Giovanni did as he was told. The countryside here was lush green with plenty of farms and acres of grassland with roaming cows and horses. Giovanni watched them as he drove by. Rolling green hills wasn't exactly the type of scenery he'd become used to the past few years.

Rosen checked the address on a slip of paper and then told him to turn right onto a residential street. He directed him through a maze of neighborhoods before they reached a dilapidated white home with a truck in the driveway.

"Here it is," he said.

Giovanni parked at the curb and turned the car off. Rosen checked his pocket to make sure he had his badge and FBI ID and then said, "Let me do the talking."

With that, Rosen got out of the car, and Giovanni followed him. They walked up the driveway and opened a chain-link fence. Just as Giovanni was closing it behind him, barking startled him. A black lab sprinted around the corner right at them.

Instinctively, Giovanni reached for his sidearm.

"Easy," Rosen said.

The lab stopped about five feet away and barked but didn't come any closer. Rosen walked right in front of it onto the front porch, and Giovanni hesitated and then did the same. He never took his eyes off the dog, even when it had turned away.

"It's just a lab," Rosen said. "You got some jittery reflexes there."

"I just got startled is all."

"Well, take it easy. I don't need the paperwork of shooting some poor guy's dog."

A few moments later, a man answered the door. He was heavyset and wore a flannel shirt tucked into some jeans with a wide belt buckle. He looked through thick glasses at them, from one man to the other.

"Can I help you?"

"Mitch Bullock?" Rosen said.

"Yeah."

"I'm Special Agent Arnold Rosen, and this is Agent Giovanni Adami. We're with the Federal Bureau of Investigation. We'd like to ask you a few questions if you don't mind."

"What's this about?"

"It's about Nathan Archer."

Bullock stood silently for a moment, his eyes passing between both men again. Then he nodded and opened the door wider. "You may as well come on in, I guess."

Giovanni followed Rosen in. The home was clean but filled with so many decorations and religious paintings that it appeared cluttered. One entire wall was taken up by a painting of Moses receiving the Ten Commandments on Mt. Sinai. Another wall had a life-size portrait of Christ rising from the tomb. Over the television were various medals and commendations. Several were from the military.

Giovanni scanned all the paintings and decorations, but Rosen took only one quick glance.

"So," Bullock said, settling into his couch, "what about him?"

Rosen sat down across from him in the living room. He put his arm on the armrest and tapped each of his fingers against it before speaking. Giovanni had seen him do that on his lap when he sat down in his car.

"I understand you were the one that discovered him?" Rosen said.

"Discovered and then killed. But not by choice." Bullock slid his finger along a scar on his cheek. "He did that to me when I asked him to come down and talk to me."

Rosen nodded. "It was great police work. I read the initial reports."

"Why do I sense a 'but' coming on?"

Rosen grinned. "But in a small county, there's no one to look them over. Especially when it's the sheriff writing them. You don't have an internal affairs department like most major police departments."

"You saying I'm a liar?" he said sternly.

"No, absolutely not. I'm just saying no one ever asked you questions about your reports. I don't care about anything in there except one thing: How'd you find him?"

The sheriff was quiet a second, glaring at Rosen. "I wrote that in the reports."

"You wrote that you had an anonymous tip that he worked at a hospital and had scratches. But you never identified the tip or how they knew."

"Wouldn't be anonymous if I identified them, now would it?"

Rosen kept his grin and glanced up to the shelf of medals above the television. "Vietnam?"

"Yup," the sheriff said, leaning back.

"Me too. You wanna know something I learned in Vietnam? The government is full of shit. And there were two shooters that killed Kennedy."

The sheriff, though he looked like he was trying not to, smiled. "Because every infantryman knows the body falls in the direction of the shot. And with Kennedy that means he was hit from a direction different than Oswald and then hit again from another direction."

Rosen shook his head. "When I was taught that in basic and thought back to the assassination, I couldn't believe how much they lied and didn't even care. And this wasn't some guy off the street. They covered up and lied about how a president was killed."

"Damn shame. That young man had a lot of potential."

Rosen leaned forward. "Don't be that government, Mitch. Don't cover things up. People need to hear the truth."

The sheriff looked flustered. "Why do you even care who the anonymous tip was? It was years ago."

Rosen leaned back. "You retired after this case. Early retirement. Something in the case caused you to do that. And a man with those medals up on his wall wouldn't back down because he was cut. We've all been cut, and we move on. Something else happened. What was it?"

The sheriff sighed. "Why are you here, Agent Rosen? What do you care about a long dead case?"

"Because I've got six young women killed in the same identical fashion over the past six months. Think about that, Sheriff. One woman a month. Killed in an identical—not similar, *identical*—method as the victims of Nathan Archer. And then I read through your reports and find some anonymous tipster, so I'm wondering if there's some connection. Maybe the tipster can help me, too."

The sheriff rose and said, "I need a beer. You guys want a beer?"

"No, thank you."

The sheriff hobbled into the kitchen. Giovanni could see a cane leaned up against the wall, but the sheriff didn't get it. Instead, he used the wall for balance. A fridge opened, and he heard the top of a can pop before the sheriff came back in, this time stopping and leaning against the wall.

"The most important thing for me is that my cases not get reopened. If I tell you what you want, all them defense attorneys with clients I've put away are gonna be combing through my cases lookin' to get their clients out."

"You and I are from a different time, Mitch. Where a man's handshake was better than a contract. I give you my word as a man; I will not reveal anything you tell me." He glanced to Giovanni. "And neither will he. If he does, I will contradict him on the record and say that he is mistaken."

The sheriff nodded. "Was a young girl, Sarah King. She was Amish, up there in the community in Lancaster. She left when she was seventeen. Ran away, I think. Ain't seen her since."

"The girl knew who Nathan was?"

The sheriff hesitated. "Not exactly."

"What then?"

He sipped his beer. "She said one of the victims talked to her… from the grave."

Giovanni looked at Rosen, who didn't move. He kept the sheriff's gaze and then said softly, "You used a psychic?"

"I don't know what she was. All I know is, she helped me twice. The first time, her and her daddy came walking into the Sheriff's Office and asked to see me." He grinned, his eyes on the carpet. "She sat in a chair in my office, and her feet couldn't touch the floor. She was just kicking them and had this smile on her face. We'd found a body in the river, and her dad told me she had something to tell me about that. We thought it was an accident."

"What'd she say?"

"She told me the body belonged to a man who jumped in on purpose. That his wife left him and he lost his job and didn't want to live anymore. But he forgot to leave a note. So he wanted me to deliver a message to his wife."

The sheriff downed some more beer. Giovanni looked at Rosen, who wasn't even blinking. He seemed much more interested in this than Giovanni thought he would be. Most grizzled federal agents abandoned all superstition, including religion. The things they saw tended to preclude, in their minds, an all-loving, merciful God, or the supernatural.

"She told me," the sheriff continued, "that the wife needed to look in a locker he'd rented at the gym for a month. Locker 114. That the locker was in the women's locker room under her name. I didn't think anything of it, and I didn't even deliver the message. I thought it was ridiculous." He drifted off a moment. "There was a news report a little bit after that, maybe five weeks. The gym had a policy to stick everything from abandoned lockers in the lost and found. When they emptied locker 114, they found a gym bag full of money with a, like, Post-it note. It just said, 'I'm sorry, Grace.' Grace was the wife's name. The name the locker was under." He shook his head. "Was a hundred grand in there. Grace got it eventually, with a call from me. Damnedest thing I ever seen… Until I took her to see one of Nate's bodies."

7

It was evening by the time Sarah exhausted herself on the treadmill. A straight hour and a half of jogging. The muscles in her legs were weak, like Jell-O. Each step was an exercise in concentration so she wouldn't just collapse on the gym floor.

When she was done, she got on the exercise bike and cooled off. The cool-off was an important step, like a gateway back into the real world. She needed that time to brace herself.

The gym showers were strong, and the water bounced off her flesh as it massaged her aching muscles. She closed her eyes and pretended she was sitting under a waterfall as the warm water rushed over her, calming and soothing her. No one else around. Just her and nature.

When she was through, she changed into jeans and a tight black T-shirt. As she was changing, she heard two women speaking close to her. They were discussing one of their husbands and whether he had a wandering eye. Without asking for it, an image flooded her mind. A man with dark hair and dimples, a tattoo of a sun with rays coming off of it on his left shoulder. He removed his wedding ring before getting into a bed with a woman who was nude.

Sarah finished quickly and left the locker room, trying to focus on something, anything, else. The woman deserved to know, but everyone deserved to know the secrets all the people in their life kept from them. And Sarah, without wishing it, knew them. She wouldn't be able to explain them to everyone. That's what she told herself when that twinge of guilt stung her, reminding her that she could help the woman with a sentence. But then again, no one ever believed her anyway. They just believed what they wanted to believe.

Sarah stopped just outside the locker room. She stood still for a long time, though she wasn't sure how long. Turning around, she saw the two women stepping out, talking about something else.

"Excuse me," she said. "Your husband has a tattoo of a sun on his shoulder, doesn't he?"

The woman looked at her friend and then back to Sarah. "Yeah? How did you know that?"

"He's cheating on you with a blond woman. Blond and dark eyes. It's happening in hotel rooms, so you can probably see it on his credit card statements."

Without waiting for a response, Sarah immediately turned and marched away. The woman said something behind her, but Sarah didn't hear it. She just quickened her pace and was out of the gym before the women could catch up to her.

Sarah jumped into her car and sped out of the parking lot. Her work wasn't too far from here, and she thought she would get there early and maybe have a few drinks before starting her shift.

Pink's was as upscale as bars went, and the theme—the color pink—was on prominent display everywhere. From the neon sign out front, to the suit coats the bouncers had to wear, to the name tags the bartenders displayed on their chests. At first, the place seemed glitzy to her, something like an old Hollywood Playboy party or something. But night after night of Pink's wore on Sarah, and she realized how sensitive she was to her environment. She had been trying for the past year, unsuccessfully, to land a job that involved less interaction with other people but paid relatively the same. The problem was that bartenders could clear two hundred fifty bucks a night for five hours of work. No other jobs she could get without an education offered anywhere near that.

The bouncer, a large black man with tattoos on his neck, smiled when he saw her. "How are ya, Sarah?"

"Good, Catcher. How you been?"

"Can't complain." He stepped aside, letting her enter. "Bit early, ain't it?"

"Thought I'd catch up on some side work."

"I bet."

Sarah knew they called him Catcher because he'd played for the Mets as a relief catcher nearly a decade ago. Though he said he hated the nickname, she knew he secretly liked it. His career had ended because of an injury, not because it'd run its course, and he always regretted not being able to play longer. She knew all this about him in a fraction of a second the first time she met him.

Though evening had fallen, it wasn't yet dark, and the dimming sunlight coming through the bar's windows gave her an eerie feeling. Something about being in bars in the middle of the day didn't sit well with her.

"Hey," she said, coming behind the bar. The woman back there, Jeannie, was stocking the liquor bottles in front of a large mirror.

"Hey yourself. What're you doing here so early?"

"Oh, just bored. Didn't have anything else to do."

Sarah lifted a bottle of Jose Cuervo and poured herself a shot, filling the glass to the brim. She swallowed it, enjoying the warmth of the liquid down her throat and into her belly. She poured another shot and took it with her eyes closed. When she opened them, Jeannie was staring.

"What?" Sarah said.

"You know what. Your shift hasn't even started."

Sarah took one more shot and then slapped her hands together and hooted like a frat boy. She grabbed Jeannie's hands and spun her around. "Don't be such a grump. Our job is to party."

Jeannie kept a stern face for only a few moments and then began dancing with her behind the bar. Sarah spun her and dipped, their faces nearly touching, before she pulled her back up and began helping her stock.

The night wore on, and the bar grew packed. The music was so loud sometimes she'd have to wear earplugs, but not tonight. Tonight, she wanted to feel it right down to her bones.

The drinks were poured quickly. Despite the fact that she'd probably had six or seven shots in the past four hours, Sarah was really good at her job. At least she thought so.

A party of four guys was at the end of the bar, and with each round they bought they gave her a twenty-dollar tip. One of the men was handsome, his muscles bulging underneath a gray V-neck shirt. His hair was styled, and his eyes glimmered when the roving strobe lights hit them in just the right way. He'd been smiling at Sarah the entire night.

"Hi," he shouted over the music as she poured them another round.

"Can I touch your hair?" she shouted back.

He nodded. She tapped it. It was hard, almost immobile from all the product he had in it.

"You'd look better with dry hair. Watch."

She ran her hands through his hair, mussing it up. The wet look faded, and his hair wasn't up as high. It looked naturally styled now rather than plastered in place. She reached down and washed her hands in a sink underneath the bar.

"How is it?" he said.

"Look for yourself," she said, stepping to the side so he could see himself in the mirror behind the bar. The man evaluated his hair from all angles and nodded.

"Not bad. You a stylist?"

"No, just an observer of culture, I guess."

"What time do you get off?"

"Two."

"You wanna grab a drink afterward?"

"Why would I leave a bar to grab a drink?"

The man thought a second. "How about something to eat?"

"How about coffee?"

He tapped his hand against the bar. "Coffee is perfect. I shoulda thought of that."

"You can make it up to me later."

Sarah poured two shots, one for him and one for herself. She lifted her shot glass, and they tapped them against each other as the man said, "Salud."

The shift lasted another two hours. Toward the end, Sarah was thoroughly drunk. By her estimation, she'd had at least ten shots. She gulped down water and Sprite to help flush her system, but it didn't seem to be helping much.

She and Jeannie got to go on break at the same time, and they went out back to smoke. The back alley was quiet, only the dull thump of the bass coming through the walls. On the other side of the alley was a sushi restaurant, and sometimes the garbage stank like fish back here, but most nights it was bearable.

Jeannie lit a cigarette and handed it to Sarah. She didn't smoke, but whenever she drank enough, the urge came to her and she'd have a cigarette or two. Odd what alcohol did, she thought, considering that most nights the smell of cigarette smoke in the bar made her gag.

"You goin' home with that guy?" Jeannie asked.

"Maybe. We're gonna have coffee and see what happens."

Jeannie inhaled deeply, the cigarette tip glowing a bright red. "I'm taking out that one guy. The one that's been bugging me for like three weeks."

"The guy with back hair poking out of his shirt?"

"He doesn't have back hair. It's just like… I don't know… manly hair."

She shrugged. "To each her own, I guess."

"You don't think he's cute?"

"He is. Except he has back hair poking out of his shirt."

She smirked. "You're such a bitch."

Sarah puffed at the cigarette. "What are you guys doing? Maybe we should make it a foursome date?"

"He's taking me back to his place. He has this huge hot tub, and we're just going to hang out and—"

Sarah didn't hear the rest of the sentence. An intense pain radiated suddenly through her head. So powerful it was blinding, drowning out all sound and sight. Her fingers went up to her head, and she bent down as though she'd been punched in the gut.

She saw it there. The hot tub. Jeannie was in her underwear, and they were kissing. The man said he would get drinks for them. He walked into the kitchen and crushed up a white pill and put it in a wine glass. He walked back out and gave it to her.

Sarah saw the entire night—the torture and penetration with inanimate objects, like a lamp and pliers. He needed them passed out for that. They would never consent to the pain otherwise.

In the morning, they would wake up in the park or at the front of a hospital if the injuries were severe. Then he would never go to that bar again.

"You okay, hon?" Jeannie said.

"I'm fine. I just need a sec," she said through gritted teeth.

"It's that tequila. I keep telling you to—"

"You can't go with him, Jeannie."

"What?"

"He's going to drug you in the hot tub. He needs you drugged. You can't go with him. Promise me you won't go with him. Promise, Jeannie."

"I've already gone on a date with him, Sarah. He was a perfect gentleman."

"No, no, you have to promise me you won't go with him. Please. Please!"

Jeannie was stunned into silence a moment before she said, "How do you even know?"

"I know. I know... please, you can't go with him." She grabbed Jeannie by the arms. "Listen to me. He is going to rape you. You can't go with him."

Jeannie tossed her cigarette and looked Sarah in the eyes. "You okay, babe?"

The pain was fading into the background. Like some horrific memory that was slowly subsiding into the unconscious to be brought out again at another time. "I'm fine."

"Sweetie, I know there are things in the world that are weird, but that's too much."

"Jeannie, listen to me, as a friend. Please do me a favor and do not go to that man's house."

Jeannie held her gaze awhile and said, "Okay, as a friend, I won't go."

"Thank you."

She checked the clock on her phone. "Why don't you take off? I'll cover the rest of your shift."

"No, I should finish."

"No, no. You go with your guy and get some coffee."

"Thanks, Jeannie."

She began walking back inside when she realized she had nothing in there and their hours were kept on the honor system. She stopped and began walking out of the alley toward her car. It felt like she was in a haze, as though pushing through a thin soup. Everything appeared blurry, and her movements were slow. Her body seemed detached from her, as though she were another person watching everything happening to her.

"You sure you're all right?" Jeannie yelled out behind her.

"Fine. I'll see you tomorrow."

Sarah got to her car and leaned against it. The images came like a powerful current, overwhelming all her senses. Usually, through years of effort, she had come to control them. But when she drank or when she was off guard and relaxed, they could push themselves into her consciousness with a force she could never prepare for.

The last thing she felt like doing right now was getting coffee. She inserted the key into the lock and heard someone behind her. She jumped and gasped, startling the cute guy from the bar.

"Sorry," he said. "I'm really sorry."

"No," she said, her hand to her chest, as though that would calm her racing heart down, "no, it's my fault. I'm just jumpy."

"I saw you leaving. It's cool if you don't want to grab coffee. I just wanted to see if maybe you wanted to do something tomorrow. I mean, I figured you were tired or something."

"No, it's not that. It's just… You know what? Maybe I could use the company. Coffee would be great."

8

Sarah knew she shouldn't be driving, but the coffee shop was far away. As she sat in her car and debated, the man came back up to her window and said, "Hey, I don't think either of us should drive outta here. There's a cab right there."

"Sure."

The man held the cab door open for her, and she climbed in. He got in right behind her and gave the driver an address to the nearest coffee shop, a place called Rose Garden.

"I don't even know your name," Sarah said.

"Michael. You're Sarah, right?"

"Yeah, how'd you know?"

"Your name tag."

"Oh," she said, feeling silly for not realizing she was still wearing it. She snapped it off and slipped it into her pants pocket. "I don't think I've seen you there before."

"No, it's my buddy's bachelor party, so we started the night out here. They're heading off to a strip club, but I've never liked those places."

"Yeah, right," she said with a smile.

"No, seriously. My mother, briefly, just in college, had to do that. You know, single mom, my father ran off, left her without a penny and all that. So, no, I can't go there. I just keep thinking the girls are forced to be there to feed their kids at home, and it makes me feel bad."

"Well, either you're really sweet or you're really a scumbag to make something like that up."

He grinned. "Guess we'll never know for sure."

The coffee shop was crowded, like most places in Philadelphia near Pennypack Park. Most of the city was deteriorating with drugs and crime, but certain spots shone as brightly as Los Angeles or Manhattan. This neighborhood, which Sarah had chosen to live and work in very deliberately, was one of the best in the city.

They stood in line and ordered two coffees. Sarah had hers black without any sugar or cream. They grabbed a table by the window, and Michael pulled out her chair for her.

"I've never actually been in here," he said.

"I like the feel of the place. It's mostly college kids. They have a real… kind of optimism about the world, ya know? Like it hasn't changed that about them yet."

"Or maybe they're just naïve?" he said.

"Yeah, maybe. Either way, I like it."

"So are you from here originally?"

Sarah sipped at her coffee. It was hot to the point of burning her tongue, but she didn't mind. "No, Lancaster County. Born and bred," she said with a sigh she didn't mean to give.

"Really? Farm girl, huh?"

"You could say that," she said, staring into her coffee.

"I've never been."

"So what about you?" she said, wanting to get the spotlight off of her.

"Oh, I'm a Philly boy. Pretty boring actually. I've never really been outta the East Coast. Boston's as far as I've been."

"I've always wanted to travel. I've never been out of the state."

"Really? Not even to, like, New York or DC?"

She shook her head. "Nope. Philly seems far enough from where I grew up. But I've been seriously playing with the idea of maybe moving to California."

"How come?"

She shrugged. "Just the sunshine, I guess. I'm really sensitive to weather. And the beach. I really want to lie around on the beach."

He sipped at his coffee, grimaced, and then pushed the cup away. She could tell this wasn't the ideal first date he'd had in mind.

"Can I ask you something, and will you promise not to get mad?" he asked

"I guess so. That's not really something I can promise, though," she said.

"Fair enough. But try not to get mad 'cause I'm just curious."

She sipped at her coffee again. The temperature had gone down enough that it was enjoyable. "Okay. I'll try."

"Did you really beat up another girl to get that job?"

She snorted, nearly spitting up her coffee. "Who told you that?"

"That other bartender. The male one, not the woman."

She shook her head. "I didn't beat her up to get the job."

"Then what happened?"

"She attacked me and accused me of sleeping with her boyfriend. We just happened to be up for the job at the same time."

"So did you?"

"Sleep with her boyfriend? No, I didn't. She was thinking of someone else. But she didn't realize that until after."

He smirked, playing absently with some sugar packets on the table. "He said you put her in the hospital."

"She took a swing at me, and I raised my arm. She hit my elbow and, like, broke one of her fingers, I guess. That's hardly my fault."

"Well, it's a cool story. I don't think you should change it."

She smiled, swirling her coffee with her finger. "You wanna get outta here?"

He looked stunned for a moment and then nodded. She took his hand, and they ran out into the warm night air.

At sunrise, Sarah woke with an epic headache. Her face, neck, shoulders, hips, and legs all screamed. She rolled out of bed and realized she was at home. Looking over her shoulder, she saw Michael with his face planted firmly in the pillow, asleep. This was why she preferred to be out at their place. She couldn't very well leave him here to go through her things.

He stirred, realizing she was awake, and tried to reach for her. She brushed him away and got up.

"Where you going?" he said with his eyes still closed.

"The bathroom. You better get ready, too. I have some stuff I have to do today."

"Oh, wow. I'm getting kicked out already, huh?"

"Not kicked out. I just have some stuff I need to do. I'll call you tonight, though."

"Ouch. I'm guessing I shouldn't be waiting by the phone for that one."

She stopped and smiled. "No, probably not. Look, you're a nice guy, but I'm just not ready for anything serious."

"Yeah, I figured. I better, ah, get going then."

She walked into the bathroom and turned on the shower. She heard him come to the door, but he didn't say anything. She heard footsteps, and then her front door opened and closed.

Sarah stared at herself in the mirror and exhaled. Michael was a perfectly good man. What was it about her that pushed them away so quickly? A piece of her felt like it was rotting. Something deep inside her that she couldn't find and excise. It was hidden, but it was powerful.

Before Sarah could get into the shower, her phone rang. She stepped out of the bathroom, making sure Michael was gone, and then answered it. It was a call from the bar.

"Hello?" she said.

"Sarah, it's Trevor. Hey, I know it's your day off, but I was wondering if you could come in tonight?"

"Sure. Somebody call in sick?"

"Yeah, you could say that. Jeannie's in the hospital."

Her stomach dropped. "For what?"

"I don't know. I got a call from her mom saying she's in the hospital and she can't make it to work for the next few days."

"Do you know which hospital?"

"Hahnemann, I think. Why?"

"I'll cover for her. Thanks."

Sarah hung up, threw on some sweats, and ran out the door. She realized halfway down the hall that she'd forgotten her keys and had to run back and grab them.

9

Giovanni Adami was woken by the sound of his doorbell. He was nude, the way he preferred to sleep, and he stumbled out of bed and slipped on his boxer shorts. His apartment was small, just a studio with a kitchen the size of a closet, but the view out his living room window was a park across the street. He glanced out of it now and saw the sunshine glimmering through the leaves before he answered the door.

Agent Rosen stood there looking sternly at him. "You not up yet?"

"It's only eight."

Rosen brushed past him into the apartment. "Gotta get up early and go to bed early. It's the only way to stay healthy. Get dressed. We're meeting with someone. You got a cat?"

"How'd you know?"

"I'm allergic."

Giovanni walked to his closet, which was in the same room as his bed and the couch, and pulled down a black suit with a white button-front shirt. "Who we meeting with?"

"Melissa Archer. Nathan's mother."

"Yeah?" he asked, going into the bathroom to brush his teeth.

"Yeah. I want to know if he had any cousins or close friends that he would have shared his life with."

"You think that's who it is? Someone close to him?"

"Who knows? A lot of times copycats are just psychotic stalkers that become obsessed with a particular subject. So it could be that. But those are much more difficult to find. First, you exclude the impossible. Then whatever's left, no matter how improbable, must be true."

"Mickey Parsons would always tell us that," Giovanni said as he brushed.

"Yeah, helluva agent. You were lucky to have him in the academy. I was actually his partner for about a year. He had a logic about this… insanity we see every day. He could just… make sense of it."

"I heard he retired."

"Yeah, well, we're all headed down that road."

"Spock said that too, you know."

"Who?"

Giovanni looked back at him. "How old did you say you were?"

"Just hurry up."

Giovanni finished brushing and put on his socks and shoes. He ran a brush through his hair and put on his watch and holster.

"Why do you live here?" Rosen asked.

"What do you mean?"

"It's not the best neighborhood. You can afford something better with what the Bureau pays you."

"Our entire job is moving around. I don't want to fall in love with a place only to leave it a few years down the line."

Rosen nodded as he scanned the apartment. "Makes sense, I guess. Let's go. I'll drive."

Unlike Giovanni's car, Rosen's was the standard-issue sedan, a Ford the Bureau kept in the motor pool at least five or six years past its prime. But the interior and exterior were spotless, and as Giovanni got in, Rosen took out a handkerchief and wiped at a spot on the windshield before getting in and pulling away.

"So what about where you live?" Giovanni asked.

"The condo is just a rental because it's close. I have a house in Fairfax. When you get as close to retirement as I am, they don't move you around anymore. You just kind of run out the clock."

"You always been in Behavioral Science?"

"No, I started in Organized Crime. But they shuffled me around a few times after September Eleventh. This is just kind of where I landed."

"Really? I thought most agents fought to get in here."

Rosen grinned. "Only the new ones, who don't know better. We have more requests for transfers than any other division. You know why?"

Giovanni shook his head, though Rosen wasn't looking at him.

"It's because most people don't want to know what's really going on in the world. If they knew, truly knew, how much danger we're in every day, how could they live? Take these cars flying past us. With the kinetic energy they're producing, they could demolish this car. Disintegrate us to nothing. And the other drivers might be mentally ill, they might be sick, they might be angry, not paying attention… they may even want to kill someone. But no one thinks about that when they get into their cars. There are things we can't explain and just stay blind about. In Behavioral Science, a lot of that is exposed. This isn't for everybody."

Giovanni stared out the window and thought back to his days in Iraq. A young man had been firing on their position from across a street. They lit him up from all sides. When his unit got over there to look at the bullet-riddled corpse, the "young man" turned out to be a ten-year-old boy. The rest of the unit didn't care, or at least pretended they didn't. But Giovanni stayed behind, staring at the mangled body. The boy's eyes were open, his head tilted toward Giovanni as if glaring at him accusingly. That face had never left him. It was always there.

The neighborhood Melissa Archer lived in was primarily small family homes in a typical suburban setting. No liquor stores on the corner, no markets with bars up on the windows. The neighborhood appeared safe, the type of place you'd want to raise a family.

They parked on the curb, and Rosen had his eyes locked on a brown house with shutters closed over all the windows. An overly large padlock hung from the gate to convey that whoever was inside definitely didn't want to be disturbed.

"Follow my lead," Rosen said as he got out of the car.

Giovanni fell behind. Technically, Rosen wasn't his boss—just an agent with seniority. But he had a leadership quality about him that told Giovanni he had a lot to teach. Still, Giovanni wondered what exactly Rosen had done not to be promoted further. With his time in the Bureau, he should at least have been a special agent in charge of a field office, if not higher.

Rosen got to the gates and eyed the padlock. He glanced around to make sure no one was watching and then hopped the three-foot fence.

"Um…" Giovanni stammered.

"What? We're not searching her house. I just want to talk to her."

Giovanni looked both ways and then hopped the fence, too. He strolled up to the porch, making sure no neighbors had just seen them.

"What're you so nervous about?" Rosen said.

"We're trespassers."

He snorted. "Please. The NSA's reading congressmen's email, and hopping a fence makes you nervous."

Rosen pounded on the door far more aggressively than he needed to. The whole situation made Giovanni nervous. He was too new to understand all the rules, and definitely too new to be breaking them. The last thing he needed was a black mark in his file already.

A woman came to the door and said, "Who is it?" without opening.

"FBI, ma'am. We'd like to ask you a few questions about Nathan if we could have a minute of your time," Rosen bellowed.

A long silence followed, and then the rattle of chains and the clunk of locks sliding open.

Melissa Archer was petite, almost frail. A woman probably in her late sixties or early seventies, her hair was still a deep brown, but the spots on her skin betrayed her age. Giovanni noticed her hands were trembling.

"Yes?" she said.

"Ma'am, I'm Special Agent Arnold Rosen, and this is Special Agent Giovanni Adami. We're investigating a string of homicides that we believe you may be able to help us with."

Ms. Archer looked from one to the other and back. "Oh dear. Well, come in."

They entered her home. The first thing that struck Giovanni was how bare it was. Not a decoration or photo anywhere. This woman was at the end of her life, but there was nothing here to remind her how she had lived.

The furniture was covered in plastic, and as the two men sat down, the covering crackled as if it had never been used before. Ms. Archer was preparing something in the kitchen and came out a moment later with cookies and juice.

"I'm okay," Giovanni said.

Rosen took a cookie and a glass of juice. He drank a sip before taking a bite of the cookie. "I'm sorry about what happened with Nathan," he said after chewing.

"He was my boy. I have two girls, too. One's in San Francisco, and the other is in Canada. As far away from this town as they could get, I guess."

Rosen nodded as though he knew exactly what she was talking about. "Nathan was a good-looking boy."

"Oh, he had a lot of girlfriends. They were always coming in and out of the house. I kept telling him that it wasn't proper for a young man to have so many girlfriends, but he would just say, 'Mom, that's just how it's done nowadays.' He loved going on dates."

Giovanni wondered how many of his dates ended up in some ditch. Though three bodies were attributed to him, Giovanni knew it took a while for these types of perpetrators to be caught. The real number, he guessed, was probably double that.

"Did he have any close friends?" Rosen asked. "Anyone that was over here all the time? Maybe they had sleepovers. Things like that."

She shook her head. "No. Nathan always preferred girls to spending time with boys. He didn't play sports or anything like that. When he wasn't on his dates, he liked to keep to himself."

Rosen took another bite of the cookie and placed the rest down on a napkin that Ms. Archer had put in front of him on the coffee table. "Ms. Archer, can you think of anyone in Nathan's life that would want to copy what he did? Perhaps an uncle, cousin… anyone."

"No. Why would anyone want to do that? I'm not delusional, Agent Rosen. I know the evil my son brought into the world. But he was still my son. I can't stop loving him, no matter what he's done."

"I understand," he said solemnly. "Could you do me a favor? If you think of anyone that might, I don't know, walk in his shoes, could you give me a call? This man has killed six young women so far. We need to stop him, Ms. Archer."

"Of course. Please leave your card, and I'll call if I think of anything."

As Rosen was taking out a card, Giovanni scanned the steps leading upstairs. Dirty shoeprints came in from outside, the backdoor in the kitchen, and headed upstairs.

"Does anyone else live here?" Giovanni asked.

Ms. Archer looked surprised—maybe because he hadn't spoken the entire time. "No. It's just me now. My husband left us when Nathan was a child. When he was gone, it was just me and Nathan."

Giovanni nodded, a gnawing sensation in his gut, and he realized he felt bad for Melissa Archer. That her son would put her through what he put her through, not to mention the mothers of the victims he took from the world.

Rosen stood up, and Giovanni followed. They said goodbyes and thanked Ms. Archer for her time. As they walked to their car, Giovanni glanced back at the old house and saw her watching them through the shutters of a window.

"We done for the day?" Giovanni said. "I got some paperwork back at the office."

"Almost. One more stop."

"Where?"

Rosen took out his cell phone. He dialed a number he had saved in his contacts and said, "Yeah, Steve, this is Arnold. I need a skip-trace done on a Sarah King. I don't have a middle name or birthday, but she'd be twenty-one or twenty-two now. From Lancaster County… Yup. Thanks."

"Seriously?" Giovanni said.

Rosen sat on the hood of the car and looked down the street to where a few children were playing. His eyes fixed on them a moment, and he began to grin.

"You have any kids?" he asked.

"No, not married," Giovanni said.

"Best and worst thing in life. I have a son. I don't know where he is. Last I heard he was bartending in Las Vegas."

Giovanni joined him on the hood. "You don't talk?"

"No. He… forgot to call me on Father's Day last year. He said it was 'cause he just forgot, but that's not why. He's got a drug addiction. Heroin. Me and his mother saw it early. We tried everything—every program, every method, tough love, no love, over-loving… nothing did it. The drug won in the end."

"I'm sorry."

He nodded. "Yeah." He exhaled through his nose. "Try and explain drug addiction logically to me, Giovanni. People willingly destroy themselves and everyone around them. It's inexplicable. There are just some things you can't explain."

"I don't believe that. Everything has a cause. An explanation."

"When I was ten years old, and this dates me, but when I was ten, my brother and I shared a bunk bed. On July third of 1971—and I remember that date because it was the day before Independence Day and we were supposed to drive to Lake Mead for that. But I woke up on July third, and I saw my brother asleep in his bed. I went and peed in the bathroom we shared, and I came back out, and he was sitting straight up in bed, as white as a ghost. And all he said to me was, 'Jim Morrison's dead.' We were huge fans of The Doors back then. There wasn't a radio or TV in our room. There's no way he could have known that. It didn't even hit the States until later that day. News didn't travel as fast as it does now."

"How'd he know?"

"He said he saw it in a dream. Jim Morrison lying in a cold bath, his heart not beating. That memory has stuck with him his entire life. It changed his life, actually. There were things he could never believe in that he started believing in because of that." He looked Giovanni in the eyes. "You may not have had a moment like that yet, but I think the universe has a lot of mysteries we don't know about. And if there's a chance this girl can help us save some lives, why wouldn't we do it?"

Giovanni didn't really have anything to say to that. Instead, he kept his eyes forward, on the children playing. After a few moments, Rosen hopped off the hood and got into the driver's seat. Before Giovanni got in, he looked over the Archer's home one last time. She wasn't at the window anymore, and the shutters were closed again.

10

The tires screeched as Sarah slammed on her brakes. The hospital parking lot was full, so she just stopped at the curb and hopped out. A valet there gave her a ticket, and she handed him the keys and rushed inside.

The hospital was like all hospitals and made her uncomfortable. Lots of people died in hospitals, and if she didn't control it, they would flood inside her mind. Images of people gasping their last breaths, screams of pain, the quiet sobbing of those left behind.

"Excuse me," she said to the help desk volunteer. "I'm looking for a Jeannie Kehr. She's here recovering from surgery."

Sarah didn't remember being told about the surgery, but she knew it was true. The surgery occurred the night before, when she was brought in to stop the bleeding.

"Room 303. Take the elevators up, and check in at the front desk."

The elevators were slow and stopped on the second floor. Impatience welled up inside Sarah, and she didn't even know why. There wasn't anything she would be able to say or do. She wasn't a doctor or a therapist. But at least she could be there for her friend.

The elevator finally stopped, and she raced off. She quickly checked in at the front desk and then found room 303. Jeannie was in bed, her mom sitting on a stool next to her. They were both watching television, though Sarah could tell neither one of them was paying attention to it.

Jeannie's face was heavily bruised, her left eye nearly closed with swelling. Her lips were cut, and her nose was swollen and bandaged. Her right wrist was in a cast.

Jeannie's eyes slowly drifted over to where Sarah was standing. The white in her eyes hardly showed due to the burst blood vessels. Sarah didn't say anything. She felt tears and tried not to show it. But Jeannie started crying.

Sarah stepped inside the room. She wanted to put her arms around her friend, to tell her that it would be all right, that she would survive and move on. But she couldn't. Jeannie was sobbing uncontrollably now.

"You knew," she mumbled, "you knew."

"I'm sorry," Sarah whispered. "I'm so sorry."

"Why didn't you tell me?"

"Jeannie, I did."

"You could've stopped me. You could've taken my keys."

Sarah rushed to the bedside and tried to hold her hand but Jeannie pulled away. "I'm so sorry. I should've done more to stop you. I'm sorry."

"Get out."

"Jeannie, no," she said through tears. "No, don't do that."

"Get out!" she screamed.

Sarah felt the cold stare of her friend's mother. They needed someone to blame right now. Life had thrown them intense pain, and they didn't know what to do with it. People rarely did. If it helped them, Sarah would take the blame.

"Okay. I'll leave."

Jeannie was crying, and her hand came up to her eyes. "You're a freak. You're a freak!"

The words cut and startled Sarah. She swallowed and wanted to say something, wanted to explain, but no explanation would come. All she could say was, "I'm so sorry."

"Get out!"

Jeannie's mother said, "You're upsetting her. Please leave."

Sarah turned and ran out of the room, tears streaming down her face. She bumped into a nurse and mumbled something that sounded like "Excuse me," but she couldn't be sure. The hallways looked the same in both directions. She felt vertigo and had to lean against the wall a moment. Her heart was racing, and she was getting tunnel vision. Putting her hand over her eyes, she began to breathe deeply, trying to calm herself.

It took a few moments, but her heart began to slow. She wiped the tears away and continued down the hall and out of the hospital.

Sarah sat in her car and cried for a long time. She wouldn't be able to face Jeannie again. How could she? Maybe Jeannie would calm down, and Sarah could explain, but what explanation could she give that would satisfy her? Jeannie believed Sarah had known about this beforehand and hadn't done everything in her power to stop her. Sarah could say she was drunk that night and tried her best to talk Jeannie out of going, but she knew there were no apologies that could be made.

She started her car and pulled away from the front entrance. She realized she'd forgotten to tip the valet, so she stopped and, still crying, gave the man a few dollars.

She'd driven halfway across the city when she'd finally calmed enough to control the tears. She needed to see the ocean right now. The way the sunlight reflected off the waves, the sand underneath her feet. This was the hottest time of year, and soon winter would come again, and with it the cold and the dark.

California called to her like a beacon. She knew that was where she would end up. Something about the sunshine and the people. Maybe even Hawaii. Anywhere that had plenty of sun and a relaxed environment.

She parked in the lot by a strip of beach called Champaign Cove overlooking the pier. Sarah got out and strolled down the sidewalk to the sand and took off her shoes. When she first left Lancaster County, she had never seen an ocean, other than a picture in an outdated textbook. The beauty of it took her breath away. Since then, she'd come here whenever she needed a moment to herself to think.

She buried her feet in the sand and brought her knees up to her chest. Wrapping her arms around her legs, she felt warm and protected. She closed her eyes and let her mind focus on the sound of the waves, the way they crackled against the beach. Seagulls scavenged for scraps on the sand, and their squawks made her grin. They sounded so innocent, devoid of any malice or deception. It seemed sometimes like everything people did was a deception, even to themselves. Maybe especially to themselves.

And that's when she saw it.

A man on a boat with a child. The man was strangling the child, and the child was trying to scream. It jolted her eyes open, and the child was there, in front of her. Pale with a red throat and eyes that had hemorrhaged and bulged.

"No," she said. "No."

She closed her eyes. The boat was still there. From the man's tube socks, his messy and wild hair, thick mustache, and the Journey song from the '80s on the radio, she knew what she was seeing had happened decades ago.

Sarah opened her eyes. The child was gone.

She took a deep breath then let it out slowly and watched a few waves lap. She told herself the beauty wasn't gone, that it was still there and she was enjoying this moment, but she knew she wasn't. So instead of forcing herself to stay, she rose and walked to her car.

11

The restaurant was a fast-food hybrid place. Somewhere that had the appearance of a sit-down restaurant but really just fried up the food as quickly as possible and didn't have wait staff.

Giovanni stood in line behind Rosen, who was eyeing the menu like a child in a toy store. Rosen decided on the double cheeseburger and then mumbled to himself that it was bad for him and said he would get a salad. When their turn came, he ordered the double cheeseburger. Along with fries, a Coke, and a slice of pie.

"What would you like, sir?" the cashier asked Giovanni.

"Just a salad with whatever you have that's fat free."

Rosen looked at him.

"What?"

They sat down in a booth, and Giovanni looked over the families in the restaurant. Some seemed to be having a lot of fun, playing with their children and joking around. Some were quiet and ate in silence. Others had children who looked terrified to do anything without permission.

"You sure you just want a salad?" Rosen said.

"Yeah."

"I'm worried about you."

"What?"

"I don't know. You've got a cat and order salads."

"My manhood's secure. I like cats. Dogs are so needy."

He nodded. "That's true, I guess. Although they're more loyal. They'll die for you. You better believe when you really need him your cat isn't going to be there."

"Like when?"

"I don't know. Like when you have a giant mouse attacking you. Or Jehovah's Witnesses at the door or something."

Giovanni chuckled. A woman walked in just then, looked at him, and smiled. He smiled back.

"She's cute," Rosen said.

"Yeah."

"You gonna talk to her?"

"No."

"Why not?"

Giovanni leaned back in the booth. His back occasionally ached from an injury in high school. "I'm not interested right now. Relationships complicate things."

"You ever been married?"

He nodded. "I have."

"What happened?"

The order was called, and Giovanni was relieved. He went to get it and brought the tray of food back to the booth. He took a napkin and tucked it into his collar, hoping the subject had passed.

"So?" Rosen said, shoving a fry into his mouth. "What happened?"

"We divorced."

"I know, Sherlock. Why?"

"It's not something I like talking about."

He shrugged. "Suit yourself."

A moment crawled by in silence.

"Did she pass?" Giovanni said.

"Who?" When Giovanni didn't say anything, Rosen looked at him. "Oh. Yes. Pneumonia. A really brutal bout. She was already ill, and it just hit her. She fought like hell, but life had other plans."

Giovanni took a bite of salad. The leaves were wilted, and the dressing tasted slimy. He pushed the salad away and pretended to wipe his lips with a napkin but really spit out the leaves. He crumpled the napkin and placed it off to the side.

"She cheated on me," he finally said. "When I was in Iraq."

"Oh," Rosen said, looking up. "I'm sorry."

He shrugged. "It's a little weird we're going to visit a psychic," he said, changing topics.

Rosen didn't respond as he took a bite of the burger, grease dripping down onto the tray. "I don't know what she is. She could've been in on it for all I know. But she had something to do with catching Nathan Archer, and I think we need to follow up on that. Never leave a lead hanging out there. You never know what's going to get you a collar. A lot of this job is just pure luck."

"Mickey Parsons didn't think so."

"Mickey's a fluke. I'm talking about the average run-of-the-mill agent. You and me."

71

The woman who had smiled at Giovanni sat down with a group of friends. She kept looking over at him with a grin and then away shyly. She was cute, dressed conservatively, and appeared to have a normality that the last few girls he'd been on dates with hadn't. One of them, in fact, upon finding out he was a federal agent, told him that he should've told her that at the beginning, and then she took off without saying goodbye.

But he knew what it would lead to. The inevitable conversation of when they would move in together. Giovanni couldn't move in with anyone. Some nights, he woke up screaming. Once, he had pulled out his sidearm and fired a round into the wall. That wasn't something he wanted to bring somebody else into.

Rosen's phone buzzed. He checked it and read through a document as he bit down on his burger with his free hand. "You ever heard of Pink's?"

"No. Why?"

"It's the bar Sarah King works at. About a half-hour drive. Let's finish up and hit there first."

Giovanni saw Pink's first and pointed it out to Rosen. Something about the way bars looked in the daylight made him uncomfortable. As though something people liked to keep hidden had revealed itself. He stared at it for a moment before turning to Rosen, who was flipping through his phone, his face contorted in bewilderment.

"What is it?" Giovanni asked.

"Just don't have much of a history for her. The first thing we have is a driver's license at eighteen. Nothing before that."

"Maybe she was a good girl who didn't look for trouble?"

"There are usually credit reports and things. She didn't even have a Social Security number."

"Didn't have one, or we couldn't find it?"

"No, she was never assigned one. Not until two years ago."

"Weird."

Rosen shrugged. "There are a lot of groups that consider themselves separate from the United States and don't participate in any of that stuff." He slipped his phone into his pocket. "Let's go. I could use a drink anyway."

As they walked, Giovanni scanned the surroundings. Pink's was in the industrial section of the city, which had the cheapest rents for the amount of space needed and therefore nothing decorative. All the buildings were functional and nothing else.

Pink's clearly wasn't open yet, but Rosen peered through one of the darkened windows. "I see people inside." He pounded on one of the heavy metal side doors and then paced while he waited.

Giovanni leaned back on a railing along the side of the building, probably the remnants of some fence. It was times like these he wished he still smoked. Not for the buzz, but just for the action. Something to fill the dull moments between events. He'd had to kick the habit to keep the fitness requirements for the Bureau, and Mickey had told him it didn't look professional. He said it could give people the impression that you didn't have control over yourself. Giovanni didn't know if that was true, but he stopped smoking anyway.

73

A large man in a tight T-shirt that looked as if it might split at any second appeared at the door, eyeing them suspiciously. Rather than speaking, Rosen just showed him his badge. The man's eyes changed, along with his facial expression. Filled for a moment with anger, and then fear. Bars and clubs dreaded law enforcement more than anything. One or two vice busts, along with the enormous administrative fines, and a single weekend could mean the difference between staying open and filing for bankruptcy.

"How can I help you?" he said in a deep voice that reminded Giovanni of Barry White.

"We were hoping we could speak to Sarah King if she's here."

"Nah, tonight's her night off. My manager Trevor's here, though."

"No, it's not about bar business. I have her home address. We'll try there. Thanks. Oh, how about a drink?"

"Now?"

"Sure, if it's not too much trouble."

The bouncer hesitated a moment and then nodded. He held the door open for them, and Giovanni followed Rosen into the dark. The bar was large, with two separate dance floors and serving counters separated by a single door in a wall made of glass, presumably so each half of the bar could see the other. Stairs led up to the second floor and a balcony where people could stare down at everyone else. Velvet furniture was thrown around randomly, and a massive mirror behind the bar took up almost the entire wall. Rosen leaned against the bar and said, "How 'bout a Coors?"

The bouncer said, "Sure." He took a bottle from underneath the bar and placed it in front of Rosen before popping the top off.

"Nothing for me," Giovanni said. "Thanks."

The bouncer nodded and stepped away. Far enough that, Giovanni knew, he could still hear what they were saying.

"You sure?" Rosen said.

"I'm good." He turned around, facing the dance floor. "I remember coming to places like this," Giovanni said. "Back when I was outta high school. My friends and I would try to pick up girls and take them home for the night. We struck out probably ninety-nine percent of the time, but man, that one percent made up for it."

"You still go out?"

"No. I don't like how loud it is."

Rosen nodded. "I was married at nineteen. Never got to experience the single life." He scanned the bar. "But I tell you, things have seriously changed. This is all anonymous and dark. It used to be about meeting new people and having good conversations." He drained his beer in a few gulps and laid a five on the bar. "Ready?"

"Yup."

They headed out, and Rosen threw him the keys. "You drive."

"Where we headed?"

"Just two miles up the road. She likes to live near where she works apparently."

Giovanni pulled away and into traffic. It seemed like there was a stoplight on every corner, and even though they were traveling only a couple of miles, it took nearly twenty minutes. Giovanni let his mind drift rather than focusing on the traffic. One car cut him off and then tried to swerve into the next lane over and nearly got clipped.

"It's that one," Rosen said, ignoring the near accident.

75

The apartment building was rectangular and brown, nothing special or out of the ordinary. The bits of grass before it were yellowed, but the trees engulfing it were green. Giovanni parked at the curb, and the two men stepped out of the car.

The interior of the building smelled slightly of mildew, and the carpets had stains—enough to be noticeable but seemingly not enough to warrant a cleaning. Several apartments were crammed in on each side of the hallway, and Rosen checked his phone before walking up two flights of stairs and knocking on one of the doors.

Giovanni stared out a window at the traffic while they waited. Some sort of medical clinic was across the street, their wall adorned with graffiti. Next to that was another apartment complex with paint peeling off the exterior.

"Nobody's home," Rosen said. "I'll leave my card. We can try again tomorrow."

Just as they were taking the stairs, a door opened. Giovanni glanced back to see a man coming out of an apartment across the hall from Sarah King's.

"Excuse me," Rosen said. "We're looking for Sarah. Do you happen to know when she'll be back?"

"Couldn't say. She works nights."

"Ah."

"Who are you guys exactly?"

"We're with the Federal Bureau of Investigation. We needed Sarah's help with something. You don't happen to know where she could be right now, do you?"

"No, sorry. Well, there's a bar around the corner she's at sometimes."

"Which bar?"

"Habituals. It's the flat kinda square building."

"I appreciate that. Thank you."

"No prob."

Rosen looked at Giovanni and said, "Couldn't hurt. Let's walk."

12

Darkness swallowed the figure at the desk. The room was cement walls with a single rug, the desk and his chair, and a fridge. In the corner was a water pipe that ran from the ceiling down through the floor and into the bowels of the house. Handcuffed to the pipe was a young woman in a nightie.

He looked over at her. The woman's head was bobbing up and down, the drugs still dulling her. The only illumination in the entire room was the florescent lighting on the ceiling.

"Please…" she mumbled. "I wanna go home. I just wanna go home."

"Whores don't speak unless spoken to."

"Just let me go. I promise I won't tell anybody anything. I just… I just wanna go home."

The man exploded out of his chair and rushed at her. He slapped her across the mouth so hard she fell over, caught by the handcuffs on her wrists, which cut in and made her bleed.

"Whores don't speak unless spoken to!"

The man stood over her, his eyes blazing with fury. His chest was heaving, hoping she would say another word so he could cut out her tongue. But she didn't. She sobbed quietly. The man relaxed and returned to his desk. He picked up the small brush and began working again.

"Are you hungry?"

She hesitated. "No, I'm not hungry."

"Thirsty?"

"Yes."

The man lowered his work again and rose. He went to the small fridge in the corner. Inside were several bottles of sports drinks and some casserole he had made. He dipped his finger in the casserole and tasted it, closing his eyes as he savored the flavor.

He took one of the sports drinks and opened it, brought it over to the woman, and put it to her lips. She sipped at it softly.

"There," he said almost gently. "Drink."

A quarter of the bottle was gone when he stopped. He capped it and stared at the woman. She would be considered beautiful by conventional standards. Her breasts were coming out of her nightie, and it aroused him, but it wasn't time. Not yet. He reached down and pulled the nightie up to cover the breasts.

"You have my permission to sleep."

As the man turned to get back to his work, the woman shouted, "How the fuck am I supposed to sleep!" She pulled at her handcuffs, swearing and spitting, trying her best to break free. The man calmly walked to his table and looked over his tools. He grabbed the pair of scissors.

"What're you doing?" she said. "Stop. Stop!"

He cut out just the first half of her tongue and threw it on the floor beside her. Blood poured out of her mouth, and he watched it awhile as she cried and screamed. Then he returned to his table and meticulously cleaned the blades of the scissors.

In front of him was what appeared to be a mask but was not. The face was dried and stretched, as were the others up on the wall in front of him.

The man picked up his brush and began his work again. The woman was trying to scream, but he didn't mind. There'd be plenty of that soon enough.

13

Sarah sat by herself in the corner, away from the windows and the other people in the bar. She didn't feel like talking right now. All she wanted to do was drink, and forget. But the more she drank, the weaker her will became, and the images began to take over. It was as if it exposed a crack in her mind, and the weaker her will, the larger the crack.

She motioned to the waitress for another drink as two men walked into the bar. The place was dimly lit, not the type of establishment meant for hanging out and socializing in. It was a place to get drunk and nothing else. These two didn't look like they wanted to get drunk.

One was older with pure white hair. The other one was young and handsome with a chiseled face and high cheekbones. They spoke to the bartender for a moment, and the bartender looked over at Sarah before the two began walking over to her.

"Sarah King?" the older man said.

She looked past them, as though ignoring them would make them go away. "No."

"You're not the Sarah King from Lancaster County?"

"No."

He hesitated. "I don't believe you."

She exhaled as the waitress brought another drink. Sarah thanked her and gulped down half the glass without tasting it. "Who are you?" she said.

"I'm Agent Arnold Rosen with the Federal Bureau of Investigation, and this is Agent Giovanni Adami. We were hoping we could talk to you for a minute."

"About what?" she said, not looking up from the table.

"About Nathan Archer."

Sarah froze. Her eyes slowly drifted up, and she stared at the two men. "I don't have anything to say about him."

Rosen sat down at the table next to her, and Giovanni followed. She suddenly felt uncomfortably boxed in.

"Even if I told you that the same type of murders have started again?"

"Same type?"

"Six months ago we found the first body. Torn apart like she'd gone through a meat grinder. And the face had been removed. Same as Archer."

Sarah didn't move or say anything. Every bit of concentration she had went toward fighting off the flood of images and sounds trying to worm their way into her mind. And she couldn't tell if they were memories or something else.

"I can't help you with that," she said.

"See, we were told that you had a hand in catching Nathan Archer. But the sheriff wasn't exactly too clear on how you did it."

She looked the old man in the eyes. His eyes were steely, showing no trace of what was going on inside. But the younger one had soft eyes. Eyes that took in what he saw and sympathized with it.

"I didn't do anything."

"Are you sure? Sheriff Bullock seemed to think differently."

She shook her head. "Nope. Sorry to disappoint."

The younger one, Giovanni, said, "I told you. Let's go."

Giovanni rose, but Rosen stayed put. He stared at her, as if trying to read something about her from the way she wasn't looking at him.

"Can you do what I think you can do?" he said, quietly enough that Sarah was certain the younger one couldn't hear.

"Please leave," she said.

Rosen nodded and then rose. "I'm sorry."

With that, the two agents left the bar. Sarah watched them until they were gone, and then she stood up and left some money on the table. She had to go cover Jeannie's shift.

Pink's was unusually packed. Sarah worked the bar with two other bartenders, but it didn't seem like they had enough staff. She didn't have time to mingle or drink. All she could do was mix the drinks, take payments, and keep the bar reasonably free of clutter.

"Hey, gorgeous."

She looked up to see a man with a Penn State T-shirt standing in front of her.

"What can I get you?" she said.

"What time do you get off?" he said. "'Cause I'd like to watch."

83

He chuckled, but Sarah gave him an icy stare. "I don't find that funny."

"What? Listen, my buddy over there said you were good to go."

Sarah glanced back to where he was pointing. A group of men huddled in a booth. One of them looked familiar, a man from her past whom she'd slept with.

"So what time you get off?" he said.

"I'm not interested."

"Hey, I'm just askin' what time you get off. And in case you didn't notice, you're not the hottest bitch here."

She moved to turn away and get to another customer when he grabbed her wrist. "Hey, I'm talking to you."

A single image came to her mind. This man sneaking into a window in high school. Another boy was in bed, and the man got undressed and entered the bed.

Sarah said, "Closeted gay men don't usually hit on me. Maybe one of the male bartenders would better fit you."

"Fuck you, bitch."

Sarah ignored him and continued with the drinks. The man walked back to the table, and the group of men laughed, glaring at her. She felt her face get hot and wanted to be somewhere else, but there was nowhere else to be. So instead she just told Trevor she was taking a five-minute break and would be right back.

Sarah grabbed a beer and went out to the back alley. She leaned against the wall as she twisted off the top of the bottle and tossed it into the nearby dumpster. It missed and bounced on the ground. She walked over and bent down to pick it up when she heard someone behind her.

She turned, startled, and saw Agent Rosen casually strolling toward her.

"What're you doing here?" she said.

"I was inside and saw you duck out here. It's quiet," he said, looking around, "but not exactly sanitary."

"What do you want, Agent Rosen?"

"Just call me Arnold." He leaned against the wall, his hands in his pockets. "The sheriff struck me as a man who believed in miracles. His entire house was nothing but religious paintings."

"Really?" she said, taking a sip of beer. "He wasn't that religious when I knew him."

"When was that?"

"Last time I saw him was about six years ago, when I left Lancaster County."

"Why did you leave?"

Sarah ambled over to the wall across from him and leaned back, letting the bottle dangle in her fingers. "Trouble at home, wanting to see the world… You name it, I guess."

Rosen nodded and was quiet a moment as he watched a pedestrian walk past the alley. "Do you have it, Sarah?"

"Have what?"

"You know what."

She didn't say anything.

"What do you see when you look at me?" Rosen said. "Be honest."

Sarah looked him over. She took another sip of the beer. Allowing one thought to enter her mind, she saw a woman in a hospital bed. The woman turned to her and said something. It wasn't a full picture. It was more akin to turning on a faucet and then immediately closing it, letting only the smallest spray out.

"I see your wife."

Rosen's mouth fell open. It only lasted a moment, and then he gained control of himself again. "What about her?" he managed to get out.

"She says that the blanket was warm enough. I don't know what it means."

Tears welled up in Rosen's eyes, and he had to turn away. He paced around the alley, acting as though he were lost in thought. But Sarah could see he was fighting back the tears.

"A few days before she passed," he said quietly, "I brought her a blanket. She was unconscious at the time. But I still talked to her. I told her I was worried that the blanket was too thin and wouldn't keep her warm."

Sarah didn't say anything. She thought back to the last time she saw her mother. The shame and guilt on her face as she turned her back on Sarah.

"How long have you had this gift?"

"Gift?" she scoffed.

"It's a gift, Sarah. Don't let anybody tell you different."

She sipped her beer and looked out of the alley at the cars passing by. "You see those shows on TV, and they show the dead as full of light and love. That they're there to tell us things and let us know they love us." She looked him in the eyes. "Do you know what the dead actually are? They're angry. They're angry, and they're jealous that we're still alive. And they take it out on anybody who can see them. Murder victims are terrified and lash out because they don't know what else to do. This isn't a gift. My life has been a nightmare since the day I was born…" She trailed off, leaning her head back against the wall. "A waking nightmare. I can't wake up."

Rosen was quiet a long while. He finally said, "My grandmother taught me that just because you don't believe in things doesn't mean they aren't real. She lived in a world filled with ghosts and demons. With possibility. But she wasn't bitter. She said every day she looked for a way to help people. On this side or the next."

She was silent a moment before finishing off her beer and throwing the bottle into the dumpster. "What do you want from me?"

"I want your help. The person who did this, I think, will keep doing this for a long time. He's smart, and completely detached from any human emotion. He won't stop, Sarah."

"Do you know how many people die every day? I can't help all of them."

"No, but you can help the ones that are being killed by him." He took out his card and slipped it into her hand. "Please call me if you change your mind."

Sarah watched Rosen walk out of the alley and go around the corner. She was alone again, in the dark.

She sighed and went back inside the bar.

14

As the crowds began leaving the bar around two in the morning, Sarah finished her side work and wiped everything down. Bottles were replaced, the tills were counted, and she helped some of the other staff make sure the tables were clean before the maintenance crew came in the morning to clean the floors.

"You doin' okay?" Trevor asked from behind the bar, where he was filling in a spreadsheet.

"I'm fine." Sarah used a fresh rag to wipe down a table. "Why?"

"I know you visited Jeannie. Do they know what happened?"

She stopped what she was doing and sat down, moving the rag aside. "She was raped."

"Shit." He grabbed a bottle of whiskey and brought it over to the table with two tumblers. He poured a couple of fingers in each and pushed one toward her. They clinked glasses and downed the drinks.

"Do they know who?"

"This guy she'd been seeing for a couple weeks. She's pretty beat up, Trevor."

"Did they find the guy?"

"I don't know."

He shook his head. "I don't understand that urge, man. To beat up on a woman. I mean, how could you feel good about yourself doing something like that? I just don't get it."

"That's because you're a good person. It's hard for good people to understand how bad people think." She exhaled loudly. "I'm gonna go if you don't need anything else."

"I'm good. Thanks for covering."

"Yup. See ya tomorrow."

Sarah left the bar and sat in her car for a few moments. She debated going home but then started her car and did a U-turn, heading toward the hospital.

When she got there, parking was wide open. She stopped in front of the building and stared at it. There was no telling how Jeannie would react this time. But Sarah didn't care. This was what friends did.

The hospital wasn't busy, and the quiet was the most unnerving thing. Sarah could hear the televisions that were on in various rooms, the beep of machines, the creaking of a cleaning cart as it rolled down the hallway.

She found Jeannie's room and poked her head in. No one was around to stop her, and no one asked questions. She wondered if that was normal for this time in the morning or if the nursing staff that was supposed to be watching the front desk had stepped out. Sarah had no experience with hospitals and didn't know. She'd only been to one once, two years ago after a car accident. It'd been the oddest experience of her life to have machines hooked up to her.

When she was young, about two years old, she'd almost gone to a hospital. She'd had a fever so high that her parents thought she might die. Her mother wanted to take her into town to the hospital, but her father refused, saying it was God's will that she be sick. She didn't remember the incident, but her mother later told her that she had, briefly, died. That her heart had stopped and they'd thought they'd lost her. And then, just as quickly, she gasped for breath and screamed.

Jeannie was asleep. Sarah didn't want to wake her but didn't want to leave, either. Taking quiet steps, she came next to the bed and sat in a chair, staring at her friend. Some of the bruising had actually increased around her face, though it was dark and Sarah couldn't really tell, but her face did have a sort of shadow over it. Sarah gazed at it a long time before she noticed that Jeannie's eyes had opened.

"How did you know?" Jeannie asked, in almost a whisper.

Sarah fidgeted, wishing she had something other than her car keys to roll around in her fingers. She stared down at her hands. They appeared rough and scarred compared to other hands she'd seen on girls her age. Since the time she was six years old, she'd been working on the farm and in the home.

"It's just something I've always had, Jeannie. I'm sorry I didn't try harder to stop you."

"It wasn't your fault. I didn't listen. I thought that… I don't know. I don't know. I'm so fucking stupid."

"No, you're not. You hear me? This is not your fault in any way."

"I don't think anyone else will see it that way. I was in his hot tub. I would've had sex with him. I was planning on it. And then I passed out. When I woke up, I was naked in front of this hospital. He broke my arm, my nose… I had to get stiches everywhere, Sarah."

She looked up at her friend and then back down at her hands. "I know."

"I just feel so stupid." She began to cry softly, and Sarah reached out and held her hand. After a minute, Jeannie stopped but didn't have the strength to wipe the tears away. Sarah did it for her.

"Did you call the police?" Sarah asked.

"No. Who would believe me?"

"I believe you."

She shook her head. "I'm not going through that. They'll tear me apart in court. I was drunk and naked and willing to have sex with him. And I can't look at him—to see him sitting there smiling at me…"

Sarah dipped her head low. She couldn't think of anything to say. No other words seemed to come to her, so she just said, "You're stronger than you think you are."

Jeannie looked at her. "What is it exactly? This thing you have?"

"I don't know."

"So, what do you do with it?"

"Nothing."

"Seriously? You don't play the lottery, or go to Las Vegas, or anything?"

Sarah grinned. "How about you get better and we'll go get rich in Atlantic City?"

Jeannie chuckled softly. "I don't think I want to do anything but lie in my own bed for a long time... I'm sorry I said those things."

"You don't have to apologize."

Jeannie closed her eyes and took a deep breath, gripping Sarah's hand tightly. "You should do something with it, Sarah. I don't understand it. But you could've helped me if I would've listened to you. You should be helping other people."

"It doesn't... It's not a pleasant experience for me."

"When is helping people ever easy?"

With that, Jeannie seemed to drift off. The only sound in the room was the soft hum of the machines and the beeping of her heart monitor. Sarah rose, bent down, and kissed her forehead. She left the hospital with her hands in her pockets and her head down. Something in her pocket poked her finger. She pulled it out. It was the FBI agent's card. Looking it over, she slipped it back into her pocket and went out to her car.

15

Arnold Rosen woke up to the sound of his iPhone playing soft ambient music. He loved modern technology. He remembered the old days of waking up to the horrendous beep of a regular electric clock, or even worse, the ringing bells of the old alarm clocks before digital took over the world.

He turned his alarm off and got out of bed. The first thing he did was go to his dresser and slip on his wedding ring. He stared at it a moment and then went about gathering his clothes before his shower.

The water was hot, and it steamed up the bathroom the way he liked. His wife used to yell at him and tell him that it would cause mildew, but she never told him to stop. She would just come over quietly and open the door to let the steam out, pecking him on the cheek before she left. Now he left the door open anyway.

He toweled off afterward, dressed, and went down to have breakfast. He cooked a few sausages and some eggs in a frying pan and ate quietly at the table before getting his sidearm and putting on his suit coat. Even though he preferred not to wrinkle the coat by driving in it, he had never been a big gun person and didn't feel it appropriate to show off his gun in public. No matter how responsible the gun owner, a gun out in public made people anxious, and he didn't want to impose that on others.

As he was driving down to the field office, his phone buzzed. A number he didn't know. He answered after turning down his stereo.

"Hello?"

"Agent Rosen?"

"Yes."

"It's Sarah King. I would like to come down and speak with you today if that's okay."

"Of course. I'm at the DC FBI field office. Do you need the address?"

"I can google it. Around noon okay?"

"That works."

Rosen hung up. He didn't ask any questions as to what changed her mind. That's not what he needed right now. All he needed was her in his office so he could show her the photos of the girls.

When he got to the field office, he rode the elevator up and was buzzed in. A receptionist sat behind bulletproof glass and waved to him. He waved back. He walked past the cubicles where the younger agents set up shop and found his office. The first thing he did was pull out the photos of the six murdered girls, all labeled across the top with the title "Blood Dahlia"—a play on the original Black Dahlia killer but even more vivid and gruesome.

He hung the photos up behind him with Scotch tape, exactly where someone sitting in front of him would be looking. Then he cleaned up what little clutter was on his desk—just a few papers—leaned back in the chair, and decided he needed a few minutes of quiet before anything else. Though he had a few other cases assigned, they could wait. It was best to focus on one case at a time, though limited resources sometimes made that impossible.

Giovanni poked his head in. "Hey."

"Your top button's undone."

"I know. I button it when we go out. Don't like things right against my throat." Giovanni walked in and sat across from him. "You sure you want to look at those every day?"

Rosen glanced back to the photos. They weren't the autopsy or DMV photos. The FBI had collected recent photos from the families, primarily headshots, and all the girls were smiling and appeared full of life.

"They're not for me. They're for Sarah King. She's coming in at noon to meet with me."

"For what?"

"I think she's changed her mind about helping us."

Giovanni glanced over the photos and then looked quietly at Rosen for a moment. "You sure you wanna do that?"

"Why?"

"It seems weird."

"It is weird. But what the hell about our job isn't?"

Giovanni shrugged. "Have you run it past Kyle?"

"No."

"I think you should."

Rosen leaned forward. He picked up a pen on the desk in front of him and began tapping it against his wrist. "Probably best to inform him after we've made the bust."

"I'd feel a lot better if we informed him now."

Rosen exhaled. "I'll do it when Sarah gets here."

Giovanni raised his eyebrows as though too lazy to shrug his shoulders, and he stood up. "Up to you. I think it's a mistake, though. We'll look desperate, consulting a psychic."

"Do you have any idea who the Blood Dahlia is?"

"No."

"Then we are desperate. Because I guarantee you he's got the next victim picked out, if he doesn't have her already."

"I'm just sayin'."

Rosen watched Giovanni walk out. *The kid was right.* He had to be losing it to bring in a psychic. That's the kind of stuff dinky sheriff's departments in the South did, not the FBI.

But Giovanni hadn't seen the bodies yet—what the Blood Dahlia did to them. Rosen, in his nearly twenty years with the Bureau, had never seen a killer this bad before. He didn't care how desperate it looked. He would work every angle he could.

The day ground by slowly. Rosen found himself working his other cases but glancing at the clock every fifteen minutes. He'd been writing a supplemental narrative on the murder of a young boy in Richmond, Virginia, and realized he'd misspelled the word "trouble" as "treble." He stopped typing and saved the document before getting up to go find some coffee.

97

The break room was stocked well, and he found some coffee, cream, and a croissant. A few other agents were milling around, joking about a case they were working. They nodded to Rosen but didn't say hello. He took his coffee and croissant back to his office and ate at his desk.

By the time noon rolled around, he felt a ball of anxiety in his stomach. He didn't know what to expect. Was this just crazy? Should he just phone Sarah and call this whole thing off? Before he could decide, the front desk buzzed him.

"Yeah?" he said.

"Sarah King here for you."

"Send her back, please."

A minute later, one of the staff led Sarah back to his office. Rosen stood and shook her hand. "Glad you could make it," he lied. He wished suddenly that he hadn't visited her.

"I want something for my help," she said as she sat down.

Rosen sat down across from her. Sarah's eyes didn't even glance up at the photos. He felt foolish for putting them up.

"Okay," he said. "What do you want?"

"I want a job. A real job. Something that can turn into a career."

He nodded. "Well, what can you do?"

"I can find the people you're looking for."

He leaned back in his seat, thinking that if he acted relaxed he might actually feel relaxed. "Why the sudden change from not wanting anything to do with us to wanting to work for us?"

"I don't want to end up a bartender when I'm sixty. I want something more. I left my entire family, my entire people… I want that to mean something. I have no education and no skills… except this. This is the only thing I can do."

"I'm still not exactly sure what *it* is. Do you hear things? See things?"

"It's different all the time. Sometimes a bunch of pictures come to me. People, places—things like that. There's sound sometimes, and other times there's not." She looked down at the desk, shifting in her seat. "And sometimes I see people that have… crossed. And they tell me things. But not always. Sometimes they try to attack me. Others just cry. It's different for each one."

Rosen didn't say anything for a long time. "Are there… some here?"

"Yes."

Rosen swallowed. "In this room right now is a dead person?"

"Not really a person anymore, but yes. I can push them out of my mind when I want to, if I really concentrate. But I'm not right now."

An icy chill went up Rosen's back. He didn't want to know who was in his office. "Sarah, I think this may have been a mistake."

She looked at him incredulously. "You bring this to me, and then when I say I want to help, you're turning me away?"

"I just don't know how it's going to look. People might start questioning me, maybe even questioning other cases I've worked. This isn't accepted practice."

"You put those pictures up there for me to look at. Which means you wanted me here at some point. What's changed?"

"I just have had time to think about it. I don't think it's the right fit."

She nodded and rose, glancing over the photos. "You know they're alive when he cuts their faces off, don't you?"

He was silent a moment. "No, that's not accurate. The autopsies all said they were done postmortem."

"No. He stops their heart first so no blood pumps in their body. But he does it in that minute afterward while they're still conscious. They feel it." She glanced over the photos one more time. "Goodbye, Agent Rosen."

Sarah turned and left, leaving Rosen looking up at the photos. He rose and quickly took them down.

16

Sarah ran out of the FBI's office in tears. It was stupid of her to try to use… this. Her mother had never called it a gift. No one in her life had ever called it a gift because it wasn't. It precluded a normal life, normal relationships. It felt naïve to think she could use it to help people. Maybe her father had been right all along. Maybe it wasn't a fluke or an act of God. Maybe it was, as her father had told her, from the devil.

She bumped into somebody, and she gasped and nearly fell over. Giovanni Adami grabbed her.

"Whoa, sorry," he said.

"No, it's my fault," she said dismissively. "Excuse me."

"Sarah, right?" he said as she tried to walk away.

"Yeah."

"I'm Giovanni."

"I know."

"So, you leaving already?"

She tucked a strand of hair back behind her ear. "Yeah, Agent Rosen said you didn't need me."

He nodded. "I'm sorry. I think it's for the best. We bring you in, and people will start questioning our judgment."

"That's what I've been told," she said with a sigh.

"Look, I'm open to stuff, but you have to admit, bringing in a psychic on a serial homicide investigation is pretty out there. And no disrespect, but it's all guesswork. We both know you don't have any magical powers."

"Have you ever seen a baby tuna fish?"

"Um, no."

"But you don't doubt that they exist, do you? Even though you have no real evidence that they exist. For all you know, they could be hatched from eggs as adults. But you believe in them anyway. We believe in a lot of stuff there's no evidence for. If you believe in a soul, then you have to believe it goes somewhere when we die."

"Maybe. What I don't believe is that there are people who can communicate with those souls once they've gone."

She nodded. "I better go. Nice seeing you."

"You too."

As she got into her car, she looked back and saw him watching her.

When she turned the car on, she stopped, rested her head against the wheel, and just breathed. Alcohol was the only thing on her mind right now. She didn't want to get drunk. Not really. She wanted to fight, but nothing else made sense right now.

Her shoulders heaved, and without an ounce of effort on her part, the tears flowed out of her. She cried about a life she could've had, one that was taken from her. She cried for her life now, which seemed to be little more than loneliness. And she cried because she didn't know how to change that.

After a few minutes, she wiped the tears away. As she was about to pull out, she noticed Giovanni standing next to her car. She rolled down her window.

"You okay?" he said.

"Fine."

He glanced over at a car pulling in. "Why do you want to help on this?"

"I don't. I asked for a job."

"A job?"

She nodded.

"Do you wanna get a cup of coffee? There's a café on the first floor here."

She wiped the rest of the tears away. "Sure."

The café was a little shop with pastries and three options for coffee and a few more for tea. She ordered tea while Giovanni got a coffee, and they sat down on the patio underneath an umbrella. The day was warm, and the umbrella provided a nice, cool shade. Sarah could see some birds hopping around on the ground, looking for crumbs.

"Do you know how hard it is to get a job at the FBI?" Giovanni said. "Even our staff have to go through a background check, a two-day polygraph, several interviews…"

"I could help."

"How?"

"Those cases that you can't do anything on. Where you've hit a wall. What do they call them?"

"We have an open-unsolved room where we keep the cases that go cold."

"Yeah, the open-unsolved cases. I could help on those. The ones where no one else can do anything."

He nodded. "Even if you could, why would you want to? Arnold thinks you can see the dead. If you believe that, why would you possibly want to see murder victims? I can't imagine they're too happy."

"It depends. Some of them want justice. Others have gone crazy. They're mindless... It just depends."

He sipped his coffee and set the cup back down, absently running his finger along the rim. "When I joined the Bureau, they had me assigned to the forensic accounting division. That's what my undergraduate degree is in, accounting. So they thought I would like that. We checked bank accounts and ledgers against deposits and checks written. I thought I would quit my first day."

"Why didn't you?"

"Because I knew something better would come up. If I just stuck to it, I knew they'd give me something better. Well, as it happened, the forensic accounting division was moved, and I just kind of floated around for a few weeks. My boss assigned me to Behavioral Science just a few days ago. I'm not even sure what the hell I'm doing. Arnold says there's this whole other world that people don't see that we do, and that it's gonna change me."

"You think it will?"

"I don't know. Maybe."

"It won't."

"Why not?"

"Because you've already seen so much death."

He paused for a moment and then drank some more coffee. "How do you know?"

She hesitated. "I just know."

"You think you see something, huh?" he said, trying to suppress a smirk. "Well, let's hear it. What do you see?"

Sarah didn't like his tone. He was handsome and pleasant up until then, and she didn't understand why he needed to mock her. "I see a little boy filled with bullet holes. He's crying because he doesn't know where he is."

Giovanni's face went completely slack. Sarah thought he turned white, but it could've been the way the shade played off his face. He sat in silence a long time, unmoving, his eyes locked onto hers.

"How did you know that? Did Arnold tell you I served in Iraq?"

She shook her head. "I'm sorry. I shouldn't have said that. Forget I said anything."

The tea was warm and went down smoothly. She savored it, allowing it to calm her nerves. This, just talking to someone else, felt better. Even though Giovanni looked like he might faint any second.

"Did the boy say anything?" he asked after a long silence.

"No. One of the bullets went through his throat, so his voice wouldn't come out."

Giovanni swallowed and stared down into his coffee awhile. "We were in Fallujah. Our position was fired upon, and we fired back. It happened every day. We were used to it. We went over there, and we'd hit this boy. Maybe ten years old. He'd been the one firing on us."

105

"No," she said. "It wasn't him."

"What do you mean?"

"It was some man. Someone with a beard and one of the white hats that doesn't have a brim. He'd been shooting at you guys. When you started shooting back, he shot the boy first and threw the gun on him. I think he was hoping you'd find the body and not pursue him."

Sarah looked back at the birds. They'd found a few crumbs and were dipping their heads quickly, eating as much as they could before something took this opportunity away. Somehow they knew that good things didn't last forever.

"If you're making that up, you're a serious asshole," he said.

"I'm not making it up. I told you what I saw."

He leaned back in the chair. "I still don't believe it. I was in a news story once. You could've googled me. Is that what you did?"

She shrugged. "Believe what you want, Giovanni. I'm not here to prove myself. I was here for a job, but it looks like I'll have to find something else. Something away from bars and booze. Maybe I could work at a school library or something."

He chuckled. "My high school librarian was an eighty-year-old woman who threw books at us. You don't seem like the type."

She smiled. "Yeah. You know when I first saw a library, I was amazed. All these books that anyone could read. And then I discovered the internet and Wikipedia."

"When was this?"

"About five years ago."

"You discovered the internet five years ago? Were you living in the Arctic or something?"

"Almost. An Amish community. That's where I was born."

"So what happened? You went out on your little world pilgrimage and decided you didn't want to live on a farm anymore?"

"It's called rumspringa, and no. I did rumspringa when I was sixteen and decided I wanted to stay."

"Then what happened?"

She watched her tea, the way the fluid sat still as glass when she didn't drink it. The color was rich, and even the smell warmed her… but she couldn't help a thought that crept into her mind: *it would be better with a little whiskey.*

"I was thrown out."

"Really? For what?"

She looked at him. His eyes were dark brown, speckled with bits of green. They took her in, and he didn't move when she spoke. He actually listened to what she had to say rather than just waiting for his turn to talk.

"Maybe we can talk about that some other time," she said. "The day's so pretty. I don't want to think about that stuff."

He nodded. "Okay. How about we talk about what other jobs we could get you outside of the library?"

She smiled. "I'd like that."

17

The body was wrapped nicely in the tarp. In the back of the van, he'd also stuffed several paint cans, brushes, rollers, buckets, and anything else that prying eyes would think a work van should contain. Daniel Wolfgram never used any of them of course. Manual labor wasn't something he enjoyed.

Wolfgram lifted the body off the floor and heaved it onto his shoulder. He had to take a moment and balance himself because of the weight, but once he got a feel for it, it wasn't difficult to walk. He made his way out of the kitchen and to the back of the driveway. Glancing around to make sure no neighbors were out, he quickly shoved it into the back of the van. The body flopped like a side of beef. He tried to contort it further, making it look out of shape. He piled a few things on top of it and then scanned his neighborhood again before shutting the van's doors.

Wolfgram climbed in to the driver's seat and adjusted his rearview mirror, catching a glimpse of his own eyes. When he was a child, he had been told you could hypnotize yourself by staring into your eyes long enough. He had tried it once and lasted several hours. But no mystical experience came. All that he gained for those several hours was a realization that his eyes didn't look like other people's eyes. They were emptier, without the emotion and tears he saw in the eyes of the other kids at school.

As he started the van to pull away, his neighbor George came over and waved.

"Daniel, glad I caught you."

Wolfgram smiled widely. "How are ya, George? How's Maddox's flu?"

"Better now. He was throwing up for a day straight, but then his fever just broke last night and he's on the mend."

"That's good to hear."

"Yeah, thanks. Um, anyway, the reason I stopped you, we're having that little get-together tomorrow and I wanted to make sure you got our invitation."

"I did. Unfortunately, I can't make it."

"You know, I don't think Debra's gonna be okay with that. She invited her sister specifically to meet you."

"I… don't think I can make it, George. I'm really busy right now."

"I get that, but listen, Debra's sister is hot. And if you ever tell Debra that, I'll kill you."

George laughed at something that was apparently funny. Wolfgram grinned, though he didn't understand what it was that was so humorous. Humor had always been lost on him.

"Debra invited her just to meet you. You can't ditch."

He hesitated. He wondered if anyone would notice if he just reached out and slit George's throat right now. "Okay, I'll be there."

"Great. See you tomorrow then."

"Tomorrow."

Wolfgram waited until George had walked away before he glanced at the body in the back. He turned back around, started the van, and pulled out of his driveway.

His neighborhood was about as cookie-cutter, family-friendly as you could get. Wolfgram was the only single man on the block, and several of his neighbors tried setting him up on dates. They didn't understand someone who preferred to be alone. It was alien to them. Just as wanting a family and children was alien to him.

The van rounded the corner and headed up to the freeway. Wolfgram checked his GPS and made certain he was headed the right way.

This was glorious, his magnum opus thus far. The excitement tingled in his belly, and he could barely contain it.

Since a month ago, when he had learned from the local news that the FBI had taken over the Blood Dahlia murders, he had been trying to come up with a way to contact them. Something that would capture their interest and let them know he was watching and paying attention. This idea had hit him in a dream, and he hadn't been able to let it go.

The freeway was nearly empty at ten in the morning. It was the perfect time for travel, he'd found. Most people probably thought late at night was the safest way to travel when trying not to attract attention, but he'd found that that wasn't true. The bulk of DUI arrests happened at night, and any decent-sized city had plenty of police officers out looking to pull people over for the most minor traffic violations. Ten was past the morning rush but before lunch. He'd found that few officers were out on the roads.

The day was turning out to be a pleasant one, and he rolled down his window and put his fingers outside to feel the wind. A terrible memory jolted him, and he pulled his fingers inside. He remembered his father would roll the window up whenever Daniel's fingers were outside, trying to catch his fingers between the glass and the frame. His father told him it was to teach him a lesson, but Wolfgram never could figure out what lesson that was exactly.

His exit was coming up, and he could barely contain his excitement. As he drove down the off-ramp, he looked around him and into his rearview—a habit he'd purposely developed. He wanted to be aware of his surroundings at all times.

There was a surface street in a residential neighborhood he had to take for six miles, and he turned on the radio. Though no music appealed to him, he did listen to talk radio and enjoyed the energetic banter. Someone was yelling at someone else about how to solve homelessness.

The drive was quick. Too quick. Wolfgram thought he would have time to prepare, to replay the incident in his mind over and over. But he hadn't even been able to concentrate because of the anxiety and adrenaline coursing through him.

Only three quick turns through a maze of residential neighborhoods and he was there. The home was nice. Large, with an immaculate lawn. He parked up the block. Far enough away that none of the home's neighbors would notice his van.

Once stopped, he put on a blond wig with long hair that came down to his shoulders. The boots were in the seat next to him. They had built-in inserts—custom made by him—that added six inches of height without anyone else being able to notice. And because of their design, they didn't even affect his balance that much.

Next were the fake tattoos. The most prominent was on his neck, a skeleton. The tattoo was bright red. The most memorable color to the human mind. They were placed on transparent sticky plastic. He had to just press them against his skin for about half a minute, and they would stay there at least a day, or until he could wash them off. They'd been designed by a tattoo artist in Florida for people who wanted to wear their tattoos around for a few days before committing to a more permanent decoration.

Wolfgram looked himself over in the mirror, adjusting a few hairs, and then stepped out. The day was warm, and the sky a clear blue. He walked around the van to the back and opened the doors. The first thing he got out was a dolly. He examined the neighborhood slowly, going from house to house and looking in all the windows. A car was coming up the street, and Wolfgram didn't make eye contact as they rolled by. When the sound of the engine had faded, he pulled out the body.

Crumpled and heavy, it barely stayed on the dolly. He had to lean the dolly far back to make sure the body didn't tumble off. Then he stacked a few rollers and paint cans on it before shutting the van doors and heading down the sidewalk back to the house.

The neighborhood was the type of place where couples had a lot of dogs and no children. He saw lawn signs supporting liberal issues and bumper stickers with phrases like "9-11 was an inside job" were plastered on a stop sign.

Wolfgram looked both ways before crossing a street. The home wasn't far now.

As he rolled down the sidewalk, a woman stepped outside her house and turned to lock her door. She glanced to Wolfgram but didn't pay much attention. He smiled to her and nodded, and she nodded back. As he walked past, he memorized the address numbers on her house.

The home he was here for was two houses down now. He had to stop a moment and just make sure he wasn't being followed. It was amazing there was no security here, or police, or even a camera on the street corner. There was nothing protecting any of these people from him.

He rolled down the sidewalk and quickly turned toward the house. Pulling the body out, he lifted with his legs as he heaved it up and onto his shoulder. Before taking the stairs up to the porch, he looked around again.

The porch had some furniture: a side table and two chairs with a swinging bench on the other side. He stepped to the swinging bench and plopped the body down. He made it sit as upright as possible. Until now, the body had appeared crumpled and loose. Now, the outline of a human female was clearly visible.

Wolfgram turned and began casually walking back to the van.

17

As soon as Rosen walked into the field office building, he knew something was wrong. One of the younger agents looked at him just a little too long. Nothing really revealing, but enough that told Rosen something had happened last night and that everyone had already heard about it.

When he stepped off the elevator on his floor, his suspicions were confirmed. One of the secretaries came up to him and said, "Kyle needs to speak with you, Arnold."

"What about?"

"You haven't heard?"

"Heard what?"

"You really need to get a TV."

"I will. What is this big secret I'm supposed to know?"

"Somebody dumped a body on the director's front porch."

Rosen stared at her, unable to say anything for a moment. "Which director?"

"Gillian, Arnold. She got home and saw a body sitting on her swing bench."

"Shit," Rosen said, his eyes drifting to Kyle's office.

He tried not to panic. It could be anything. Some nutjob digging up corpses at the cemetery. He'd had that once before, a case in New Mexico. Two high school students thought it'd be funny to dig up corpses and arrange them in inappropriate poses around the high school.

But somehow, he knew that was not what it was. His gut told him this was something much, much worse.

He marched to Kyle Vidal's office. Giovanni was already sitting there. Rosen walked in and shut the door behind him. He sat down across from Kyle and waited for him to speak first.

"You've heard?" Kyle said.

"I did."

"I don't think I need to tell you what it looks like when a body is dropped off on the porch of the director of Behavioral Science. It makes me, and it makes the Bureau, look bad."

"Do we know who the victim is?" Rosen said, avoiding the bait that would just lead to him getting criticized for something he couldn't have possibly controlled.

Kyle exhaled, rubbing the bridge of his nose. He looked tired, Rosen thought. Kyle had probably been informed and called into the field in the middle of the night.

"Not yet. I've been getting updates, but you'll have to get over there yourself."

Rosen nodded. "We're on it."

As he went to leave, Giovanni followed him. Kyle said, "And Arnold?"

"Yeah."

"She's missing her face."

He hesitated at the door. "I'll handle it."

"You better. PR is something the Bureau's really concerned about lately, with all the NSA information leaks. Everybody already dislikes us. They can't think we're incompetent, too."

Rosen nodded and left. He waited until they were down the hall before he asked, "When did you find out?"

"This morning," Giovanni said. "Someone posted it on my Twitter feed."

"This isn't good. I've never seen someone so brazen. I mean, we've gotten notes and things before, but nothing like this."

Rosen pulled out of the parking lot and was silent as he drove to the interstate. Only when he was nearly there did he realize he didn't know exactly where he was heading. He'd never been to Gillian Hanks's house.

"Find out where it is, would ya?"

"I know where it is. Take the sixty-six up to Falls Church."

"How do you know where our boss lives?"

"I was invited for a party once."

Rosen glanced over. "What kinda party?"

"I don't know. Just something welcoming new agents to the field."

"Oh."

The interstate was relatively clear, and Rosen got into the far left lane, weaving between a few cars before settling into the middle lane. The drive was long, and he felt like talking, but Giovanni seemed completely preoccupied by his phone.

"Those things will rot your brain."

"What will?" Giovanni asked.

"Being on your phone that long. It's not natural."

"How do you know? Maybe this is how our brains were meant to work."

Rosen glanced out the window. A minivan with several screaming children passed them by, easily going thirty miles over the speed limit. "I sometimes wish I could pull people over," Rosen said.

"You got an attachable siren in here, don't you?"

"That's not what I meant. I meant it'd be a massive headache to do it. I'd have to come testify in traffic court, and Gillian would be wondering why the hell one of her special agents, that should be chasing murderers, is pulling people over for speeding. Just one of my pet peeves, though. People speeding with children in the car."

"Whoa."

"What?"

Giovanni was silent a moment. "Someone on the scene posted a picture of the victim. It's bad."

"Who posted it?"

"I don't know. Maybe someone walking by. It's in the comments section of an article about it on the *Post*."

"Shit."

Another fifteen minutes and Rosen found the exit near Falls Church. The town was quiet and picturesque. He saw a diner with a sign in front that said, "Smile, Mother Earth is Watching!" The streets were narrow, and the main road cutting through town seemed to go all the way from one end of the valley to the other. Giovanni directed him until they came upon a scene like a circus.

At least four news vans were already there, lined up just outside the police tape. Several people from the local Sheriff's Office were there, as were the coroner's people. Rosen parked away from them, hoping to avoid any reporters, and he and Giovanni got out of the car and hurried up the sidewalk.

They ducked underneath the police tape and showed their badges to someone from their office who let them through to the house. Luckily, Gillian was out. He hoped she was at the office. Something about her had always unnerved Rosen—the way she would look into people with that icy stare of hers, as though she could tell the instant she was told something that wasn't one hundred percent truthful. But, as far as Rosen was concerned, she was the best criminal investigator he had ever seen. Better even than Mickey Parsons. Something about the way she thought was so outside of normal bounds that he had a feeling crime scenes didn't look the same to her as they did to everyone else.

Rosen walked to the porch and saw the body slumped in the swinging bench. The corpse was still wrapped, but the head was exposed, long strands of blond hair on a faceless skull. He glanced at Giovanni, who was staring at the sight unblinkingly.

"You okay?" Rosen said.

As if snapping out of a trance, he blinked and said, "Fine."

Rosen walked up to the porch as one of the Bureau's forensic techs photographed the scene. Another was using red string to determine blood trajectory from a puddle by her feet. Rosen could tell immediately that the blood had dripped down her leg onto the porch, and there were no blows to the woman to determine trajectory from. But he figured the tech wanted to do every single thing possible.

After a few seconds, the tech determined the same thing Rosen had and wrapped up the string. He turned to another tech and said, "The blood is dripping down from her leg. She has some injuries we can't see."

"Her tongue's cut out, too," the other tech said, snapping another photo.

Rosen hadn't noticed. He slipped some glasses out of his pocket, glancing around to make sure no one saw, and put them on. Leaning close, he could see clearly that the woman's tongue had been slashed about halfway down. The edges of the cut were clean. He used something sharp.

"ID?" Rosen said.

"Not yet," the tech with the camera replied. "They cut off her fingers, so no prints. We'll have to do it with the teeth."

Rosen nodded. He looked around at the crowds just beyond the police tape. A young deputy from the Sheriff's Office stood sipping coffee out of a paper cup, and Rosen went over to him. "Deputy, clear these people out, would ya? This is my boss's home."

"Sure thing."

Rosen turned back to the body and leaned against the porch, letting the techs work. They would reconstruct what happened—how the body was laid down, how it was carried, and probably how far. But he didn't care about that much. What he cared about was why someone would do this. The killer had to have known the entire FBI's resources would be unleashed to find him. An insult like this couldn't go unanswered. So he either had to be really crazy or so confident they couldn't find him that he didn't care. Either way, it gave Rosen a tight feeling in his gut.

"We're dusting for prints," the tech said. "Looks like it's just some garbage bags spread over her body. That type of plastic holds prints pretty well."

Rosen watched as two techs peeled off the garbage bags, revealing pale, almost waterlogged, skin underneath. "I don't think you're gonna find anything."

18

Liberty Park was a lush green this time of year. The trees were tall, providing shade to the joggers circling the park. A few people were out with their dogs, and some were throwing a Frisbee around on the massive lawn between the man-made pond and the gazebo.

Sarah King walked casually under the trees. She let the cool morning breeze flow through her hair. The pond water wasn't the cleanest, but it wasn't exactly dirty either, and the way the sunshine shimmered off of it reminded her of the lake near her home when she was growing up. The only body of water she'd seen until she was eighteen years old.

"Where are the ducks?"

She turned to see Giovanni Adami standing behind her, his hands in his pockets.

"How'd you know I was here?" she said.

"Would you believe me if I told you I was psychic?"

She grinned. "No."

"Then it's a block from your house, and I decided to drive by and give it a shot."

He began strolling next to her, watching the way the sunlight reflected off the water. She noticed that his shoes were freshly shined, and she wondered if he did that every morning.

"I come here to walk and clear my head. It's usually empty except for the joggers."

"It's nice. Better than the one close to my apartment."

"Did you grow up around here?"

"No," he said with a chuckle. "I grew up on a ranch in Arizona."

"You're kidding."

He shook his head. "Nope. My dad was a rancher, and I grew up with the whole bit. Breeding cows, wrangling horses, raising chickens… Of course that's impossible now. The big corporations have taken over, and the small ranchers are all outta business. It's scary how little people know about what they're actually eating. My dad and I always wanted to change that."

"You sound like you care about it."

"I do. It's my passion."

She looked at him, trying to imagine him in overalls getting up at four in the morning to wrangle a calf. No matter how hard she tried, she couldn't see it. "The FBI isn't your passion?"

"No. It was just a logical step after the army and being a beat cop. I joined to get out of my small town, and now all I can picture is going back. The worst thing that ever happened in my town was that my uncle may or may not have urinated off the roof of city hall when they increased our property taxes."

She chuckled. "Sounds like a charming place."

"There are trade-offs, though. The only thing in town was a Walmart. People on dates would literally go hang out at the Walmart because there wasn't anyplace else to go." He was silent a moment. "But compared to the stuff I've seen now, that seems like paradise." He stopped and looked at her. "How'd you know about that boy?"

"I told you. I saw him."

"He's following me around?"

"No. I just saw a flash of what happened. It was in my head; he wasn't here. But I saw that he was scared and didn't know where he was."

"Can you control when the flashes come?"

She nodded. "Sometimes. I've been working on keeping them out. When Agent Rosen convinced me I should help you, I let them in a little, and it's been hard keeping everything out again. When I open myself up to it... it's overwhelming. I feel like there's another world layered over this one." She started walking again, and he sauntered alongside her. "I read once about these schizophrenics that would complain of hallucinations, and I thought that's what they were. I thought I was just crazy. But I think the difference between a crazy person and me is that I'm right most of the time. If I wasn't, I'd be locked up, too."

Giovanni watched his feet a moment on the wooden planks as they crossed a bridge over the pond. "I um..."

Sarah saw a woman in bell-bottoms holding a child. They were somewhere in an apartment, the sun bright outside the windows. She was singing to it, and as the child fell asleep, the woman planted a kiss on its forehead.

She hesitated and then said, "You want to ask about your mother, don't you?"

He looked at her as he stopped again and leaned back on the railing of the bridge, as though he couldn't keep his own bodyweight up anymore. He didn't speak for a long time, and Sarah got the impression that he couldn't speak. So she let him gather himself.

"She killed herself when I was ten. For a long time, I thought it was my fault. I thought I'd done something… Like she didn't love me enough to stick around."

"I…"

She stopped as she saw the woman sitting in a chair, the same woman that had been holding the child. Now the woman was taking a handful of pills and washing it down with a bottle of brown liquid. She was in pain. So much pain that she screamed herself hoarse. The pills weren't putting her to sleep like she thought. They were tearing her up on the inside.

The woman flopped down onto the floor, writhing in agony and vomiting, before her eyes darted up, as though catching Sarah peering in on her.

Sarah closed her mind as fast as she could. The scene sent ice through her veins, and she didn't want to see any more of it.

"What?" Giovanni said. "What did you see?"

"She killed herself with pills," she said, looking down at the water. "She went peacefully. No pain," she lied.

He nodded. "I knew about the pills. But I'm glad to hear that she wasn't in pain. You know when you're a kid you forget that your parents are people too. That they have their own hopes and fears… their own demons. So when something like that happens… I don't know. I don't know what I'm trying to say."

"When something like that happens, they stop being your parents and they become just a person. A fragile, confused person."

He nodded sadly, staring out over the water. "Something's happened. That's why I came down here." He shyly looked at her. "Aside from wanting to see you."

Sarah felt herself blush but couldn't tell if it showed. "What happened?"

"I'll show you."

Sarah kept her eyes forward or out her window as Giovanni drove them down to Falls Church. She noticed that he preferred to keep one finger on the steering wheel, his hand resting on his lap. His head lay back on the headrest as though he were sleeping. It seemed almost like a forced relaxation.

As she was looking at him, she noticed the scar sticking out from the sleeve on his right arm.

"What happened there?" she said.

He saw where she was looking. "Old knife wound."

"You were in a knife fight?"

"No, I wish that was it. My stupid brother had a hunting knife and slipped on the porch and fell into me. It went through one side of my forearm and out the other." He drove a moment in silence. "So how come you can see some things but not others?"

"I thought you didn't believe in it."

"I didn't say I've changed my mind. I'm just curious."

"I don't have control over it. It doesn't work that way. It comes when it wants and shows me what it wants. Sometimes I can keep the images and sounds out, and sometimes I can't."

He looked at her and then back at the road. "I don't think I could handle giving up control like that."

"Nothing in life is easy. That's what my dad always used to say."

Giovanni changed lanes as they approached their exit. "You talk to him much?"

"Not in years. He doesn't have a phone, so the only way is for me to drive down there. I think I make them uncomfortable. I'm like a reminder of their failure with me."

"I doubt it's as bad as that."

"You don't know what the Amish community is like. Technology isn't just frowned on; it's evil. In their eyes, I've rejected God to go out into a world of sin."

"You think you could ever go back?"

She shook her head. "I don't want to. I've gotten used to the noise of cities drowning everything else out. I don't want to lose that. But sometimes I just miss the simplicity. Everything's good or evil there. There're no gray areas."

Giovanni took the exit, and before long, they were pulling up to Gillian Hanks's house. He parked in the driveway and turned the car off.

"There were news vans here, but it looks like they're all gone."

"Is there a..." Sarah said, trailing off.

"A body?"

"Yeah."

Giovanni shook his head as he looked out past some police cruisers. "No, that was removed hours ago. Right now it's just forensic people going through the house and searching the neighborhood for anything we can use. They'll probably be gone in a couple of hours, too."

She looked at him. "Why did you bring me here, Giovanni?"

"I just... this is a big deal. That house belongs to my boss. Everybody's boss, actually. The director of Behavioral Science. Somebody dumped a corpse on her porch. There's a lot of pressure, and Agent Rosen doesn't think there're gonna be any leads. He thinks this guy is too smart. So I figured, why not bring you up here?"

"What do you want me to do?"

He shrugged. "I don't know. Just look around and tell me if you see anything, I guess."

Sarah stared out of the windshield at the home. The neighborhood was pleasant and quiet. The streets were clean, and under the open blue sky, the sunlight rained through the trees, speckling the sidewalks.

Stepping out of the car, Sarah opened her mind. But only slightly. Just enough to let something in. But nothing came. No impressions, no sounds or images. Nothing but her own thoughts.

Giovanni had come around the car and was waiting for her on the lawn. As she joined him, she focused her mind, and still nothing came. Not a drop of feeling. She began walking toward the house, and he followed. Giovanni hung his badge from a chain on his neck. One of the Sheriff's Office people eyed them but didn't stop them.

Sarah stood directly in front of the home, staring up at the empty windows. The pleasantness of the home had turned to something more sinister now that she knew what had occurred here. The sites of murders were always dark places.

Some places had a light, airy feeling, like a children's park or an elementary school. These were places that Sarah could spend a lot of time in. They made her feel pleasant, and a calm euphoria would melt over her.

But some places had the opposite effect. She'd once gone into a cemetery because she'd taken a wrong turn. The place instantly filled her with grayness so heavy that she couldn't move. Her legs, arms, even her head seemed to stop responding, and the car went off the paved road and hit a tombstone. It took the paramedics to pull her out of the car and get her away from there.

Though the feeling of light and warmth she had initially felt was gone, replaced by something colder, it still didn't feel like death. It didn't feel like much of anything.

"Sorry," she finally said, after several minutes of standing in silence. "I just don't see anything."

"Let's go up on the porch."

She followed him up the steps, and he stopped near some porch furniture. A side table, a swinging bench, and two patio chairs.

"It happened on that bench," he said. "That's where Gillian found the body."

Sarah hesitated a long time, staring at the bench as though it could somehow speak to her. She took a step closer and rested her hand on it, but still nothing came to her. She felt foolish now but didn't want to show it. So instead she scanned the porch as though looking for something.

Finally, she said, "I'm sorry. There's nothing here."

He nodded. "Thanks for coming anyway. Come on, I'll give you a lift back."

19

The basement needed to be cleaned. Wolfgram cleaned it with undiluted bleach that he bought at a store a hundred miles from his home. It was unlikely that someone buying large quantities of bleach would be on law enforcement's radar, but you never knew.

He wore overalls and a breather mask as he mopped the floor. The mop, once white, now was a dull brown from soaking up blood. Though, eventually, the bleach would take the brown out.

As he got to the corner, he saw something on the floor. Wolfgram bent down and picked it up. It was a tooth.

He smiled to himself and placed the tooth in his pocket.

The cleaning took a good two hours because he liked to go over everything at least three times. The chains and cuffs were detachable from the pipe, and he took them off now. A ventilation shaft on the wall opened up, and just to the side he'd built a small storage area. He placed the bleach and his cleaning equipment inside. The bloodied mop, the cuffs, and the rags would be thrown away.

Once the basement was clean, he stood in the center of the room and looked around. When he'd bought this house, the basement had actually been finished and carpeted. It took almost six months and twenty thousand dollars to make it what it was now: a soundproof chamber.

Wolfgram checked the clock on his phone. It was nearly time for George and Debra's party. He headed upstairs.

The clothing he chose, though not expensive, was immaculately clean. He lay it all on the bed and showered before putting everything on. Then he slipped on a sports jacket and stared at himself in the mirror. He needed a haircut, but it wasn't something he enjoyed, so he always put it off until he couldn't put it off anymore. Other people touching him sent quivers of anxiety through him.

On the wall of his bedroom were several firearms. He debated taking a pistol with him to the party but then thought that was too obvious. He checked his hair one more time in the mirror and then left the house.

George and Debra Katz's home was one of the largest ones on the block. Something Wolfgram had heard one of the other neighbors refer to as a "McMansion." Several cars were out front, and the front door was open. He could hear music coming from the backyard.

A slight shiver went through him. Social situations weren't his specialty. Though he could get by with a few comments and witty stories he'd memorized, on a fundamental level, he didn't relate to people in any meaningful way. When they were stretched out nude in his basement, he thought they just looked like skinny pigs. No more, no less.

Putting on his best smile, he strolled into the home. Voices and laughter were coming from the backyard. The home was well decorated, and everything was clean. They had an eclectic style, made up of all the trinkets and artwork they'd bought on their twice-yearly vacations to exotic spots around the world.

Wolfgram rounded the island in the kitchen and looked outside. At least twenty people were there, lounging in lawn chairs or the clean wooden benches the Katzes had set up. Debra came over and smiled. "So glad you made it, Daniel."

"Thanks for the invite. Smells great."

"Barbecue's roaring, so go grab whatever you like." She took a step closer to him and said, "My sister Dara's the one in that chair right over there."

Wolfgram looked where she was pointing. A woman in checkered shorts and a blue blouse sat in a chair nursing a beer. Her legs were long and brown, and her hair went past her shoulders. She was quite lovely, and it stirred something in him that he didn't want awakened right now. He looked away, searching the faces of the other guests to see if he recognized anyone. The only person he knew was another neighbor from across the street, an older man Wolfgram knew as Kim.

Wolfgram grinned and nodded as he walked past the guests to the table laid out before them. He eyed the various foods but found almost nothing edible. He ate only organic vegetarian food, and the only thing even remotely close was the salad. He placed a few leaves on a plate, got a bottled water, and turned to find someplace to sit.

George motioned for him to come sit next to the sister. Reluctantly, he did so. The woman was speaking to someone else, relaying a story about something that had happened to her in graduate school. Once the story was over, George said, "So Dara, this is Daniel Davies. He's our neighbor up there just to the west."

"Hi," she said with a wide smile.

Though Davies was not his real surname, he had stuck with Daniel and now regretted it. It would have been better to have a completely fictitious name.

Wolfgram grinned and thrust out his hand. She shook it, and he said hello, focusing on the sensation of touch. It was an odd thing to be touching her willingly, to feel her skin against his without her recoiling. He didn't know if he enjoyed it or not, but it certainly wasn't unpleasant.

"So Debra told me you're a math professor?" she asked.

"Yes," he said.

"Wow. That's amazing. What drew you to that field?"

He glanced away but knew that eye contact was appropriate, so he forced himself to look at her. "Numbers are simple."

"Really? I couldn't think of a harder subject for me."

"Not simple that way. They're simple because they don't have any motivations. They are purely themselves. Honest. And they're consistent. They never change just because they want to or because you want them to."

"Hm, I guess I never thought of it that way."

George chimed in, "Dara's a nurse."

Wolfgram turned to his plate of lettuce and took a bite. The lettuce tasted like chemicals, and it sickened him, though he didn't show any reaction. A long silence had passed, and no one said anything. Wolfgram knew it was getting uncomfortable, so he said, "That must be interesting."

"It has its moments. As a whole, people are on their worst behavior when they're sick, so there's that to deal with. But you get to do some good."

"Mommy, can I go play with Tom?"

A young boy had run up to Dara. Perhaps no more than nine years old. Daniel watched him, surprise showing on his face for only a moment before he forced it away. She seemed much too young to have a child this old.

"Where's Tom's?"

"Next door," George said. "They're good people."

"Okay, but you come back and check in with me every fifteen minutes, Jake, okay?"

"Okay," the young boy said, scampering off.

Dara, for some reason, seemed embarrassed, and Wolfgram couldn't guess as to why.

"He's cute," he said.

"He's my life. His dad ran off before he was born, so it's just been me and him ever since. Do you have any kids?"

"No," he said, shaking his head. "I never married."

"It's the best part of life, but it's hard. It sometimes feels like if anything happens to him, I would just die. It's like I'm standing on the edge of a cliff every day hoping I don't fall over."

Wolfgram watched the boy run around the house and to the neighbor's. "That's a poetic way to put it."

She shrugged. "It's just hard sometimes. You know, trying to raise a child in this world. It seems like the culture wants to make everyone shallow, promiscuous alcoholics. Like that's cool somehow."

"Gibbon said that every empire rots from within before it falls. We attribute their demise to outside forces, but it's always internal."

He looked sheepishly at her, not knowing how she'd respond. Most women he had seen romantically, when he spoke of Gibbon or Rousseau or his myriad of other influences, immediately lost interest.

"Didn't he say that morality, not culture, is what determines if a civilization falls?"

He grinned. He was about to reply when George said, "I'll leave you two nerds alone."

When he had left and Wolfgram was alone with her, she said, "I think they're trying to set us up."

"Yes. Is it working?"

She smiled. "It is."

20

Evening fell quickly, but Sarah didn't feel like going in to work. She called Trevor and told him that she wasn't feeling well. The last place she wanted to be right now was in a crowd of drunken twentysomethings with music so loud it made her ears hurt.

Instead, she showered and decided to have a nice dinner by herself. There was a sushi place nearby that had some of the best J-rolls she'd ever had. The thought put a grin on her face, considering they were the only J-rolls she had ever had.

Even now, years after leaving her community, she felt like an ant exploring the world for the first time. Though she'd left her father's farm, she hadn't left Pennsylvania. The sliver of world she knew had grown, but it was still just a sliver.

As she headed out the door, she debated calling Giovanni. He was amiable to be around. He had a softness to him that a lot of men didn't have. She didn't feel threatened with him and felt that he wouldn't deceive her just to get into her pants.

Sarah took a deep breath and then dialed the number. Giovanni answered on the third ring.

"I'm glad you called," he said.

"Oh, you have me programed into your phone?"

"It says 'Miss Cleo'."

She laughed and then snorted and felt like she was ten years old. "Sorry."

He chuckled. "What're you doing right now?"

"I was about to go get some sushi."

"Oh, yeah? Hot date?"

"No, by myself." She waited a moment, and he didn't say anything. "You're not making this easy."

"I'd love to," he said.

The sushi restaurant was called Ginza's and sat between a hotel and an office building. Across the street were cheap motel rooms with their weekly rates listed on the marquee. Sarah parked at the curb and waited a few minutes to give Giovanni time to show up. She watched a couple walking into the restaurant holding hands. The man was smiling and leaving soft kisses on her cheek.

Sarah saw the man at a table somewhere at night. He was sitting with another woman, holding hands in much the same way, leaving kisses on her fingers. They both had wedding rings on, but they weren't married to each other.

She looked away from them and tried to focus on something else, a tree or the sidewalk or the building itself. Closing your mind was like a muscle that needed to be flexed, but it seemed to grow more difficult over time rather than easier.

After a few minutes, she saw Giovanni sauntering up the sidewalk. Only then did she realize she hadn't seen him in normal clothing. He wore a T-shirt and jeans, nothing fancy, but something had changed in how she perceived him. He seemed more vulnerable somehow.

As she got out of the car, he came over with a grin on his face.

"Hope I'm not intruding," he said.

"Nope."

He held the door open for her. "I was just gonna make a grilled cheese at home, so I'm pretty psyched for some good sushi."

"This place is great, but I couldn't tell you if it's good compared to anywhere else. I've never *had* sushi anywhere else."

"The little dives always have the best food."

A woman who didn't speak English sat them, and a waitress came over a bit later. They ordered a few dishes to share.

Sarah asked him about his college years, about his time in the army, and how he ended up joining the FBI. The one topic she stayed away from was his childhood and his mother. The wound, no matter what age, would never heal for him. She could see it in his eyes, and it amazed her that what a parent did thirty years ago could still affect someone so profoundly.

"Tell me more about how you left the community," he asked as the waitress brought their food.

"It wasn't exactly my choice. I was forced out."

Giovanni dipped some tempura in a brown sauce and wolfed it down. "How?"

She felt a gnawing anxiety in her gut. She had never told anyone this story before and wasn't sure she should share it. But looking up at him, she knew he wouldn't judge her for it.

"When I was seventeen, our preacher was giving a sermon about sin. He was talking about the evils of lust. And I saw something when he was talking. It was a young girl. I knew her, actually. We were almost neighbors. I knew her family. I saw her in his bedroom when his wife wasn't home. He would rape her and then tell her that if she told anybody, she would be cast into hellfire. The girl was only like ten.

"I went to my father and told him what I saw, but he said I was wrong. Our preacher was a good man and couldn't possibly be doing something like that. But I knew I was right. I talked to other people about it, and everyone said the same thing. They told me to leave it alone. But whenever the preacher spoke, I saw into his bedroom. Saw the girl crying and begging for him to stop. So I did the unforgivable sin in that community. I went to the government for help. I walked to a police station and told them about it."

He was silent a moment, his eyes not moving from hers. "What happened?"

"They came down to interview the preacher at his house. They found some child pornography under his mattress and put him under arrest. He confessed to the rapes later. There were other girls, too. None of them came forward until later."

"But how did you get kicked out?"

"The preacher was a well-respected man. One of the most powerful in the community. His wife was furious with me. She said I was a whore of the devil. I think that's actually what she called me. People felt betrayed, and they needed someone to blame. So they blamed me, and said I had worked with the devil to set him up. They told my father either the whole family could leave or I could leave." Her mouth felt dry, and she took a sip of water. "My own father told me to leave and never come back. My family didn't want anything to do with me."

He chewed a moment before saying, "Whoa."

She exhaled. "Yeah. So anyway, that's my sad story. But it could be worse. If I hadn't been forced out, I never would have seen *Breaking Bad.*"

He grinned. "That's a good way to look at it."

Despite the subject matter, she smiled. It came easily around him. The waitress came by and asked if they needed anything. She considered ordering some beers or sake but changed her mind. Around him, she realized, she wanted to be sober.

21

The night seemed to go too swiftly. Whenever Sarah was having fun, she noticed that time flew by so quickly that she couldn't tell what time of day or night it was. But when something unenjoyable had to be done, every second seemed to drag on forever. That feeling seemed common to most people, but when she was growing up in a secluded community, it had never been apparent to her.

After sushi, they went out for drinks. Giovanni ordered wine.

"Do you want a glass?" Giovanni shouted over the din of the bar's music.

"No, thanks. I'll stick to diet soda."

Conversation was impossible in the bar, and since she wasn't drinking, there was no reason to stay. Instead, they just strolled around the neighborhood and looked into the various shops. It seemed like something from an era that no longer existed. Small cigar stores, clothing shops, antiques... they were all crammed next to bars and clubs in a section of the city no larger than a square mile. A hip, younger area that Sarah fell right into. The energy of youth was something she craved, something that had been lacking in her life for seventeen years.

"This fits you," Giovanni said.

"What does?"

"The city. I can't picture you on a farm."

After their walk, they stood near Sarah's car and talked. Just this, talking, wasn't something that she had done in a long time with anyone but Jeannie. And even that was superficial. They never dove into themselves or where they saw their lives leading. With Giovanni, it seemed to just fall into place.

He didn't try to kiss her as they said goodbye, and she respected that. Usually, men would flirt with her with their wives or girlfriends right in front of them, and she knew that, if she wanted them, she could have them. She didn't get that sense with him. He was more reserved than most men. She got the impression he would rather be alone than with another person.

On the drive home, she couldn't help but grin. He was handsome but not pretty. Not dolled up or overly muscled like most men she met. He was smart but not an intellectual. Giovanni struck her as a man that took action before anything else.

When she got home, the apartment was empty and dark. She'd closed the blinds earlier, and no light was coming in. The first thing she did was open all the blinds and stare out onto the city. Philadelphia was such an odd mix of wealth and poverty. It seemed as though the middle class were completely disappearing and all that remained were these two polar extremes, neither one of them understanding, or wanting to understand, the other.

Sarah watched the traffic and the moon and the apartments across the street for a long while. Normally, she would be drunk by now. The truly odd thing was how much she had missed. The way the moon bathed the city, and the city lights that sparkled like golden stars spread out before her. She tended to miss everything around her when she was drunk.

Walking into the bedroom, she stripped and then hopped into the shower. The water was hot. When the neighbors ran their showers or dishwashers at the same time, the hot water would run out and she would have to finish her shower as quickly as possible. But right now was the perfect time. The other people in her building were young couples, and they were all out right now.

After her shower, she lay in bed and had some fruit and cheese. The television was mindless entertainment, but that was what she wanted. It filled the empty space with noise and light and gave her the impression that she wasn't alone.

Within a couple of hours, she began drifting off. She flicked off the television and curled up with her body pillow. Taking a deep breath, she debated saying a prayer. For the first seventeen years of her life, she had her father standing over her, reciting a prayer with her. When she was too sick or putting up a fight, he would do it for her. She remembered how much she looked forward to those prayers with him and how much she could use them now.

But the words just wouldn't come. Too much pain too recently. So instead she thought about the things she had to do tomorrow. Get some groceries and go to work and call Jeannie to check up on her. All the mundane things other people took for granted gave her purpose and direction.

Within a few minutes, she was nearly asleep. In that twilight where sleep is imminent.

And that's when the pain pounded into her skull so forcefully she screamed.

The fiery agony radiated through her head, as if a bullet had been fired inside her brain but didn't have the velocity to leave and just bounced around.

Sarah fell to the floor, curled up into a ball, screaming.

She saw walls. Bare cement walls and darkness—pure darkness, except for a lamp at the end of the room. Next to the lamp was a face. A man sitting there, watching a young woman. He rose and walked to her and ran his hand along her face. The woman was crying uncontrollably, begging him to let her go, but he didn't even seem to notice.

The pain grew in intensity, and Sarah wrapped her hands around her head, squeezing so tight she thought she might crush her head. Anything to get the pain to stop.

Suddenly, she saw something else. The man rose again from the desk, a pair of scissors in his hand. He went to the woman and cut out her tongue. Blood sprayed down over the woman's chin and onto the man's pants, but he didn't care.

Sarah could see what was on the desk the man had been sitting at: a face. A human face that had been severed and dried. Hanging on the walls were a lot more.

And then the ache shot through her in one forceful hammering, and as abruptly as it had come, it stopped.

She was left on the floor sobbing. The tears ran down her cheeks, and she wanted to wipe them away, to ignore what had happened. To show it that it didn't control her. But she couldn't move. Every ounce of strength had gone to fighting the pain, and she had nothing left, not even the mental energy to keep thinking about it.

After a few minutes, she had calmed down enough to climb back into bed, unsure whether sleep would come tonight or not.

22

Though most of the agents around had gone to lunch, Arnold Rosen stayed behind and stared at the phone on his desk. The lab was supposed to get back with an ID on the corpse that had been found on Gillian Hanks's doorstep. Lunch could wait.

But watching the clock inevitably made it go slower, and he got up and paced the room awhile. Then he crumpled up paper and shot baskets into his waste bin, which occupied him for a good five minutes or so. Surfing the internet grew boring after about ten minutes, and he didn't belong to any social media sites, so the number of things he could actually do to kill time was limited.

Finally, mercifully, he thought, the phone rang.

"This is Rosen."

"Agent Rosen, it's Steve."

He pulled out a pen and got a notepad from his desk. "Give me something good, Steve."

"Got a match for you. Claire Robison from Harrisburg. I'm sending the address and next of kin along in the email. Should be getting it in a minute. Twenty-two years old, lived with both parents."

"Remind me to get you a good Christmas present."

"Get me a good Christmas present."

Rosen hung up and checked his email. Though he needed to wait only a few minutes, it seemed much more agonizing than waiting for the phone to ring before. When it arrived, he read the biographical information and rushed out the door. He checked the cubicles and saw Giovanni writing a report on an unrelated case.

"Agent Adami, let's go. We got something hot."

Harrisburg was over two hours from DC. Rosen let Giovanni do the driving. After a certain age, he found, concentrating for long periods of time became more difficult. But Giovanni was humming along to a song on the radio, oblivious to the fact that his youth was a major advantage in nearly every realm.

"You seem in a good mood," Rosen said.

"I am. I had a date last night."

"Yeah? Who was she?"

"Sarah."

"Sarah, as in the psychic Sarah? The one you told me would ruin our reputation if we associated with?"

"And I still think it would. But that doesn't mean I can't have dinner with her."

Rosen glanced at a liquor store out the window. Though it wasn't yet ten in the morning, it was busy. "She's cute. If I was thirty years younger, maybe I'd give you some competition."

"Oh, it'd be no competition."

"Really?" Rosen said with a grin. "Son, I was in the dating game when you were pooping your pants. Don't downplay experience. Besides, it won't last."

"Why do you say that?"

"Two people who meet in law enforcement is one too many. There's something about this case that you're working that won't be there when it's over. When the investigation is done, you'll both go your separate ways."

Giovanni glanced to him. "You sound like you know from experience."

"I do. Before I was married, there was a victim of an attempted rape. This was back when I was a detective in Detroit. I spent a lot of time with her. We grew close. Started dating. When we finally caught the bastard, he took a plea deal and went upstate for fifteen years. The relationship just fell apart after that. I was a reminder to her of one of the worst experiences of her life. It'll be like that for you two. After this is over, you'll both be thinking of this case when you look at one another."

"She's not part of the case."

"I know, but that's how you guys met. It's part of your history now."

They drove most of the way without speaking again, just listening to music. They had to stop for gas once, and Rosen used the bathroom in the gas station. It was one of the ones that were around back and filthy, like it'd never been cleaned. As he was walking out, he saw Giovanni giving cash to a homeless man who was begging in front of the gas station.

Once back on the road, Rosen said, "I usually don't do that as a policy. Too many schemers."

"I give to the veterans."

Rosen looked at him and then back out at the road.

Harrisburg wasn't a quiet town. It'd grown since Rosen had been here last, almost twenty years ago. As the state capital, the city spread out around the government buildings in the city center, the most prominent being the capitol building itself.

As they exited the interstate, their GPS led them through congested downtown Harrisburg and through the winding suburbs. The run-down home they were looking for had a dying lawn guarded by a rusting fence with a "Beware of Dog" sign, though Rosen didn't see a dog anywhere.

They got out of the car and walked up the driveway to the house. The weather had gone from sunny to overcast, giving everything a gray pallor. Rosen could tell it was going to rain soon.

He knocked, and a short while later, a woman answered. She was thin to the point of being unhealthy, with thinning hair. Her beige sweater was frayed at the sleeves.

"Are you Mrs. Mindy Robison?"

"Yes."

"Ma'am, we're with the FBI. We're investigating the disappearance of your daughter."

"Yes," she said in an upbeat way, as though hoping for good news. "I, ah…"

Rosen had never, in the nearly twenty years doing this, been able to break bad news to good people. It was a skill he just didn't have.

"I'm sorry," was all he said.

The woman didn't move. Tears ran down her face, but she made no attempt to wipe them away. She didn't appear to notice.

Rosen stood in front of her and didn't speak. He would wait until she was ready. Giovanni couldn't even look at her. He had to look behind them at the passing traffic.

"If you need some time, I understand. But we'd like to ask a few questions now."

"What happened?"

"May we come in?"

She nodded and held the door open for them. She walked into the front room and sat on the couch, absently playing with her fingers, her eyes staring at a spot on the wall. The tears continued to flow, but she wasn't really sobbing. Rosen wondered if she was on any medications that dulled her senses.

"I prepared myself for the worst," she said. "But you can't prepare yourself for something like this. Not really. It feels like my heart has been ripped out, Detective."

Rosen was about to correct her but instead sat down and quietly took in the home. Photographs filled every space on the wall. Mostly of children. In one photo, he counted seven kids and wondered which one Claire was.

"She was our middle child," the woman said. "She was troubled. Into drugs and things like that. Ran with the wrong people. But I never thought anything like this could happen."

Rosen nodded. "It's my understanding you tried to file a missing persons report, but it was denied, is that right?"

"Yes. She had run away before. Several times. The police here knew about her, and they said they would keep an eye out. So I didn't go through the whole process, didn't push for it. Maybe if I had…"

"No, filing or not filing a piece of paper in a filing cabinet would not have done anything to prevent this, Mindy. This was like lightning striking. Something that we have no control over."

She swallowed. "How did she…"

"She was murdered."

"How?"

Rosen thought of how to phrase this. In truth, she'd probably bled to death. But he wasn't about to tell her mother that. "We're not a hundred percent certain yet." *True enough*, he thought.

"I see." She drifted off a moment and then said, "When can I see her?"

"We can probably have the body returned to you for burial within a few days. She's being processed for evidence right now, and an autopsy will be performed."

Mindy nodded and didn't speak again. Rosen looked at Giovanni, who shrugged.

"Mindy," Rosen said softly, "is there anything you can tell us that will help us catch who did this? A list of people she was spending time with that maybe she shouldn't have been, anyone calling her at odd hours, anything like that?"

She shook her head. "Claire didn't involve me in her life at all. I'm sorry. I couldn't even tell you who her best friend was. She came here to sleep and then would leave and not return for two or three days at a time."

"Was she dating anybody?"

"If she was, she never told us about it."

Giovanni asked, "Was she employed?"

"I don't know. I don't think so. She would sleep for twelve or fifteen hours a day sometimes. I can't imagine she held a job with that schedule. She took classes at a local college every once in a while, but she always eventually dropped out."

"Do you have a current photo of her?"

She thought a moment. "I may. Let me look for it."

As Mindy left the room, Rosen said, "Looks like we're not getting anything here."

"How could she not know anything about her daughter?" Giovanni whispered.

"Because sometimes they want nothing to do with you. And once they hit eighteen, you have no control over it."

Mindy walked back in holding a phone. She showed a photo on it to Rosen. A young, very attractive woman had her arm around an older man with a potbelly.

"That's her father. I can just text you this photo if you like."

"I would. Here's my card. It has my cell phone on it. And please don't hesitate to call if you think of anything else."

Rosen stood up and took in the living room one more time. He got the impression that a lot of memories were stored here, and maybe not all of them good. As he walked to the door, Mindy followed him. She didn't say goodbye as she shut the door behind them.

"She was odd," Giovanni said as they were walking back to the car.

"She's medicated pretty heavily. Probably mixed it with some booze."

"So what now?"

"There's some link between Claire and all the other girls. She was different somehow. For all the others, he followed the pattern of the Black Dahlia. This one he didn't. He cut her up and dropped her off on Gillian's porch. Why?"

"Maybe he's just messing with us."

"Well, clearly, but there has to be a reason. He could've done that at any time."

Giovanni's phone rang. "Gonna take this."

"Sure."

As Giovanni spoke on the phone, Rosen sat on the hood of the car. It was starting to drizzle now, and he felt the raindrops on his face and watched the way they spattered on the pavement and made a polka-dot pattern in the dust. Storms cleared the air, as if violence could wash everything away. Off in the distance, Rosen could see a storm moving toward them. The gray-black clouds crawled over the city and dumped their contents over people who ran indoors.

"Hey," Giovanni said, "that was Sarah."

"Yeah?"

"She said she wants to talk to us. You feel like grabbing lunch?"

"Sure, lead the way."

23

Sarah entered the café and got a table by the windows. The rain had soaked her shoulders and hair, and she brushed it off as well as she could. She actually didn't mind the rain, which was probably why she didn't own an umbrella and kept putting off buying one.

She asked the waitress for a coffee. As the rain pounded down, several people ran in from their cars. Some of them were young, probably in high school. She remembered herself at that age. She had been put to work in the home, with some light work in the fields. Though there were dances and family functions, she remembered feeling a deep loneliness. Not as acute as it was now, but still there, just under the surface.

Sometimes she wondered what it would have been like to go to a dance or share an awkward first kiss with a boy. Her first real kiss was a drunken waste in the back room of Pink's. She didn't even remember what the man had looked like. When she lost her virginity a couple of months later, she'd been so drunk that she fell asleep during the sex. Her boyfriend at the time was so upset that he left and never spoke to her again.

Those were firsts that she knew she would never get back. They were gone forever, and she'd wasted them for nothing.

Giovanni opened the front door. His hair was wet and in his eyes. Agent Rosen was right behind him with an umbrella and a raincoat. He struck her as someone who'd have those things ready at all times. Giovanni saw her and came over. The two men sat down.

"Hi," he said with a grin.

"Hi."

Rosen leaned back in his seat and folded his arms. "What did you need from us, Sarah?"

"I saw something."

"What?"

"After Giovanni took me to that porch, I—"

"You took her to Gillian's house?" Rosen said, turning to Giovanni.

"Just to look around."

"You were the one who said we shouldn't have her on the case."

Sarah hadn't known that, and from the blush in Giovanni's cheeks, she could tell he hadn't intended to tell her.

"I just looked at it," she said. "I didn't talk to anyone or touch anything. But later, when I was going to sleep, I think I saw… him."

"Him who?"

"The man you're looking for. The Blood Dahlia."

Rosen tilted his head slightly. "And what did he look like?"

"Slim and white. I couldn't really see him because it was so dark. But I saw what he did. He keeps them chained in a basement. This one, he cut out her tongue with a pair of scissors. She was screaming at him, and he just took the scissors and did it."

The two men looked at each other.

"What's he doing with the faces?" Rosen said, placing his elbows on the table.

"He's making them into masks. I don't know why. But this girl, I saw her clearly. She had a tattoo on her forearm. It's like a tribal tattoo, and there was some red right in the middle. He usually cuts them out but he was so excited he forgot to do it with her."

"What else did you see?"

"Little things. A house somewhere. He wants to appear as normal as possible, I think, so the house is in a family neighborhood. I saw kids in the background."

"Anything else?"

She shook her head. "No. But I was there in the basement. I saw that. It looks like he made it specially, just for this."

Giovanni said, "Can I talk to you for a second, Arnold?"

The two men rose and took a few steps away from the table. Sarah could still hear them speaking but pretended that she couldn't.

"I never told her about the tongue," Giovanni whispered.

Rosen looked at him in silence for a moment. "You sure?"

"Yeah. And the body was gone when we got there. No way she could know about that tattoo."

"Did she have a tattoo?"

"I don't know."

Rosen nodded. "Only one way to find out."

Sarah sat in the back of the car as Giovanni drove. Rosen was talking on the phone to someone from the Medical Examiner's Office about visiting the body. The person was being difficult, and finally Rosen just told them that he would arrest them and then look at the body anyway. That must've worked, because then he just said, "Good," and hung up.

"What's the difference between a coroner and a medical examiner?" Sarah asked. "I've heard you refer to both."

Rosen said, "You have to be a pathologist—a doctor who specializes in studying corpses—to be a medical examiner. To be a coroner, you just have to be elected to the position. Sometimes they're doctors from other fields, but in some of the smaller counties in the South and Midwest, I've seen coroners who are just the town mechanic or farmers, and they want the job."

"Who would want that job?"

"Exactly. Except that it pays more than a mechanic or farmer."

The Medical Examiner's Office was in a white building that looked like an office building, but several other medical offices were located there. Sarah saw two dentists and a family practitioner.

After they parked, Giovanni opened the door for her. They walked into the building and across the hall to a single door with a sign that read, STATE MEDICAL EXAMINER.

Checking in with the front desk got them three visitor's passes, and then they were led back to the refrigeration units by a portly man in a white lab coat who was texting while he walked. He ran into a mop that leaned against the wall and turned bright red but didn't stop texting.

The refrigeration unit was a wall of what looked like chrome filing cabinets. The man counted out from the near end of the lowest row and pulled the handle of the middle one. Inside was a body covered with a white sheet. The man, without gloves, pulled the sheet off.

Sarah winced and looked away. Giovanni immediately said, "Hey, what the hell?"

"Sorry. I thought you wanted to see it."

Giovanni turned to her. "You okay?"

She nodded. In what felt like a feat of strength, she looked back at the body.

The blond hair was still intact, as were the ears and neck. But the face was completely removed. The mouth was slightly open, and she could see that the tongue had been cut off about halfway down.

"Pull the sheet down all the way, please," Rosen said.

The man did as he was asked. On the girl's right forearm was a tribal tattoo in black ink. In the center was a red diamond.

Rosen nodded to the man, who covered the corpse back up and pushed it into the refrigeration unit.

Rosen exhaled loudly, his hands on his hips, as he looked from Giovanni to Sarah. "Well," he said. "I guess you're hired. Welcome to the FBI."

24

Daniel Wolfgram sat on his front porch and sipped homemade lemonade. It was tangy with just a hint of alcohol from the bitters and gave him a warm feeling in his stomach. The one memory from childhood he could actually reflect on with joy was lemonade.

Though Daniel loved his mother, or at least as close to love as he could muster, his father was nothing but a memory of pain, like an electric shock going through Daniel's body whenever he thought of him.

As punishment when he was a young boy, his father had made him do bare-knuckled push-ups on cement, and, if he couldn't complete the number he was given, his father would put cigarettes out on his back. Wolfgram remembered the sting more than anything else—that initial sting when his skin would stink and burn. After a few seconds, the nerve endings would burn as well, dulling the pain.

One day at school, his teacher noticed a cigarette burn on his neck. He wasn't sure what happened after that, just a flurry of meetings with counselors and policemen, but it ended with his father losing custody of him and spending time in jail.

Wolfgram was taken out of the home and placed with a foster family. They were nice enough, initially, but they'd had eleven foster children already. Each one provided $150 per month, which back then was a good bit of money—the only real concern the foster parents had. With eleven other children vying for what little attention they gave, Wolfgram, quiet by nature, was left to himself.

That was where he discovered mathematics when he was eleven years old. It was actually at the insistence of a neighbor—a kindly old man named Gregory. The old man seemed to understand that Wolfgram wasn't like the other children. One day, he'd bought him a book on dinosaurs. Wolfgram was brought to his home to accept it. As he was flipping through the book, he noticed another book on the history of mathematics open on Gregory's desk.

Gregory, himself a professor of philosophy, thought the young boy was looking at the portraits of the great mathematicians in history who were in the book. Intuitively, the eleven-year-old Wolfgram began playing with algebra and read the chapter on Leibniz and the founding of calculus. He began running the sample problems in the book on a Post-it Note on the desk, with Gregory hanging over his shoulder watching. Wolfgram thought he was just having fun and didn't understand the old man's reaction. But Gregory kneeled down to eye level and said, "Daniel, I'm going to give you some problems to do, okay?"

Wolfgram agreed. A textbook was given to him. Within minutes, Wolfgram was solving problems of logarithmic differentiation. And time seemed to stop. He didn't remember how long he was at Gregory's house, but it was long enough that night had fallen. He had gotten through most of the textbook, well into topics covered in a third-semester college class.

The next day, Gregory came over to speak to his foster parents. Wolfgram listened in from the top of the staircase. He didn't remember most of the conversation, but certain bits of it stuck out to him. He remembered his foster father saying, "We can't afford it," over and over.

Gregory told them, "Well, *I'll* pay for it."

What they had been discussing was putting Wolfgram into a gifted school, someplace where he could be with other children like him, ones who cared more about ideas than football.

But that wasn't what life had in store for him. The week before he was supposed to start his new program, at about ten o'clock one night, his foster father came into the bedroom where Wolfgram slept with four other children and informed him that he was leaving. That they had too many children and needed to, as he'd said, "Get ridda some."

The real reason was apparent to Wolfgram even at that age: the man was jealous and insecure. He didn't want one of his foster children, who were clearly there only for the government paycheck they received every month, to succeed in life when he had failed.

The next day, Wolfgram was shuffled to an orphanage while awaiting his next placement. Within a month, his father was granted custody again. Two years later, his father lost custody permanently due to severe child abuse and neglect, primarily from a single incident where he strapped Daniel to a pipe in the basement and whipped him until he nearly bled to death.

The course his life had taken reminded him of an aphorism he'd seen, something like "Short and evil have the days of my life been." Now he wished he'd remembered who had said it.

The cell phone in his pocket rang. He pulled it out and didn't recognize the number.

"This is Daniel."

"Oh, Daniel, hi, this is Dara. From the party."

"Yes, I remember. How are you?"

"Good."

"How is your son, Jake?"

"He's fine, thanks. He's at his karate lessons right now. Um, listen, Jake's going out of town with my parents this weekend, and I don't really have any plans. I was just wondering if maybe you wanted to do something?"

Wolfgram grinned, and he didn't know why. "Yes, I'd like that."

"Okay. Do you wanna get dinner somewhere?"

"Sure. I'll find someplace good. I can't tomorrow, but is Saturday all right?"

"Yeah, Saturday works."

"Great. I'll pick you up. Just text me your address."

"Okay, see you then."

Wolfgram hung up and stared at his phone. He'd attempted romantic relationships before. One had been with another professor at the university. He'd taken her home and played some of his favorite pornography for her. She was revolted and left. That was a lesson that couldn't have been learned any other way, he concluded.

If he was going to fit in and blend with other people, he had to act like them. He couldn't be honest with anyone.

He rose, glanced around his neighborhood, and went inside his home. He had other matters that were more pressing than a date.

25

Sarah watched as Kyle Vidal tapped his fingers against the desk. The man was handsome and younger, somewhere between Rosen and Giovanni. He had shifty eyes, though. She got the impression that he wasn't someone you could fully trust.

"You guys are kidding me, right?" he said.

Rosen cleared his throat. "No."

"Do you even realize how ridiculous this is, Agent Rosen? Do I look like some backwoods hick spotting UFOs in swamps?"

"No."

"I'm sorry, I didn't hear you."

Rosen seemed embarrassed, but the only indication was a slight blush in his cheeks. "No, you don't seem like that, sir."

"Then why the hell are you sitting here with a carnival sidekick and pitching it to me like we just landed Sherlock Holmes? Do you have any idea what the media would do if they knew you had taken her to a crime scene? How do you think Gillian is going to react when she finds out that you took a fortune-teller to her house?"

Giovanni spoke up. "She's not a fortune-teller."

"I wasn't talking to you," Kyle said, his voice raised.

Kyle continued that way for a few minutes. It seemed degrading for Rosen to be yelled at by someone nearly fifteen years his junior. But he was quiet and professional. Giovanni, though, was beginning to raise his voice and fidget.

Sarah was quiet. Behind Kyle's desk were floor-to-ceiling windows, and she stared out of them onto Fourth Street. She couldn't see much, but on the roof of a small building across the street, a man sat on a lawn chair reading a book.

"Well?" she heard someone say.

Kyle was staring directly at her. "Excuse me?" she said sheepishly.

"I asked why you think we should pay you a salary to consult on cases when you have no education, no training, and are a liability to this entire division."

Sarah swallowed and looked down at the desk. She wasn't used to being on the spot like this and didn't particularly enjoy it. "I don't know."

Kyle glanced at Rosen and Giovanni. Rosen looked away, but Giovanni held Kyle's gaze. It was sweet of him to want to protect her. A man hadn't done that since her father, when she was a child.

In a flash of forced relaxation, she opened her mind.

Slowly, almost imperceptibly, thoughts came to her. They began in the front of her brain and seemed to ease their way to the back of her skull like a flowing stream. Then it filled her head until she had nothing but the images and sounds, and the pain behind her eyes that pounded like a jackhammer against her head.

The conversation came first: a woman and Kyle standing in a kitchen. The woman was in sweats and had makeup running down her face. She'd been crying for awhile. Her arms were folded, and she was leaning against the sink.

Kyle was against the refrigerator. He'd been crying as well. Sarah, if she concentrated, could hear what they were saying. The voices were thick and laced with emotion, but she could just make out enough of the conversation to know that the woman was leaving.

And then another scene replaced it: Kyle standing over her grave. He appeared older but not by much. An entire family was gathered around the site as a priest read from the Bible. The woman was in the casket.

Her eyes opened, and she looked up from the casket.

The woman stared at Sarah and began speaking.

Sarah opened her eyes, ignoring the deep, stabbing pain in her skull. "You don't want to ask me about this job," Sarah said to Kyle. "You want to ask me why your wife left you."

"Excuse me?" he said. "How dare you—"

"She wants you to know that the drunk driving wasn't your fault. That it was her fault, and she would have done it whether you two stayed together or not. She doesn't want you to beat yourself up about it." The pain made Sarah grimace, and she had to take a moment to attempt to push it back. Kyle was silent the entire time, his eyes wide and moist. "And," she continued, "she wants you to marry Cynthia. She's a good woman and will—"

Kyle jumped to his feet. "Get the hell outta my office!"

Rosen said, "Kyle, calm down. This is what you wanted to see."

"Get out, now. All of you."

Sarah rose and nearly fell over. Giovanni grabbed her and held her up. He wrapped his arm around hers and led her out of the room gently. Some of the other people on the floor were staring at them, but no one said anything.

"Can we use your office?" Giovanni said to Rosen.

"Yeah." Rosen turned and looked at Kyle, who was still standing at his desk, his chest heaving. "That's why I brought her in, Kyle. We need her. I can't stop this thing without her."

26

The couch was comfortable but too short, and Sarah's legs hung over the end. Giovanni had shut the door to give her some privacy, but she didn't feel like this was private. The door was just glass. She could feel eyes on her every time someone walked by.

After a bit, the door opened, and Kyle Vidal stood there.

"Come to yell at me some more?" she asked.

He shut the door behind him and sat down in one of Rosen's comfy leather chairs. He crossed his legs and stared at her as though she were a patient in a psychiatrist's office. "I'm sorry for my reaction. That's not who I am."

Sarah closed her eyes. The light hurt and made her head throb even more. "I've had worse."

"You don't know how painful that was for me. If you're a fake, please tell me. Tell me you looked me up somewhere before you came here today."

"She wanted you to know that the photo album you were looking for the other day is at her mother's house. I can tell by your face that means something to you. So tell me how I could've looked that up."

Kyle stayed silent a moment. "Is she here now?"

"No."

Kyle nodded, staring out the windows. "It happened about three months after she left. She was driving drunk on the freeway and hit a semi that was changing lanes. Her car flipped about four times. She died instantly."

"I'm sorry."

"I never got to ask why she left. She would just tell me she was unhappy but never give me a reason."

"She had her demons, like everyone else. And I don't think they had anything to do with you."

Kyle looked at her. He grinned weakly and rose. "You don't need to go through the hiring process. You'll be a ten ninety-nine employee. My secretary will have the paperwork for you. Your official title will be as an assistant to me."

With that, he left, leaving Sarah staring up at the ceiling. Despite the pain, she grinned.

After the new-hire paperwork was filled out, Sarah took a few ibuprofen and returned to Rosen's office to meet up with Rosen and Giovanni. She lay down on his couch again as the two men sat.

"So, how does this work?" she said.

"I don't know," Rosen said. "I've never done this before. I guess we could take you to the scenes where we found the bodies, and you could tell us what you think."

"You said this was a copycat, right?"

"Yeah. Copycat of a copycat of the Black Dahlia murder."

"Maybe I should learn about the Black Dahlia first."

Rosen shrugged. "Why not? I'll get the files for you."

27

The sun was at its zenith when the files were brought into the small library at the Bureau. The shelves had mostly law books stacked on bookshelves with two long tables and several chairs spread out in the room. Sarah sat in the one farthest from the door and had a good view of the entire room. It was quiet, and dust coated everything.

Rosen brought in several thick files, some of them old and worn. He stacked them on the table she was sitting at and said, "Well, you're getting to do something a lot of people wish they could do. Go through the FBI's files on the Black Dahlia murder."

"I never heard of it until now."

"It's pretty famous. I think they made some movies, too." He stared at the files and then at Sarah. "You sure you're okay with this?"

"You don't need to worry about me. I'm sure I've seen worse."

He shook his head. "Probably not."

With that, he left, leaving her alone again in the library. The files were numerous, and she didn't know where to start. So she just started at the top.

The first file had a black-and-white photo of a pretty young brunette. She skipped the birthdays, place of birth, and the family history and came to the original reports by the Los Angeles County Sheriff's Office and the District Attorney's Office, as well as the FBI.

The Black Dahlia was a nickname given to a young woman named Elizabeth Short by the newspapers after she had been killed. William Randolph Hearst himself was rumored to have handpicked the nickname because he thought it sounded dramatic. On January 15, 1947, her body was found in Leimert Park in Los Angeles. The body had been cut in half at the waist. It was found by a young mother walking her toddler.

The body had been drained of all blood, and they determined the killer had washed it before dumping it in the park. Every inch of her seemed to be mutilated. Her face had been cut from the corners of her mouth to her ears—the reports referred to it as a "Glasgow smile." Sarah had never heard that term before, so she googled it on her phone. The name originated from gangs in Scotland who would cut their victims' mouths at the corners and then beat the victims so their cheek muscles contracted and tore their cheeks across the face, leaving a scar like a large smile.

Portions of Elizabeth Short's breasts and thighs had been removed, as had the intestines, which were found at the scene. She had a tattoo that had been cut off and shoved inside her throat. A photograph was included in the file. The body had its arms over its head and its legs spread. It wasn't a natural position. Someone, Sarah guessed, would've had to arrange her that way.

The actual death wasn't particularly detailed. In fact, the autopsy report stated she had "Female trouble." Sarah wondered if, in the late '40s, it was improper to discuss anything relating to female sexual anatomy, even in an autopsy report.

The bulk of the file was the confessions of at least forty people claiming to be the murderer, and it was in the papers on and off for the past fifty years.

The suspects were what interested Sarah. An enormous list was attached to one folder. It included politicians, police officers, actors, bankers, and everyone in between. She just skimmed the huge list rather than reading through it.

One note caught her attention. A detective in Cleveland named John St. John was investigating a series of murders known as the Cleveland Torso Murders, which occurred in the 1930s to the 1950s. The murders were just as brutal as the Black Dahlia. The killer castrated the male victims and mutilated the genitals of the female victims. He then decapitated them and cut them in half. Some of the victims had evidence of chemical burns as well.

Forensic investigation not being what it was now, most of the victims in the Cleveland Torso Murders weren't identified, and they never found the heads of many of them. Detective St. John believed that the killer in the Torso Murders had also killed the Black Dahlia and then fled Los Angeles. The suspect he was going to arrest died before they could get there.

As of right now, sixty years after the crime, the killer of the Black Dahlia, and the Cleveland Torso Murders, was still considered at large.

Sarah stared at one of the photos from the Cleveland murders. She could almost believe the victim was still alive, except for the fact that she'd been severed completely in half. The lower portion of the torso with the legs was placed away from the top portion, and most of one of the breasts was gone. Revulsion filled her, and she had to close the file. Though she felt disgust and pity, no images came to her. Sometimes, she'd found, when she really didn't want to see anything, her mind closed itself off and nothing would come to her. She wondered if unconsciously she really didn't want to see what had happened to the Black Dahlia.

"How's it coming?"

Startled, her head snapped up, and she saw Giovanni standing there. Sarah pressed the button on her phone and brought up her home screen to see the time.

"Wow, have I been in here almost two hours?"

"Time flies when you're having fun."

Sarah leaned back in the seat. "Nothing yet. Other than the fact that this is horrific."

Giovanni nodded. "It's a legendary case. William Randolph Hearst was the one pushing it in the papers. Back then, the police were in league with the reporters. The reporters would be at the police station, interviewing witnesses and fielding calls. But of course they didn't want to catch the killer—the chase was what sold papers, so they buried a lot of good evidence. They probably would've caught the sicko if it hadn't been for the reporters."

"I got that impression." She looked down at the stacks of paper. "So Nathan Archer copied this killer, and the Blood Dahlia is copying Nathan Archer?"

He shrugged. "Looks like it. Honestly, we're kinda at a loss. Arnold will never say that because he doesn't want Kyle or Gillian to know, since this case has so much press. But the killer washes the bodies with bleach and some kind of acid before he dumps them. There's no DNA, no fibers… the most we got was a tire track near one of the bodies. We ran the type of tires but could only determine it belonged to a van or truck. Which narrows it down to about twenty million cars."

"Why's he copying Nathan Archer? That's one small case in the middle of nowhere."

He shrugged. "Who knows? Arnold says there's stuff in the world you just can't explain. You have to live with the mystery."

She exhaled as she realized she would have to read these files again. "I think maybe the mystery is better than knowing sometimes."

He grinned. "Let me know if you need anything," he said, turning and heading for the door.

Once she was alone again, she shuffled through the files until she found the first one she had read and opened it again, starting at the beginning.

28

By eight o'clock in the evening, Sarah had read through the files three times. She stared at the Black Dahlia crime scene photos until they no longer bothered her. Every suspect's name had been read aloud to see if anything would occur, but nothing did. No one jumped out at her.

She wished this stupid thing, whatever it was that she had inside her, would just be like a switch that turned on and off. The hardest part was that she had no control over it, and it was hard to use it for the benefit of anything. How could she, when she didn't know when or where something would hit her?

Sarah decided three reads was enough. Whatever she had gotten from the original Black Dahlia killing was already in her head. Nothing else was going to be gained by staring at grisly photos. She closed the files, stacked them neatly in a pile, and then rose.

The muscles in her back and legs ached, and she stretched her arms out as wide as she could. Then she squatted down, feeling the deep stretch in her thighs before she stood up and walked out of the library.

Outside the windows was darkness dappled with city lights. Inside the Bureau's offices, a few agents were still typing on their computers, and a cleaner was vacuuming in the far corner, and that was it. The place was empty, and Sarah felt uncomfortable being there without Giovanni or Rosen.

One agent, a woman in a black suit with the coat slung over the back of her chair, was typing up what looked like a police report. Sarah walked up to her, blushing, and said, "Excuse me."

The woman looked at her, her face stern. "Yes?"

"Um, is there, like, a cafeteria or something on this floor?"

"No, but down the hall that way are a few vending machines."

"Thanks."

The woman turned back to her computer without saying another word.

Sarah said, "So are you typing up a report on a case?"

The woman stopped, her eyes not leaving the computer screen. "Look, no offense, but I'd like to finish this and get outta here. I don't really have time to talk."

"Oh, right. Sorry."

Sarah turned and walked around a few cubicles before she found the hallway that the woman had pointed to. She looked both ways and saw the dim glow of vending machines on the left. Giovanni was off to the right, speaking with someone. She kept her eyes on the linoleum floor as she walked to the vending machines.

Just a few days ago, she was a bartender who got drunk every night, and now she was walking the halls of the Federal Bureau of Investigation and reading fifty-year-old files about famous murders. Life sure was odd.

The vending machines had the worst food possible, nothing but greasy meat chock-full of preservatives. Sarah glanced over the selection quickly. On the bottom was a small tray of salad with a side of ranch in a pouch. She decided against it and chose some coffee in the machine next to it. She took out some dollar bills and inserted them into the machine. As the second one entered, she squealed and crumpled over, her fingers shooting up to her temples. The coffee missed the cup and spilled onto the floor.

The pounding had started again, and fragments ran before her eyes. A man in older clothing, something from a different decade, cutting a woman's face. The woman was bound at the ankles and wrists. He slashed her body and cut pieces off, throwing them around on a bare cement floor.

Then a man in more modern clothing with vivid colors was doing the same thing to another girl, this one blond. The girl begged for him to stop and screamed for help, but they were in the woods with no one else around. The woman tried to run. The man let her get only so far before he caught up again and slashed her thighs, then flipped her onto her back and cut into her face again.

The images stopped. Sarah was breathing heavily. As she pulled herself upright, she felt the trickle of blood on her face. She reached up and touched just under her nose—two streams of blood, one from each nostril.

She covered her nose with one hand and searched for some napkins. She found a roll of paper towels behind her near a sink and unrolled a few, then pinched her nose and tilted her head back, her fingers pressed firmly against her nose as she leaned against the counter.

"Hey," Giovanni said, rushing up to her with a look of concern. "You okay? What happened?"

"I'm fine. It just hit me again."

"What happened to your nose?"

She shook her head, her eyes on the ceiling. "I don't know. It's never happened before."

Giovanni stood there a moment and watched her. "I think that's enough for one day. I'll drive you home."

The car ride was pleasant. The rain had stopped and left that wet-cement smell that doused the entire city. Sarah kept her window down for the entire drive and took it in. She watched the passing shops and stores, the people on street corners hanging out on a Friday night.

"What happened exactly?" Giovanni asked.

"I saw something."

"What?"

"I saw that girl, the Black Dahlia. A man was cutting her somewhere, like in a basement. He was cutting her face. And then it switched, and I saw another man cutting another woman. Their clothes had changed, and it was more recent. Really recent. He was chasing her through the woods or, like, a forest or something. She was trying to get away from him, and he cut her thighs to stop her, and she fell. He climbed on top of her and started cutting her face—the same exact way the Black Dahlia was cut."

"In the woods?"

"Yeah."

"There was only one victim found in the woods."

"Was she blond? With blue eyes?"

Giovanni glanced at her. "Yeah, she was. You think that's who you saw?"

"I don't know."

They pulled to a stop in front of her apartment building. Giovanni put the car in park, and they both sat quietly for a moment.

"I don't think this is good for you," he said. "I shouldn't have pushed for this."

"I'm fine. And believe me, without an education, it's the best job I can get. Sixty thousand a year with government benefits is awesome. I've never had health insurance before."

"It's not good for you to see all these things. You said you've never bled after you saw something. What does it mean that you just did?"

"It's nothing. I'm just exhausted. Some sleep will fix me right up; I'm sure of it."

Giovanni exhaled and looked at her. "There are other jobs with health insurance."

"Not that need what I can do. Don't worry about me. I'll be fine." She opened her door. "Goodnight, Agent Adami."

He grinned. "Night."

Sarah stepped out of the car and shut the door behind her. As she was making her way up the sidewalk to her building, she saw a man standing out front. He had his hands tucked into the pockets on his coat. A beard and glasses covered his face, and he looked right at her.

She ignored him and went to the front entrance and input the code to get into the building on the keycode entry. The man came up to her, and she jumped and reached for the keys in her pocket, the only thing she could think of to use as a weapon.

"Hey, it's okay," the man said, holding up his hands. He reached into his coat and pulled out a *Washington Post* ID badge. "I'm Kenneth Lott. I'm with the *Post*. I'm a reporter. It's okay. It's okay."

Sarah felt stupid and tried to force herself to calm down.

"There a problem here?" Giovanni said, rushing up.

"I'm Kenneth Lott with the *Post*. I just wanted to ask you a few questions if that's okay, Ms. King?"

"What questions?" she said. "About what?"

"We were told that you were a consultant on the Blood Dahlia murders, and I wanted to just speak to you about that for a few minutes."

"She doesn't want to talk," Giovanni said.

"No," she said. "It's okay. What do you want to know?"

"You were spotted at the scene where they found the most recent victim, at Director Hanks's house. What exactly is your role in the investigation?"

Giovanni said, "Sarah, you don't need to talk to him."

"I have nothing to hide. It's fine."

Lott was shifting from foot to foot, either cold or nervous.

"I'm an assistant to Assistant Director Kyle Vidal."

"Assisting with what?"

"Just a personal assistant. That's all."

"Well, the thing is, we ran your name, and it doesn't appear that you come from a law enforcement or criminology background. What exactly is your role?"

"Hey," Giovanni interrupted, pushing between them. "You sneak up on her as she's walking into her house in the dark? Get lost. Now."

"I'm on public property. I don't have to go anywhere."

"She's an employee of the FBI, and she's feeling harassed. I said take a hike."

Lott looked from one of them to the other then grumbled something as he turned and walked away. Sarah folded her arms and stared at Giovanni.

"I don't need protection," she said.

"You don't deal with those guys. They're vultures."

"I can take care of myself and speak for myself. I have a father. I don't need another."

Giovanni stared at her a moment. "I'm sorry. I just thought… you don't have a lot of experience with those guys. They're friendly to your face then stab you in the back the first chance they get."

She sighed and gave him a soft, quick peck on the lips that hardly registered with her as a kiss at all but seemed to brighten his mood. "You're cute. But don't speak for me again."

"I won't."

The door shut behind her, and she glanced over her shoulder to see Giovanni walking away with a smile on his face. He was, in a way, adorable—like some teenager with a crush. Despite the fact that he had seen so much war and death, the worst that humanity had to offer, there was a certain naïveté to him that was endearing.

The apartment was empty and dull as Sarah stepped inside. She turned on all the lights, sat on her couch, and flipped on the television as she slipped her boots off. A *Vampire Diaries* marathon was on, and she put her feet up on the couch and leaned back.

29

Daniel Wolfgram stared at himself in the mirror.

The button-front shirt he wore was a plain solid blue. The pants were Dockers, beige. The sports coat was a simple black, no brand name. His shoes were leather but bought from a discount bin in an outlet mall. Being single and a tenured professor at Penn State, he could certainly afford better, but everything about him was designed to give one impression: normal.

From his haircut to the socks he wore, nothing stood out about him. Everything was chosen carefully to ensure that people who saw or met him remembered very little about him.

Wolfgram put the jacket on. It was nearly noon, and his class started at three—a remedial class on calculus for students in nonscience majors every Saturday. He had personally volunteered to teach the class. Though it was held at the Penn State campus, everyone from the surrounding colleges and universities was invited to attend for a nominal fee.

The van was certainly his favorite transportation, but the vehicle he drove on a daily basis was his beige Oldsmobile. The car, like his clothing, was meant to fit in anywhere and not stand out. Rather than buy a new car, he had bought a twenty-year-old car and rebuilt the engine. The scientific literature on memory indicated that older objects didn't stay in the working memory of observers for as long as newer, flashier objects did.

As always before getting in his car, Wolfgram checked the blinkers, the tires, and the mirrors, and only then did he get in and start the engine. The car rumbled to life, and he pulled out of the garage. Sunshine filled the car, but he chose not to roll down the windows, tinted at exactly the legal limit. He didn't require GPS, though he had it. He knew this city well and had driven around for hours exploring neighborhoods he'd never been to and never would have gone to otherwise. Philadelphia was large, and it had taken him years to gain this sort of comfort, but he felt that he could start driving from anywhere in the city and know exactly how to get home.

Within twenty minutes, he was in front of the white condominiums he was looking for. They were stacked on top of each other like boxes and spread out for almost half a city block. *Efficient use of space—cram as many people into living quarters as possible.* He knew that a small fire would quickly destroy the entire complex. He pictured families running around on fire as they tried to escape.

He parked in front of the condominium and would've honked, except that he enjoyed being in other people's homes. He got out of the car and knocked. Dara answered, still pulling her shoes on.

"Hey. Sorry, I'm running a little late," she said.

"No worries."

"Would you like to come in?"

"Certainly."

The condo was decorated tastefully, he thought. The pictures on the mantel of the fireplace were mostly photos of her son, but there were also a few of her sister and extended family. A glass side table held a flower arrangement next to a white couch and glass coffee table.

"Make yourself at home," she said, disappearing back into the bedroom.

Wolfgram stared at the flatscreen television mounted on the wall. He could see his reflection in it. Off to the right was a silver urn with gold trim.

"So where we going?" she called from the bedroom.

"A little place I know near downtown. You'll like it. It's Middle Eastern."

He turned to the photos. The young boy, Jake, was smiling in all of them. A few were sports photos, but there was one where he stood on a sand dune, staring off at the sunset. Wolfgram felt nothing for children and didn't understand their allure. Why people would wish to share their lives with a creature that could give very little back was beyond him.

Dara stepped out, her hair done and her tight black dress on. Much more fashionable than lunch deserved. Wolfgram grinned and said, "You look lovely," because he knew it was what he was expected to say. He then took her arm and led her out of the condo and to his car.

As they drove, he would glance at her when he thought she wasn't paying attention. Having a woman near him like this was both thrilling and uncomfortable.

"What type of music do you like?" he asked.

"Oh, just about anything. I think I have Duran Duran in my car. Child of the '80s, I guess."

Wolfgram turned on the stereo and attempted to find something she might enjoy. The closest he came was a rock station playing a song he didn't recognize.

"So, where you from?" Dara asked.

"Los Angeles, originally. How about yourself?"

"Born-and-raised Philly girl. Sometimes I think about moving, though. I mean, don't you think it's weird to be born, grow up, and die in the same place? It feels unnatural, somehow."

"Perhaps you just need to travel more."

"Maybe. It's hard with work, though. Do you travel a lot?"

"Yes."

"That must be good, right? I guess it beats getting stuck in one place like I did."

"It's a fine line—do it too much and you become a stranger in your own home."

The restaurant was a wide-open space with plenty of plants and windows. The ceilings were decorated in frescos, and every waiter had traditional Persian garb. Their waiter seated them at a table in the center of the room, and the conversation wasn't forced. Wolfgram found she liked to do most of the talking, which worked out fine, as he preferred to listen.

She spoke of her family life, of meeting and divorcing her husband, and raising a child as a single mother. The hardest part, she told him, was that it was a son. She couldn't teach him how to be a man, and she was worried that he wouldn't learn about that part of himself.

After lunch, Wolfgram drove her to one of his favorite bars. It was a karaoke bar with a grand piano in the center. The alcohol was high quality, and they had a strict dress code. They catered to a select group of people and wanted to keep it that way.

The bar was crowded, much more so than one would think at lunchtime, enough so that they had to push their way through to order drinks. They found two barstools next to each other and waited as the drinks were made. Wolfgram turned and faced the stage where someone was singing Iron Butterfly.

"I didn't picture you in a place like this," she said loudly over the singing.

"Really? Why not?"

"I don't know. You seem more like a fancy restaurant type of guy."

Wolfgram ordered more drinks over the course of an hour. He would stare at Dara when she was paying attention to what was happening onstage—the way she would smile and the twinkle in her eye.

After four drinks, they left the bar and Wolfgram drove her home. She spent the entire drive telling him about the time she was thrown out of a bar in college for fighting with her boyfriend's lover. Wolfgram listened just enough to be able to nod when he had to or ask a follow-up question. But his attention was filled with the soft touch of her hand: her fingers lay over his right hand, his left on the steering wheel.

The sensation was an odd one. He thought he should pull away but never did.

When he stopped in front of her condo, she didn't get out right away. She looked down the parking lot at a neighbor's home, a slight smile on her lips.

"I had a lot of fun," she said.

"So did I."

"Maybe we can do it again sometime?"

"Yes, I would like that," he said.

She leaned in and kissed him on the lips. "Bye."

He watched her, all the way to her door.

The kiss had been quick and probably meant nothing. Just a small display, but to him it was the oddest feeling he had ever had. A woman kissed him on the lips.

Wolfgram did a U-turn and glanced into her condo before driving away.

30

Sarah opened her door the next morning and saw Giovanni standing there, holding two coffees from Starbucks. He handed one to her and said, "Ready?"

"Yup."

She locked her door and followed him down the hallway and out to the car. Rosen was sitting in the passenger seat, busy on his phone, and Giovanni set his coffee down on the roof to open the door for her. She got in and said, to Rosen, "Hey."

"Hey," Rosen answered, still on the phone.

Giovanni pulled away from the curb, sipping his coffee. He glanced back at Sarah. When she noticed, he looked away.

"So where we going?" she said.

"Wharton State Forest," Giovanni said. "It's where we found the body dumped in the woods." He reached over to Rosen's lap and removed a file to hand back to Sarah. "That's her."

Sarah opened the file. Michelle Anand. Twenty-two years old. Her official profession was listed as "actress." The photograph of her looked like something an actress would send to agents.

"Why do you guys still use files?" she asked.

"What do you mean?" Giovanni asked.

"Just thought the FBI would be all high tech."

"The FBI's the slowest of any government agency to change. J. Edgar Hoover wanted tradition and almost nothing else. I don't think he really cared that much about results even. The tradition was what mattered. Don't you think, Arnold?"

"He was a sick son of a bitch who didn't understand a lick about the Constitution. I prefer not to associate him with the Bureau. Take this on-ramp over here."

Sarah flipped through the rest of the file as they drove. It was just… sad. That was the only word that came to mind. Michelle was a runaway at thirteen and lived on the streets until she was almost eighteen, when she met and married a much older man. Sarah could only imagine what it would take for a young girl to choose to live on the streets rather than at home. She wondered if the parents even cared when they were notified of her death.

The sprawling urban landscape turned into dense forests that she couldn't see more than a dozen feet into. Sarah stared at the trees. Nature, something she'd spent her entire life surrounded by, now made her uneasy, and she didn't know why.

Giovanni turned down a side road that quickly became so bumpy that Sarah nearly flew out of her seat. Twenty minutes later, when they were deep in the woods, Giovanni stopped the car and both men stepped out. Sarah followed, leaving Michelle's file on the backseat.

The trees engulfed the road, taking over the path beaten out by men. Not enough people traveled there to keep the road well maintained. Other than the tracks they'd just made, Sarah didn't see any other signs that people came here at all.

"Her body was found over here," Rosen said, trekking into a thicket of trees.

Sarah followed. The trees were only a few feet apart, and she had to sidestep to get through the brush. After about thirty feet or so, the trees thinned out, and they stood in a small clearing, hidden from view of the road. No one could've seen anybody back here. Trees surrounded the space like a wall.

"Body was there," Rosen said, motioning with his chin to a spot on the downhill slope of the clearing.

Sarah glanced at both men and then walked over. She wasn't sure what she was expected to do. What little control she had came only when she concentrated by herself. Standing in a creepy forest with two FBI agents watching her every move wasn't exactly the ideal situation for concentrating.

She walked down the slope about halfway and then looked back. "Here?"

"Just down a few more feet, but yeah."

She took a few steps and stopped. The clearing, in the light of the sun, could be considered beautiful. But it was so hidden from everything else, so silent, that the beauty was overwhelmed by the eeriness.

She scanned from one end of the clearing to the other and down at the grass and dirt under her boots. She kicked a rock, watching it tumble down the hill before sighing and looking around again. Turning back to Rosen and Giovanni, they were staring at her.

"Anything?" Giovanni asked.

She shook her head. Out here in the wilderness, it hit her how silly this all was. Granted, she had seen things no one could explain, but she could totally understand why some people wouldn't listen to her no matter what. Even if they were potentially in danger.

Turning around to head back and admit defeat, something caught her eye. She stopped and stared at it. Something blue in the grass, farther down the hill.

Sarah began walking toward it, glancing over her shoulder to reassure herself that Giovanni and Rosen were still there. The color was slightly higher than the ground on which it lay. As she got closer, she saw something crumpled and stretched out over a few feet.

Only when she got near did she see it was really a body.

A young woman in a blue sweatshirt. She wore jeans and white sneakers... and her face had been removed. A clean incision that ran around the edge of the skull. The torso had been cut in half at the waist.

Sarah closed her eyes tightly.

"Am I dead?"

The voice was soft, quiet. Sarah opened her eyes and stared down at the faceless upper body. The eyes were still there, blue and frightened.

"Yes," Sarah said.

"I had so much to do. I never... I never had children. I really wanted children."

Despite the revulsion, Sarah kneeled down next to the woman. With her voice hardly more than a whisper, she said, "Who did this to you?"

"I really wanted children. Since I was a little girl. I thought I would be a good mother."

"Michelle, who did this to you?"

The woman began to cry. Sarah reached out, her hand hovering above Michelle's a moment before resting on it, their fingers intertwining. Sarah could feel the cold skin against hers, the ridges of the nails as they touched her own hand. As far as she could tell, Michelle Anand was right there in front of her.

"Michelle, tell me—who did this to you?"

"He…" She began to weep. Tears rolled down her skinless face.

Sarah didn't look away this time. Instead, she swallowed and said, "I'm so sorry."

"I don't want to die." The woman grabbed Sarah's arm with both hands. "I don't want to die!"

"I'm sorry, there's nothing I can do."

"No. No! You can do it. You can stop it. You have to stop it."

Sarah felt a trickle of fear down her back. "I can't."

The woman's eyes were now blazing with fury. She pulled herself up, screaming, "You will do it! You will."

"I can't. I'm sorry, I can't," Sarah kept saying over and over.

The woman wrapped her hands around Sarah's throat, and Sarah screamed. She fell onto her back, staring at the sky, her breath slowly choking away.

"What happened?" Giovanni said, running up to her. He put his hands under her and lifted her up. "You okay? What happened? You screamed."

Sarah looked around quickly—only Giovanni and Rosen in sight. Her breathing was labored and quick, her heart pounding so furiously she thought it would jump out of her throat.

"I saw... I saw her. I saw her. She was right here."

"Who was? Michelle Anand?"

Sarah nodded.

Giovanni looked at Rosen, whose expression didn't change.

"What did she say?" Giovanni asked.

"She... nothing. Nothing that can help us. She was frantic. She knew she was dead. She knew."

Giovanni glanced up at Rosen again. "I think I've had enough of the woods," he said.

"Me too." Sarah was on her feet. It took a few moments for her to adjust and regain her balance.

As they began trekking back up the incline, they heard something. The snap of a small branch breaking.

Both Rosen and Giovanni froze.

"I don't think we're alone," Giovanni said.

Rosen was quiet a moment, scanning the line of trees in front of them. "No, we're not."

Sarah hadn't noticed anything other than natural sounds in the forest. Branches fell and broke all the time. She didn't understand why they appeared so concerned. "It's probably nothing," she said.

"Probably. Let's keep walking."

A breeze was blowing through the trees, making a soft rustling sound that Sarah had loved, like the trees were speaking to her or singing. Until now, she hadn't realized how much she had missed that sound.

Back in between the trees, Giovanni went first, and Rosen was behind her as they made their way through the sharp branches. Just as they saw the car, Giovanni dashed to the right. Rosen spun around and ran back, sprinting in an arc back behind them.

"Hey," Sarah said, "what's going on?"

Neither of them replied. Sarah felt the trees around her, the sense of calm and peace now gone. She thought of the severed torso, the fingers clawing at her, begging for help. The thought sent a shiver up her back.

Someone yelped in pain. Despite the fear, Sarah ran toward the sound. Had something happened to Giovanni? She rounded a thicket of trees and saw Giovanni on top of another man—the man from last night, Kenneth Lott.

Rosen had his sidearm pointed at the man as Giovanni slapped handcuffs on him.

"Wait a second," Rosen said, putting his sidearm away. "I know him."

"Yeah, I do, too." Giovanni said, easing off. "He's with the *Post*."

Rosen laughed. "Is that what you told them, Kenny? The *Post*." Rosen chuckled some more. "Uncuff him."

Giovanni did so, and Lott pulled away from him like a child who didn't want to be touched.

"What the hell, Arnold?" Kenny demanded.

"What're you doing here, Kenny?"

"I'm following a lead."

"What lead?"

Lott looked at Sarah and then back. "None of your business."

As Lott began to walk away, Giovanni reached for him, but Rosen said, "Let him go."

"He's not with the *Post*?" Sarah asked.

Rosen shook his head, fingering a tear in his pants from sprinting through the trees. "Kenny couldn't get coffee for the reporters at the *Post*. He works for a sleazy news and gossip website called the Skid Row Gossip. They interview porn stars and high-level drug dealers and things. Before that, he used to be a cop but got thrown off the force for taking bribes."

"What the hell's he doing following us?" Giovanni said.

"I don't know. But it won't be good for us."

31

On the drive back into the city, Sarah didn't speak. Even when Giovanni or Rosen asked her a question, she kept quiet and stared out the window. Words just wouldn't come to her right now.

She'd seen the dead before, or at least what she thought were the dead. But they were in the background, like inanimate objects almost. Hardly interacting with her.

Except for one other time: when Sheriff Bullock had brought her out to see one of Nathan Archer's victims. Sarah remembered that one clearly because the dead woman had seen her, knew Sarah was there, and could speak to her. Just like Michelle Anand had.

"I'm really hungry," Sarah said. "Can we stop somewhere?"

"Sure."

Giovanni took the next exit without a word, and soon they had parked in front of a fast-food chicken place. Next door was a gas station that seemed to cater to semi-trucks, because the parking lot was full of them. Most of the truckers parked their vehicles in back, on a wide-open lot before walking over to the restaurant.

As Sarah stood in line, she caught a glimpse of herself in the reflection cast on the glass door. For a moment, she didn't recognize who it was. The image in the glass wasn't hers. But when her general shape and then her detailed features came in, she closed her eyes and opened them again. It was Michelle Anand.

She looked at Giovanni, who was staring up at the menu. Cleary, he didn't see it. Neither did Rosen or anybody else. They'd all be panicking if they had. She was the only one.

Sarah looked away for a moment and then looked back. It didn't help. The other woman was still there. When Sarah lifted a hand, Michelle Anand would lift a hand in the glass. When she opened her mouth, Michelle would do the same.

Sarah crossed to the glass and gazed at herself, into her eyes, to see even the slightest deviation of the reflection from her movements, but there was none. The image was not Michelle… it was her.

"Do you know what you want?"

Sarah snapped out of it and looked at Giovanni, who was still staring up at the menu. "Yeah," she said, going back. "Um, just a chicken sandwich and some French fries, please."

She watched as the two men ordered for the three of them and then paid. As they left the line to wait for their order, Giovanni came over to her and said, "You sure you're okay? You look kinda pale."

"I'm fine. Just exhausted."

Sarah turned to the glass, and Michelle was gone. It was just her again.

They sat by the window, and as they ate, Giovanni said, "You think Lott's gonna run a story?"

Rosen shrugged as he took a bite of a chicken sandwich. "Who cares if he does? No one reads that garbage but celebrity news junkies."

"Not necessarily," Sarah said. "I've seen stuff run on things like that first, and then the big news outlets run it later."

"That's true," Giovanni said. "They'll pick up a story from a smaller news outlet and run with it if it's juicy."

Rosen wiped his lips with a napkin. "I've known Kenny for ten years. He's their investigative reporter on the actual news. The problem is their demographic doesn't read the news, so he doesn't get anything but a link to the story on the main website. I don't think it's a problem." He looked at Sarah. "What did you see, Sarah? What did you really see?"

Sarah didn't say anything for an uncomfortably long time. "A woman," she finally said. "Michelle."

"How'd you know it was Michelle?"

"You had a picture in the file. It was her. I mean… she didn't have her face, but I could still tell. The hair and the ears and neck. Her face was gone."

Rosen looked at Giovanni and then back. "Did she say anything?"

"She asked me if she was dead. Then she tried to get me to help her. She said she regretted not having children. I told you, murder victims are not happy to be there. They're confused and terrified, and they lash out."

"Did you see anything else?"

"I don't think so. She was wearing a sweatshirt. It was blue and said 'Penn State' across the front."

32

The offices of Skid Row Gossip were in a boxy brown building. Next to their office was a pornography studio that specialized in married couples having sex with strangers, usually just men off the street who weren't even paid. Lott had done it a couple of times himself and found it a fun distraction. He would sleep with those women anyway—what was the difference if he did it on tape? As he parked and entered the building, he thought maybe he should ask for another session.

The elevators were scratched up inside. Lott stared at one long scratch that went from the upper right corner to the lower left, as if someone had tried to cut the elevator wall in half. He leaned back and took the flask out of his pocket. Before the doors opened, he'd knocked back enough to hold him over for the next few hours.

As he walked down the hallway, he pulled a piece of gum out of his pocket. Shoving it into his mouth, he waited a moment to let it take effect before opening the door and stepping inside.

The offices were a sprawling landscape of cubicles. There were really only two offices with doors and one was for the owner who, as far as Lott could tell, owned the pornography studio next door as well. The other office was for the website's editor, Dave Sa.

Lott went to his cubicle and checked his email. Though the offices were old, and technically he could've just as easily done his job from home, he liked the busy atmosphere. Phones were always ringing, and someone was always discussing a story. A lot of their content came from independent contractors, but they had a few full-time reporters. At least, he liked to call them reporters. Two were dedicated to celebrity gossip and had the best jobs at the site. One was in Hollywood and would spend her days tracking down celebrities at the gym or grocery store and try to get an interview or a photo that no one else had. Another was in New York and tried to do the same thing.

The third reporter was Lott. His job was to follow up on any sensational crime stories. Wives who had killed husbands or their children, police chases, politicians caught with prostitutes or drugs, and most of all, serial killers.

Serial killers were always hot. But this one, the Blood Dahlia, felt different. This was a national, even worldwide, story that was happening right in his backyard. And the high-brow journalists, the ones who considered Lott and his kin bottom-feeders, weren't doing much of a job keeping up with the investigation.

Lott knew this was special when he'd found out that a body had been dumped on the front porch of the director of Behavioral Science. The gall it took to do that was off the charts. The Blood Dahlia wasn't someone strangling random hitchhikers. Lott was convinced he was something the world hadn't seen before.

Going through his email, he saw he had a message that Dave wanted to see him. Lott pulled out his flask again and took a few more sips before heading into Dave's office.

Dave didn't appear to be the kind of man who would run a place like this. He was neat and thin, with horn-rimmed glasses. Today, he was dressed in a Hawaiian shirt and jeans.

"Have a seat," Dave said in his somewhat effeminate voice.

"What's up?"

Dave finished typing and then leaned back in his chair. "Just wanted to see what's going on with that Blood Dahlia thing."

"It's actually pretty interesting. That new person that the FBI brought in, Sarah King—you remember me talking about her?"

"The one you couldn't pull up a background on, right?"

"Yeah. So they took her to two crime scenes. One was the director's house, and then they took her to the first victim, or at least the first body they found—Michelle Anand. She was killed out in the forest, and they drove her all the way there and just had her, like, look around."

"What'dya mean, 'look around'?"

"Like, literally just fucking *stand there* and look around. It was really weird."

"Hm. What else?"

"Well, I paid my contact at the FBI a thousand bucks for the background file they got on her, and she said she'd get it to me today."

Dave took in a deep breath, as if rolling the case around in his head. Though he was not a man someone in polite society would look up to or emulate, Lott knew he had a certain knack for this type of business. He instinctively understood that to be successful, you gave people what *they* wanted rather than what *you* wanted to give them.

"Well," Dave finally said, "serial killers are hot. We got over three million views on that piece you did about the body at the director's house. Keep it up. I really would like to know who Sarah King is and why she's being taken to crime scenes."

"I should know by tonight, hopefully."

Dave turned back to his computer. "Keep up the good work."

33

The night seemed to close in around Sarah as she sat in her living room. Giovanni had called, but he had work to catch up on and wouldn't be able to come over tonight. With Jeannie barely able to hold a conversation on the phone, that left Sarah by herself.

Television could entertain her for only so long before she grew restless. She tried reading a book, a biography of someone famous, but that didn't hold her interest, either. Her guts were balled up, and as anxious as she was, she wanted to be out and surrounded by other people.

She dressed in jeans and a nice black shirt that exposed her arms. Knee-high boots finished the outfit off, and though she didn't care how she looked, she checked herself in the mirror anyway.

Once outside, she wasn't quite sure where to go, so she googled all the bars near her. A couple of miles away was a place she'd never been to. She got into her car.

The bar, a place called Bricks, was more of a nightclub than someplace people went to relax and have a few drinks. The parking was between the club and a factory, and she found a spot about a block away and walked.

The night air was cool and gave her goose bumps. She ran her hands over her arms and then stopped, as though she could fight the cold just by ignoring it. She walked past several people in line at a door marked VIP, right up to the bouncer there, and said, "I'd like to go in, please."

He looked her up and down and then nodded and let her past. Most clubs and bars let women in for free because without the women, the men wouldn't go.

The club was dimly lit and had two floors. The music was so loud it hurt her ears. But being in a crowd comforted her, and it was wall to wall, so crowded she could hardly move. As she made her way across the dance floor to the bar, she caught a glimpse of someone staring at her. Her head whipped around to see who it was, but they were already gone.

Sarah leaned against the bar and ordered a Long Island iced tea: the drink that provided the most alcohol in the least amount of space, if done correctly. But when the drink came, she could tell this bartender didn't know how to mix. The drink was mostly cola and very little of anything else. Before she could complain, a man came and sat next to her.

"Hi," he said.

She didn't look at him. Instead, she sipped her drink and debated telling the bartender how to actually make it correctly. "Hi."

"I saw you from across the club. I just wanted to come and introduce myself. My name's Brandon."

"Sarah."

"Cool. Whatchya drinkin'?"

Sarah looked at him. The man was cute, with brown hair that came to his shoulders and a tattoo on his shoulder that came up to his neck. Normally, she would be flirting right back and asking him to buy her more drinks. But the words wouldn't come to her. Something was wrong that she couldn't quite understand.

Soon the iced tea was nearly gone, and she asked the bartender for a shot of tequila.

"Lemme get that," Brandon said.

After the shots, they ordered another, and another. By the fourth shot, Sarah felt much better—maybe not better, but looser, as though she could actually have a conversation with someone without unloading all of the crap going on in her head. And that's what she did with Brandon. They talked about traveling and what types of liquor they liked, tanning, colleges, and work—nothing to do with death or blood. Nothing to do with horror.

The conversation was pleasant, and toward the end she was laughing at jokes of his that weren't even funny. At some point, she wasn't sure when, he had stood up next to her and put his arms around her. At the sensation of his touch, only one thought came to her: Giovanni.

"Wait," she said, pulling his hands off, "wait. I can't."

"Come on, let's get outta here."

She shook her head. Stepping away from the bar, she said, "I can't. I'm sorry."

Brandon watched her a moment and then mumbled, "Bitch."

She turned away, humiliated and confused. The dance floor was even more packed now than it had been before, and she slipped through the crowd. Several male hands pawed at her, copping feels—something she normally would've turned around and slapped them for. But she didn't care right now. Right now, she had to get away from all these people. The exit seemed so far away that she just ducked into the bathrooms.

There was a line for each stall in the black-and-white tiled bathroom. She pushed past the lines and stood in front of the mirror, staring at herself. The faucet was already on, and she looked down to turn it off. When she looked back up into the mirror, she wasn't the one gazing back at her.

Sarah jumped back. She thought about running, just taking off right now, not looking back. But she couldn't move, as though all the muscles in her legs had turned to ice, and the pain in her head was back.

Michelle Anand stared back at her from the mirror. Her face was still missing, and Sarah couldn't look right now. Instead, she stared at the sink.

"What do want?" she said.

"You have to stop him," Michelle said.

Sarah shook her head. "I can't."

"Yes, you can."

"How?"

"You have to stop him, Sarah."

Sarah looked up from the faucet. "How did you know my name?" she whispered.

"You have to stop him. There's no one else."

"Who did this to you? Michelle, who did this to you?"

"He's the father of lies. I don't know his real name…"

"What did he look like?"

But the image was gone, along with the phantom pain in her head.

Sarah ran out of the bathroom and raced through the club. Getting out into the night air helped the nausea she was feeling but did nothing for the pain.

Jumping into her car, she looked around. She was alone. She put the key into the ignition and started it. As she glanced in her rearview, she saw Michelle Anand's faceless head staring back at her.

She gasped and screamed, but when she turned around, the backseat was empty. Sarah was breathing so hard she thought she might be hyperventilating. She put her hand to her heart and just tried to calm herself.

Once she had opened her mind up to it, the doors were much harder to close. She hadn't realized until now that each time she allowed it all in, the doors grew weaker. And the most frightening thought she had ever had struck her just then: What if the doors simply didn't close anymore? What if every moment of her life was filled with the screaming dead—with those who'd had everything taken from them and didn't know how to get it back?

That, she decided, would be a life she would not want to live.

34

Kenneth Lott woke up early, before 7:00 a.m., and had a bowl of breakfast cereal with coffee. Spiced up, of course, with just a small amount of whiskey—his favorite morning drink. He read the paper as he ate, the op-eds first, then the headline news section, and then the gossip section. Nothing terribly interesting, and certainly nothing about the Blood Dahlia, as if they had already captured him, and the news was too old to pay any attention to.

He would be the first. This story was his chance for actual journalistic credentials. In college, he'd majored in communications with an eye toward going into journalism, but the market was so tough to break into that he decided to find something else until he could find a decent job. That something else had been being a cop.

He worked for the Philadelphia Police Department, primarily focusing on DUIs. Unlike many other infractions, DUIs were never just about DUIs. A lot of the time he found drugs in the car, or the driver was wanted for burglary, robbery, or some other felony in another jurisdiction. One time he even found a prostitute tied up in the trunk of a gang banger's car. Apparently she'd sold him some weed and scammed him out of five dollars. Five dollars was enough to convince him that she needed to be kidnapped and beaten.

But the problem in Philadelphia, more than in many other jurisdictions, was that police officers were paid so little. Most new officers could expect to qualify for welfare if they had a family. It wasn't until well after he had already been forced out that the city finally upped the pay for its police force. By then it was too late—he'd already been blacklisted for nothing more than turning a blind eye to a few dope pushers who lined his pockets a few times a year.

After breakfast, Lott took a plastic bottle of Coke out of his fridge and dumped half of it into the sink. His liquor cabinet contained only a few bottles, but that was because he knew what he liked to drink: whiskey and rum. Anything else wasn't a man's drink, as far as he was concerned.

He filled the rest of the Coke bottle with whiskey and shook it up, then waited for the carbonation to settle before taking a long drink. Now he was ready for his drive.

As he got into his car, he glanced across the street. Ever since he moved in, he'd been trying to get with the single mother who lived there. She was a teacher, blond, and middle aged with fake breasts and a manic attitude. Her husband, he'd heard, had killed himself in their front room for her to find.

Convinced she wasn't around, Lott got into his car, started it, and pulled out of the driveway.

Lancaster County was only an hour away by freeway. He blared a classic rock station and rolled down his windows but decided it was too cold. Though it was summer, a storm had come through the city and left a chill behind that no one had expected.

By the time Lott took his exit and arrived in the county, half the Coke bottle was gone. He felt fine, better than he had in awhile. The euphoric haze right between buzzed and drunk. After doing what he needed to do here, he should definitely stop at a café somewhere and get some coffee. A DUI was the last thing he needed right now.

The county was farmland—green fields and trees as far as you could see. Rolling emerald hills dotted the horizon, and several roads ran around them, surrounded on either side by classic white farmhouses, churches, and homes. It looked like something from another century.

Lott didn't know much about the Amish. Though everyone thought that everyone in Pennsylvania knew about them, it just wasn't true. They hated interacting with the outside world and thought that it was a corrupting influence. On that point, Lott knew, they had the right idea—cut yourself off from all the horseshit of the world, and have a simple life working with your hands, hot food on the table, and a wife in your cold bed.

GPS was sketchy out here, at best. There were few road signs or addresses. New buildings seemed to pop up without much government red tape, which meant that landmarks weren't a good indicator of where everything was, either.

Lott drove around, having to stop once and let a horse and buggy go past him. He nodded to the passengers, but they just gave him an icy stare.

Finally, he decided he needed to stop and ask for directions. Two women—teenagers, really—were walking along the side of the road, and he pulled to a stop alongside them. They kept their faces forward and quickened their pace.

"Excuse me," he shouted. "I just need directions. Excuse me!"

The girls didn't stop, and he sighed. As he was about to pull away, he saw a man walking toward him from the fields, a shovel hoisted onto his shoulder.

"Hello," the man said. "You lost?"

"Yes," he said, relieved. "I'm looking for the home of Isaac King."

"You got business with him?"

"I do. It's about his daughter, Sarah."

The man held his gaze but didn't move or speak for a moment. "Now what would you want with Sarah?"

"I just have a few questions. Is Isaac here or not?"

The man nodded. "Down the road about a mile then turn left. You'll see homes on the side of the road. Isaac's is the one with the white barn."

"Thanks," Lott said, pulling away.

He drove on, honking and flipping off the teenagers as he zipped past them, and found the turn the man had told him about, and found the houses. Each house was spaced far enough from the others so that neighbors were nearby if you needed something but not so close that they could see into your home.

214

Behind one particularly large home was a white barn. Lott parked in front of the house. He sat in the car awhile and just watched, making certain no one else was around. Then he got out of the car and strode up to the home.

As he stepped onto the front porch, he was amazed by how sturdy the home felt under his feet. Made completely of wood, he thought it would feel flimsy and weak. But it felt as immovable as cement.

Lott knocked on the thick front door and waited.

A few seconds went past before a girl answered, maybe sixteen years old. She didn't say anything, but he could tell she was surprised to see him. He guessed they didn't get many visitors.

"Hi," Lott said.

"Hi," she said quietly.

"I'm looking for Isaac King."

"Pa's out in the barn."

Lott peeked into the home. Clean, with furniture covered in quilts and blankets, handwoven rugs on the floors. "Do you mind if I go out there and see him?"

"Hold on a minute." The girl turned around. "Ma, someone's here."

A middle-aged woman in traditional Amish clothing approached from the other room. She brushed her daughter away and stood facing Lott. She didn't hide behind the door—rather, she opened it wider, and Lott wondered if she was somehow trying to show him she wasn't afraid.

"Morning, ma'am."

"Morning," she said sternly, her lips pursed tightly.

"I'm looking to speak to your husband, Isaac King."

"And what business do you have with my husband, sir?"

"It's about your daughter, Sarah."

The woman's face instantly changed. Where it had projected strength and steadfastness before, now it softened. Her lips loosened, and her eyes widened. Lott thought he saw the beginnings of tears glistening in her eyes.

"He's in the barn," she said softly.

"Do you mind if I go and meet with him?"

She shook her head and then closed the door.

Lott stood there dumbfounded for a moment before stepping off the porch and heading around the house to the barn. Behind the house, vast open grassland stretched all the way to the other neighbor's house, probably half a mile away. Lott could imagine waking up to this view every morning and wondered if how a man started his day determined how that day would go.

The barn was white and open, with slats missing on the roof that let in sunshine. Lott poked his head in and saw a man bent down shoeing a horse. Lott waited patiently as he finished. When he let go of the hoof, Lott cleared his throat.

The man had a white beard, and even though he was in the barn, he wore his hat. He straightened and mopped the sweat off his brow with a white cloth he'd kept tucked in his pocket. When he stepped out from behind the horse, he eyed Lott a moment before speaking.

"Who are you?"

"Um…" Lott took a few steps closer and held out his hand. When he saw Isaac King wasn't going to shake it, he shoved it in his pocket. "My name's Kenneth Lott. I'm with the *Washington Post*." Lott realized as soon as he said it that King may not know what the *Washington Post* is. Didn't matter, though—*he* still preferred it.

"Reporter, huh? Well, you can talk to our preacher if you got any questions."

"It's actually about your daughter, Sarah."

Unlike his wife, King's face didn't change. He held an icy gaze on Lott and didn't speak for an uncomfortably long time.

So Lott went on. "I'd like to know what she's doing working for the FBI."

"I ain't seen her in years. I don't have any information as to what she is and isn't doing."

"Well, that's the thing, though. See, I can get background information for anybody. Anybody. But there's nothing in her background that would indicate she should be taken to murder scenes and—"

Lott stopped speaking. At the mention of murder, there was the slightest trace of reaction from King. It was gone almost instantly, but it was undeniable. King seemed to understand that Lott had noticed.

"You know why she's working for them, don't you?"

"I don't know anything. And I would appreciate it if you left my property now."

217

Lott suddenly noticed another man in the barn with them. He was across the way in another stall, younger and with shaggy blond hair. The man was holding a broom and listening intently to the conversation.

"I can pay handsomely, and all I want is a reason. Why's she working with the FBI? What can she give them?"

King turned back to his horse and bent down again as though Lott wasn't there.

"Mr. King, I can pay money."

"We don't need money. Now please leave."

Lott stood there a moment, watching the man nail a shoe onto the horse's hoof. He thought maybe the Amish would use something else, something that wasn't metal, and was slightly surprised they thought that metal shoes, nails, and a hammer were okay but a car wasn't.

Lott exhaled and turned. He walked out of the barn and wasn't more than twenty feet out when he saw somebody coming over to him. He glanced over and saw the man from the barn. The man was glancing back, apparently making sure King couldn't see them.

"How much you pay for that information?" he said, with an accent Lott couldn't place.

"Depends how good it is."

The man wrung his hands and looked back toward the barn. "Sarah's my cousin. We all know about her."

"What about her?"

"How much you pay, first?"

Lott took the man in. He was frightened of King but also wanted the money. Lott decided he wouldn't really know the value. "Hundred bucks."

The man snorted. "Shit. I can make more than that here." The man turned to walk away and Lott grabbed his shoulder.

"A thousand."

The man looked at the barn again and then nodded.

35

The daylight broke through the blinds like an unwanted guest. Rosen lay in bed and tried to go back to sleep by pulling the covers over his head. But that didn't do anything. Once sleep had left him for the morning, it didn't come back.

Accepting defeat, he swung his legs off the side of the bed and rose, rubbing his face as he walked to the bathroom. After taking a quick shower, he headed downstairs and picked up the paper from the porch and scanned the neighborhood before going back inside. As far as he knew, he was the last one on the block who still subscribed to an actual newspaper instead of getting his news online.

Rosen put the paper down on his kitchen table and made some coffee and buttered toast. He sat and unrolled the paper. On the second page, about halfway down, was a picture of Sarah King.

His heart dropped, and he got up and grabbed his keys before heading out the door.

Though Sarah was a contract employee with the FBI, she wasn't hourly. She had little reason to be in the office right now but was sitting in the café debating whether to go up. She wasn't even sure what her job was exactly. Would she actually be Kyle's assistant and doing things like making copies and sending email, or would they just take her to crime scenes and hope something popped into her head?

Sarah rose and bought a bottle of orange juice and went back to her table, the same one she had sat at with Giovanni. The sun wasn't out today, the sky overcast with dark gray clouds. The weather had always intimately affected her mood. She found she could always endure more when she at least had sunshine. Before she was done with her juice, Giovanni called her.

"Hey," she said.

"Hey. Where are you?"

"In the café downstairs. Why?"

"Better come up to Kyle's office. There's been a… development."

"What?"

"Come up and we'll talk."

Sarah hung up, threw her juice in the recycling bin, and headed upstairs. The elevator was packed with several people she guessed were agents. They were discussing some undercover operation in the vaguest terms and would occasionally glance back to her.

"He's lying," one of them whispered. "We gotta keep him in while he's still useful."

The other one shook his head. "If he's telling the truth, we gotta pull him out. It's too dangerous."

"If you're wrong, we'll lose an entire year's work."

The elevator opened on the fifth floor, and Sarah said, "Excuse me," as she brushed past the two men. Once outside in the hallway, she turned and said, "He's telling the truth. Vincent is dead."

The two men glanced at each other. "How the hell do you know?"

"Because he's standing behind you with a bullet hole in his forehead."

The elevator doors shut just as one of the men was about to ask something else. Sarah crossed the hallway and into the main area with a dim throbbing in her head that faded away quickly.

A few agents were goofing around at a desk, watching some clip on YouTube. She glanced casually at the screen. Standing over them was the female agent who had been rude to her the other night. Sarah smiled at her, but the woman turned away.

Kyle's office was empty, and Sarah debated sitting down. She decided it'd be best to wait, so she leaned against the wall and tipped her head back, staring at the ceiling.

Discomfort began at her head and shot down to her feet. She crumpled over, nearly screaming, but the throbbing lasted only a moment and left her with a single image: two children sitting on a bench with masks over their faces.

The masks were colorful, but she couldn't make out much else. The image was blurry, almost swirling. They were in a room somewhere, and their backs were to the wall.

"Hey," Giovanni said.

Sarah straightened up and ignored the pain. "Hi. So what's going on?"

"You better have Kyle explain."

Rosen and Kyle came in and sat down, leaving a chair for her. She sat, feeling suddenly like she was back in school and the teacher was about to tell her something she didn't want to hear.

"Sarah," Kyle began, "we've got some bad news." He pushed a newspaper toward her. On the page, in a large black-and-white photo, was her face. "It's in a lot of papers, and they did a piece on the morning news."

In black, bold lettering at the top of the article it said, FBI OUT OF LUCK ON THE BLOOD DAHLIA, BRINGS IN PSYCHIC FOR HELP.

"How'd they even know?" Giovanni asked.

Rosen said, "It originated on Skid Row Gossip in a piece by Kenneth Lott. It was picked up from there."

Sarah stared at the photo of herself. It was the DMV photo she'd had taken only a few years ago. She wondered if she still looked that young.

"What does this mean?" she said.

Kyle glanced at Rosen. "It means, Sarah, that the Blood Dahlia, whoever he is, may now know who you are. I'm not saying he'll even care, but he's clearly shown that he is following the investigation. That body on our boss's doorstep was a taunt. What we're worried about is that he might find you… interesting. And try to make contact."

"Make contact? You mean he might try to kill me, don't you?"

"We don't know that," Kyle said quickly.

Giovanni interjected, "Bullshit. This guy's got balls and is fucking insane. Whoever sold us out needs to be arrested."

"Agent Adami," Kyle said calmly, "we're all on the same team. Understood?"

Giovanni swallowed before answering, and it was as though he swallowed all the anger that had shown in his previous comment. "Yes, sir. I know. I'm just pissed."

"As am I. I was told you guys ran into Lott at a crime scene. That means he has someone here who pointed him in the right direction and told him when you'd be out there. We'll start an internal investigation, and I'm sure we'll find the person. But for now, nobody knows anything about this investigation outside of this room. Clear?"

"Yes, sir," Giovanni said. Rosen just nodded.

Kyle leaned back in his seat and pushed a key on his keyboard before saying, "In the meantime, Sarah, I think it best if we place you in a safe house with a protective detail. Just until we catch him." He looked at her. "I think it's the safest option."

She nodded. "Okay. If you think it'll help."

"Sir," Giovanni said, "I'd like to volunteer as the protective detail."

"You can check in as much as you like, but you two need to work this case. I want this son of a bitch's head on a silver platter."

Rosen stood up. "We'll do everything we can."

Sarah got a distinct impression from him just then. After he'd said, "We'll do everything we can," he thought, *but it's not going to be enough.*

36

Wolfgram thought the lecture went well. As the students filed out, he wondered how many of them actually saw the beauty in what they'd discussed.

Linear algebra was one of his favorite topics, and the Perron–Frobenius theorem was one of the most intriguing themes in the field. Though it had deep repercussions in probability theory and economics, the theorem was most widely used in the ranking of football teams in the NFL. *What a waste*, he thought.

As the last of the students were leaving the classroom, Wolfgram kept his eye on one—a young woman, blond with red highlights. She wore spandex workout pants and a tank top, though the temperatures had dipped in the last couple of days.

"Shannon, would you come here, please?"

She came over. Her breasts were plump and held tightly against her body by a sports bra. He could see the elastic band on her shoulder.

"I really enjoyed today's lecture," she said.

He smiled. "I'm glad. It's surprising you're not a mathematics major. You should really consider it."

"I thought about it, but I think in the end chemistry looks better on med school applications. I could be wrong, I don't know. But I'm almost done with chem, so I may as well finish."

He nodded, gathering the few notes from the lectern. "Maybe we should discuss it further. Why don't you set an appointment to come see me during office hours?"

"Okay."

Wolfgram put the papers away and lifted his satchel. He kept pace with the girl as they left the classroom. "I think you'll find medical school more competitive than it's ever been. You should have a solid backup. Do you enjoy chemistry?"

"No, not really."

"But you do enjoy mathematics. I see how you pay attention. Most students are just preparing for the exams, you enjoy the subject matter."

They walked down the hall to the front entrance, and Wolfgram turned to her. Even without makeup, her beauty shone through and made his heart beat faster.

"Yeah, I guess we can talk about it. I can stop by tomorrow."

"Sure. I'm pretty booked early, but if you wanted to come around seven in the evening, I should be available."

"I'll check my schedule. Thanks, Professor Davies."

Wolfgram watched her walk out of the building. It was brazen, bordering on careless, to want one so close to him. He normally only chose from the Saturday class because there was no attendance there, no one keeping track of who came and who didn't.

This class had only twenty people. There would be questions. All her professors might be interviewed. But that hadn't happened so far with the other class, to Wolfgram's great surprise and delight. It was then, when he realized no one was coming, that he knew he had overestimated law enforcement. They truly were fumbling around in the dark. He had a sneaking suspicion that arrests were far more luck than skill.

Wolfgram sighed as Shannon turned a corner. He hiked back through the building to his office on the second floor. Though most professors' offices were cluttered and messy, his was meticulously neat. Every pen, pad of paper, and book in its place. He couldn't stand being in the offices of his colleagues for the simple reason that he had an overwhelming urge to clean the untidiness. Chaos had never appealed to him.

He sat at his desk and flipped on his computer. First, he checked his email, then he went to his favorites list and the website for Skid Row Gossip.

Though the website was primarily trash, he had grown fond of one writer in particular: "K. Lott." The writer followed the happenings of the underbelly of the state and had kept a close eye on the Blood Dahlia murders when it seemed that the other news agencies had moved on. Even without mention of the murders, his stories were fascinating. Last week, he'd done a piece on a police officer who had shot his two toddler children, then his wife, and then himself.

The headline excited Wolfgram so much he read it several times, the last half ringing in his head over and over: BRINGS IN PSYCHIC FOR HELP.

He read the article through twice, then he leaned back in his chair and stared at the photo. The young woman was beautiful, a streak of pure white running down the side of her hair. She was far more striking and exotic than even Shannon, who Wolfgram had had his eye on for over a month now.

Psychics had always fascinated him. He had read the report generated by the Defense Intelligence Agency and the Central Intelligence Agency at the conclusion of what they termed the "Stargate Project."

Stargate had been the federal government's attempt to verify psychic phenomena. Millions of dollars had been spent between 1970 and 1995. They had brought in psychics from all over the world in the hopes that the research could yield results in the intelligence field. What they found was shocking but, of course, unappreciated by bureaucracy.

Wolfgram had gone over the matrices himself. There was a statistically significant effect of psychic phenomena in the laboratory, particularly with remote viewing, the ability to see and communicate events and places hundreds of miles away. But the results would have to be digested and analyzed for years, and the applications then developed over time. Bureaucracy didn't have the stomach for developing talent over time. It had no patience. And funding for Stargate was cut and all the research buried until GRAMA requests brought it to light in early 2010.

A psychic, and a beautiful one at that, after him... *How deliciously captivating.*

37

The house was in the middle of a neighborhood that could've been in *Leave It to Beaver*. Sarah watched it with detached curiosity. She'd never been in a neighborhood like this. The community was known as Sugarhouse and was filled with mom-and-pop stores rather than the big chains. Two of the restaurants advertised discounted family nights.

As the car stopped in front of a plain-looking home with a fence and yard, Sarah watched Giovanni. The skies had cleared somewhat, and the sun was out again. He was wearing sunglasses, but she could tell he was uncomfortable, because he kept playing with them.

"This is it. Home sweet home."

"I love it."

"Most of our safe houses aren't this nice. Kyle must really like you."

She looked at the house, the cute square windows, and the little chairs on the porch. "Do you really think I'm in danger?"

"I doubt it, but we have to be careful. If anything happened to you, we… I couldn't live with it."

Giovanni was blushing, thinking he had revealed too much. To make him feel better, she gently placed her hand on his, and they sat quietly a moment, letting the breeze blow through the open windows. The neighborhood smelled pleasant, though she could still detect the faint odor of exhaust and smog coming from the city just a few miles away.

"We better get inside and set up," he said.

The interior of the home was decorated sparsely but well. The furniture appeared to be from IKEA and without any wear and tear. There were even photos on the walls of random families. Probably, she guessed, to fool anyone who happened to look through the windows.

She threw her gym bag full of clothing and toiletries on the hardwood floor as Giovanni went through the house to find the alarm panel. He turned it off and then checked all the closets and rooms. The house was only two floors, a main level and a basement, and he was in the basement for a while. When he trudged up the stairs, he shut the basement door behind him and said, "All good. There'll be one agent here at all times with you."

Sarah flopped down onto the couch. "You sure this is necessary?"

He came toward her, placing one hand in his pocket, which exposed his sidearm in the holster. "As far as I'm concerned, it's not enough."

She leaned back on the couch. "Can you get me something then?"

"Sure. What?"

"A drawing pad and some pencils. Colored ones."

As night descended, Sarah sat at the dining table with the pad of paper in front of her. She hadn't seen Giovanni since he had dropped the supplies off, but another agent was with her—the rude woman.

They hadn't spoken since the woman had arrived, but she was clearly annoyed at having to be there. She stomped around the house and planted herself somewhere and didn't move or talk for a long time. Then she stomped somewhere else and folded her arms as if she were an older sister forced to babysit.

"You really don't need to be here with me," Sarah said.

"I've been ordered to protect the princess, so that's what I have to do."

Sarah drew for a while in silence. "Have I done something to offend you?"

"Yes, you offend me. Do you have any idea how hard I worked to get into the FBI? How long it took? How much bullshit I had to take from these Neanderthal adrenaline junkies to finally earn their respect? And you just come in and are a consultant on our most famous case in decades? What, are you sleeping with Kyle?"

Sarah hadn't expected that much venom that quickly. She sat in silence for a moment and thought about what to say.

"Do you know why I'm here?" Sarah said softly. "Because I'm a freak. They're using me. As soon as I'm not useful to them, they'll throw me aside. But I'm so desperate that I'm willing to do it, just for the chance that I might be able to change my life. I'm sorry that threatens you for some reason, but I have as much right to be here as you do."

The woman turned away, staring out the windows in the front room. Sarah could've reacted with vitriol; she could've been as angry and bitter as the woman was. But instead, she wanted to try something else. She reached out to her, opening her awareness just enough that a whisper of the woman's mind came to her. Like a brush on the shoulder.

Sarah saw the woman as a young child. She was bullied, mercilessly picked on by the other kids—and home was even worse.

Flashes came to Sarah—a mother who was in and out of mental institutions, an alcoholic father, poverty so deep that Sarah saw the young girl without a coat in the winter. She had risen from atrocious circumstances to earn her place in a bureaucracy that favored men.

Sarah suddenly felt a deep pang of sympathy for her.

"I'm sure it wasn't easy," Sarah said. "Getting where you are."

She shook her head and glanced back. The woman's face was softening. "You have no idea."

"I have some idea. I grew up Amish. Women are second-class citizens. We're married off quite young and usually don't have any say in who we marry. Then we're just used for breeding."

"So maybe you have some idea," she said.

Sarah smiled, and the woman, though not quite there yet, at least didn't frown.

Returning to her drawing, Sarah didn't even realize when the woman came up behind her and began watching her. Sarah didn't stop until the drawing was done.

"What is that?" the woman said.

"I don't know. I saw it."

"Saw it where?"

Sarah didn't know how much the woman had been told about her position as Kyle's "assistant," and she wasn't about to go around blabbing it. All she said was, "I don't know. Somewhere."

"You don't have to be coy. I know exactly who you are and why you're with the Bureau."

"Oh."

"So what is this?"

Sarah looked the drawing over. Two young boys sitting straight, their backs to a wall, masks over their faces. "I keep seeing it. Two kids with masks over their faces in a room. I can't see anything else in the room. I heard screaming the last time I saw this, but I don't know where it came from."

"Those masks are creepy."

Sarah ran her finger over them. "I don't know what they mean." She looked up at the woman. "You probably think I'm crazy, right?"

The woman sat down. Sarah could see her badge clipped to her skirt. Her name was Melanie Foster.

"No," Melanie said, "I don't think you're crazy."

"Most people do. Maybe I am. Maybe this is just what crazy people do, and sometimes they're right."

"I don't think Kyle would've hired you if he thought that. He's a bare-bones kinda guy. Life is rational thought and nothing else. Big fan of Ayn Rand. I really don't think he would bring you in if you didn't show him something special." She paused. "What did you show him?"

"You sure you want to know?" Sarah said, running the tip of an eraser over the edge of the bench the two children were sitting on.

233

"No, I guess not. But… do you see things with me?"

"Nobody from your past is here if that's what you mean."

She swallowed before speaking. "My father…"

The hostility suddenly made sense. "Is that why you've been so rude to me? You're scared I'm gonna tell you something about your father?"

Melanie looked away at the far wall in the room that held the photo of a family who were probably just actors. "If that bastard is on the other side, I hope he's burning in hell."

Sarah kept her mind tightly shut. With some effort, she kept the thoughts out. But it exhausted her. Like contracting your stomach for a long period of time. She didn't want to know why Melanie had said that, or what her father had done to her. Melanie clearly didn't want her to know, either.

"I better head back to the front room," Melanie said. "Someone will be here to relieve me around midnight. If you hear the alarm and voices, it's just us."

She nodded. "Thanks."

Melanie rose and went back to the living room. She sat on the couch and stared out the window. With a single thought, Sarah could know exactly what she was thinking, what demons lurked behind her eyes that made her the way she was and made her so frightened of Sarah. But she didn't open herself. She'd had enough monstrous thoughts for the day. Instead, she pushed the drawing away from her and headed to her room, hoping that she'd be able to get some sleep tonight without any nightmares.

38

One thing that always fascinated Wolfgram was how much information one could buy with nothing more than a credit card and a valid email address. He'd run several searches on different individuals over the years and was amazed how much was in the reports. But Sarah King's was different.

There was almost nothing in them. A modest credit score, one arrest for public intoxication, an address and phone number, and practically nothing else. The woman certainly was an enigma. No matter, though; he could get what he needed from other sources.

Wolfgram, whenever possible, preferred to be nude. He was nude now as he went about his household chores, and by the time he was done, he was ready for his afternoon nap.

His nap schedule was rigid. Every day at 4:00 p.m., rain or shine, he would take an hour nap. Not fifty-eight minutes, not sixty-three minutes, exactly sixty minutes. If he woke up early, he would try and sleep again for the remaining time. He kept a pair of pantyhose underneath the pillow, and he took one side and slipped it over his head. He wouldn't be able to sleep without something covering his face.

Exactly fifty-nine minutes later, he woke and lay in bed another minute before rising. He stretched his back and his arms, his shoulders and thighs. He had seen lions once in Kenya waking to a sunrise, and they stretched every part of themselves. He had done it ever since.

Though evening was falling, it was still light out. He had some time.

He spent it in the shower. The shower calmed and relaxed him. Sometimes he'd play opera or yoga music on the stereo in his bedroom and sit in the shower for hours, until the water ran ice cold.

But he had too much excitement buzzing within him to do that today, so the shower was no longer than usual, and then he dressed in jeans and a T-shirt with a baseball cap. In his medicine cabinet were several full makeup kits. A blue zip-up bag contained false beards and mustaches. He chose the brown beard, not quite full and not quite stubble, and stuck it to his cheeks with eyelash glue. He waited a few moments, glaring at himself in the mirror as the glue dried.

When he felt he looked just right, he left the house and got into his Oldsmobile. Twenty-five minutes away by service roads was a car rental agency. He parked in their customer parking lot and went inside.

The clerk was a young man of no more than twenty, with a buzz cut. He smiled widely and said, "How can I help you, sir?"

"I'd like to rent a car, please," Wolfgram said.

"Just need a driver's license and a major credit card."

He produced a false driver's license and a credit card. The driver's license was connected to a real man who had passed away last year. All of his false identifications and credit cards were connected to men who had passed away. The best lies, he thought, contained partial truths.

After the paperwork, Wolfgram waited by the front entrance for his car to be brought around. As he did so, his phone rang. He took it out and checked the ID. It was Dara.

He had forgotten about Dara. But there was something pleasant about her. Comfortable, not entirely revolting, like most women in his life. So he answered.

"Hello, Dara."

"Hey. What're you doing?"

"Just heading in to grade some papers. How about you?"

"Getting off a shift at the hospital. I was wondering if you wanted to grab a late dinner. I gotta run home and change, but I was thinking after."

"I can't… But maybe later tonight if you can wait that long. Perhaps ten or so?"

"Um, yeah, why not? I'll just have a snack. Let's do it the European way."

The car, a dark four-door sedan that wouldn't stick out no matter where it was, pulled up to the front of the rental agency. "I'll pick you up at ten, then."

"Okay, see you."

Wolfgram hung up and got into the car. The clerk asked him to inspect it so he wouldn't be liable for damage that was already there when he returned the car, but Wolfgram waved him away and drove off.

The freeways, unfortunately, were bumper to bumper. A giant sea of taillights. Wolfgram listened to Beethoven's Fifth and then his Sixth symphony, on the radio. Hardly the last note had played by the time he got off the exit.

A few more streets, and he was in front of Sarah King's apartment complex.

He was familiar with the building. It had an interesting allure, and he'd googled its website after he had driven by once. It had been a dormitory for a defunct college that had been a few blocks away and then turned into a mental institution in the '60s. The institution had been shut down in the '80s and turned into an apartment complex. Of all the places for a psychic to live, if that's what she indeed was, he wondered why she would choose someplace filled with what must've been so many horrific memories.

Sarah King just became even more interesting to him.

Wolfgram parked across the street and stared at the building. He knew Sarah wouldn't be here. That story painted the FBI as buffoons; there was no way it had been sanctioned by the Bureau. It had caught them off guard. Which meant they were probably concerned for Sarah's safety. Unless they were entirely incompetent, she should be in protective custody somewhere—that was the protocol anyway.

Law enforcement was quite curious to Wolfgram. He'd worked as a police officer for several years, during college. He thought he could learn about procedure, but that was not covered to the extent he had wished. Instead, he attended law enforcement seminars on forensics.

The best one he had ever seen was given by a homicide detective from San Diego named Jon Stanton. The man was teaching at the front of a large auditorium of local, state, and federal law enforcement agents. He was emphasizing the importance of observation, of not letting any detail escape the investigator's attention. To demonstrate, he told the attendees he would leave and they could move anything in the auditorium, and when he came back in, he would figure out what it was.

Several people moved some of the dry-erase markers, some moved pens or pencils, one took an item of trash from the bin in the corner, but Wolfgram one-upped them. He removed something from the auditorium entirely so that Stanton couldn't find it.

Stanton came in, observed the auditorium like a bloodhound on a scent, and determined that someone had removed a pen that was on the floor. They'd taken it outside. He then walked out the way Wolfgram had and returned with the pen a few moments later—the pen Wolfgram had thrown into a dumpster outside. It was the most incredible thing Wolfgram had ever seen.

It was from Stanton's seminars, which Wolfgram had attended four of while a police officer, that he learned the art and science of forensics—both how to find evidence and how to conceal it.

He scanned the surrounding streets and saw what he was looking for about half a block up. Two men in a sedan parked inconspicuously in front of a house. They had their eye on Sarah's complex. Wolfgram grinned and pulled away. He drove past them, careful not to look, and then glanced in his rearview.

He turned at the intersection and headed for the freeway entrance. This was just a curious diversion from his real destination.

39

The moon shone fiercely, a glowing ball of silver light hanging in a dark sky. Sarah stared at it through the shutters in her bedroom. She lay on the bed a long time, just watching it. She and the moon had always had a history.

When she was a little girl, she would run into the woods when she was hurt. Her father was a strict disciplinarian and would beat her with a belt when she misbehaved, as though she was a mule. On these nights, the dark forests were her friends, her comfort.

There was a stream near her home. Several large stones jutted out from the shore, and she would sit on them for hours and stare at the gushing water below her. Sometimes the moonlight would be so bright that she could see her reflection in it. And there, among the whispering trees and the wind that kissed her skin, she'd open her mind.

She would see things that were to come and things that had been. The dead would tell her things as though they were angels and devils sitting on her shoulders. She saw civilizations fall and cities demolished. But she also saw love and hope. She saw civilizations rebuilt and new nations formed. She saw history before her, and she was too young to know what it was. Now, in her twenties, she wished she could remember what it was she had seen. If she had kept a journal… But then again, maybe the visions would have terrified her.

Sarah stripped off her clothes before hopping into the shower. The water was hot, and she let it run over her a long while before getting out and into her pajamas, which consisted of an old sweatshirt and sweatpants. The bed was cold, and laying her head back, she stared at the way the moonlight appeared slotted on the ceiling from the beams being cut by the shutters. And at some point, as she stared, her mind began to drift and sleep overtook her.

Sarah stood in the middle of a house. Not like any house she had ever been in and she wondered how she'd gotten here. Was she sleepwalking? Was this where she had been all along?

Noises were coming from somewhere. The sounds were too muffled to know what they were. Maybe the television, maybe an animal whining to get out.

"Hello?" she said.

No answer. She stood frozen for a long time, scanning the home. Past the kitchen in front of her were sliding glass doors leading to a backyard. A small kitchen table held an empty beer can. In the living room was a flatscreen television on the wall and furniture that looked old and ragged, though it was so dark she couldn't really tell. There were no paintings or photographs up as far as she could tell.

More sounds, this time louder.

"Who's there?" she said.

No reply. The sounds continued.

Sarah hesitantly took a step in the dark. The only light was the moon coming through the sliding glass doors—a full moon, like the one she thought she had just been looking at before. She stood in the kitchen and looked around. Dishes in the sink, cupboards open, the floor sticky. Not a place that was kept clean. Turning around, she saw a set of stairs leading down to a basement. The sounds grew in pitch and then leveled off. They were definitely coming from the basement.

The downstairs was completely dark except for a dim glow at the bottom, something like an old hanging lightbulb. And the light was coming from around a corner.

"Hello? Is someone down there? Hello?"

Still no reply, though she was certain that the basement was where the sounds were coming from. Gingerly, she took the first step and then another and another. Before long, she was at the bottom of the stairs in the light.

She turned the corner and froze.

In the center of the room, a nude man lay on the floor. Prostrate, he was bleeding out of his side. Another man stood over him, blood dripping from both his hands. The man had fury in his eyes, a type of anger Sarah had never seen before. The man on the floor was whining.

The other man reached into the wound on the man's side and pulled out something slick and wet. Sarah screamed, and the man's gaze shot to her. She turned around to run, but the stairs were gone. There was nothing but a brick wall. She pounded against it with both fists, but it was immobile. Behind her, the man was grinning and took a step toward her…

Sarah sat up in bed and screamed. The darkness enveloped her. She didn't know where she was, and she crawled back against the headboard, shadows dancing everywhere before her.

The door flew open, and a man stood there. He flipped on the light. The man was bald and in a button-front shirt and tie. His gun was held in front of him, and he swept the room.

"What happened?" he said, panic in his voice.

She took a deep breath, her heart loud in her ears. "I'm sorry… I'm sorry. It was a nightmare," she said breathlessly.

The agent scanned the room and then checked the bathroom. He gave Sarah an odd look and said, "You sure you're okay?"

"Yes," she said, one hand to her head, partly from the headache that was just making itself known and partly from embarrassment. "Yes, I'm fine."

"Well, let me know if you need anything. I'm right outside."

When he had left, Sarah exhaled loudly and fell back into bed. The moon had shifted positions, and the light was in a different spot from when she had first gone to sleep. She stared at it awhile, hoping it would have the same hypnotic effect, but nothing was happening. She knew sleep wouldn't be coming again tonight.

40

The home was surrounded by neighbors, but Wolfgram knew instantly it wasn't the type of neighborhood where people got involved in each other's affairs. All the blinds were drawn, and no one was out on their porches. Though, granted, it was evening.

He parked up the block and walked back after slipping on a jacket that said, "Philadelphia Electric Company" across the back in bold lettering. A clipboard was tucked under his arm, and he glanced at the addresses on the houses as if he didn't know where he was going.

The home was not well kept. The lawn was shaggy and yellowed in spots, the windows were so greasy he could see the smears in the dim light of the setting sun, and the driveway was cracked and chipping.

Wolfgram glanced around one more time and then walked to the door. He knocked and then rang the doorbell and waited.

No sounds came from inside, no feet on floors or running down stairs. Nobody was home: even better.

He walked around to the back. Fences hadn't been put up, and that saved him having to pick the lock. He simply rounded the house and was at the backdoor. The only neighbors that could have seen him were the ones directly behind, to the south. But no one was out. The lights weren't even on.

Wolfgram took out his lock-pick set and went to work. Picking a lock was more an art than a science. He'd gone to Home Depot and bought every lock they had and then ordered the unique and rare locks from Amazon. He would practice for hours at a time, opening every combination of lock and timing himself. His fastest time yet was five seconds.

It took about triple that to open the backdoor. Wolfgram stepped inside and shut the door behind him.

Kenneth Lott sat in the darkened bar and finished his second beer. The glass was frosty, but the beer was warm. He didn't complain. He wasn't drinking it for the taste, anyhow. The beer went down quickly, and he burped. After leaving a twenty on the bar, he headed home.

The story on Sarah King had gone national, and his name was everywhere. The piece had been well written. He stayed up for twenty-six hours straight editing and reediting it. The sensational aspects had been downplayed, and the angle he had taken was that the FBI, the paragon of well-run investigations, was bringing in mystics because they were so desperate.

Only a few blocks in, Lott realized he was too drunk to drive. Debating whether to pull over, he saw the freeway entrance up the road a bit and decided to risk it.

The freeway was busy, and he weaved between the lanes a couple of times but thought that otherwise he was doing fine. The only difficult part was how many times he had to check his rearview to make sure a cop wasn't behind him.

But, despite how drunk he felt, he got home without incident. He parked in the driveway and got out, a dizzy spell hitting him and making him wobble before he took the few steps to his door. A key in a lock was not the easiest thing for a drunk person to do, and he probably spent a full minute trying to open the door. But once it was open and the familiar smell hit him, he felt at ease.

Lott kicked off his shoes and headed to the fridge for the leftover pizza from the other night, and he threw a couple of slices in the microwave while he nibbled on a cold slice. As he leaned against the oven and took a few bites, he noticed a light coming from his basement. He didn't remember going down there today, but it was possible. Or he could've left it on from yesterday.

"Damn it," he mumbled. There were few things he hated more than spending money when he didn't have to.

Lott walked down the stairs to his basement, the slice of pizza still in his hand, and saw the dangling lightbulb in the center of the ceiling. He walked to it and turned it off, leaving himself in the dark.

As he turned to leave, all he saw was a white flash, and then he felt the cool cement of his basement floor against his face.

41

"Wake up, Kenneth."

Lott was only dimly aware that someone else was near him. He thought that perhaps the voice had been in his head, so he didn't respond. Then he felt something cold on his face. The sensation startled him, and his eyes darted open, getting cold water in them, and he had to blink several times to get it out.

The man standing over him was smiling, and Lott realized he was lying on the floor. He was dressed neatly and appeared calm, almost friendly. Lott felt an enormous throbbing pain in his head and tried to raise his hand to touch it but couldn't—his hands were bound.

"I need a hospital," Lott whispered. Even his eyes hurt, and he knew he'd suffered a concussion.

"Perhaps later. I need something from you first."

"I need a hospital."

"Do try to pay attention, Kenneth. I need information."

"Please, just take me to a hospital."

The man reached down, and Lott couldn't see what he was doing. Then he felt cold against his ribs, and a pain so intense that he had never felt anything like it. It was like fire shooting inside. Lott screamed as he felt something wiggling inside him and was only dimly aware that it was the man's hand inside of his ribcage.

Something tore. He could feel it—as though the man ripped something inside of him.

The man rose back into view. "Kenneth, I need information. If you can't help me, I'm afraid you're no use."

"What—what information?" he said, panic overtaking him.

"Sarah King. I was unable to find out much about her, but you seemed to know her entire history. How?"

"The… the psychic?"

"Yes."

"She's Amish. I went to—to her house. To her father's house."

"Where?"

"Please, I need a hospital. My head is killing me, and I can't see. I need a hospital."

Pain again, agony so acute that he felt faint and dry-heaved once before the vomit shot out of his mouth. His attacker had ripped something else out of him, something that made him go numb and lose control of his bladder. He felt the urine pooling around him.

"Please," he cried, "please, let me go. Let me go. I won't tell anybody. I promise I won't tell anybody."

"Where did you find the information about Sarah King?"

"Her father's house. Some guy at the farm told me. Some fucking cousin or something."

"You will tell me exactly where her family's home is."

"Yeah, yeah," he said desperately, "I'll tell you everything. Please, I'll tell you whatever you want to know."

The man smiled. "I know you will."

"And then you'll let me go to a hospital?"

"Certainly. We wouldn't want to be considered a liar, now would we?" The man leaned down, his bloodied hands softly caressing Lott's head. "I promise I will take you to a hospital. You have my word on that."

42

The kitchen table seemed unsteady. One of the legs was too short. Sarah folded some paper towels several times before sticking them under the short leg. It didn't help much, but that would have to do.

She sat down and stared through the window at the rising sun. She had always been an early riser. On the farm, her father had woken her up at 4:00 a.m., and it had stuck. Several times a month, she tried desperately to break the habit and sleep in, but it never worked.

The coffee was hot, and there were some granola bars in the pantry. The fridge was empty except for a box of Arm & Hammer. Sarah sipped the coffee quietly as the guard who had burst into her room last night slept on the couch.

The door opened, and the alarm went off as Rosen pulled his key out of the lock. He saw the agent asleep on the couch and stared at him as the man rose, wiping the sleep out of his eyes and acting as though he had just been resting.

"Agent Hoffman. Get a good night's sleep?"

"No, sir. Just resting my eyes."

"Giovanni and I are here. You're relieved."

"Thank you."

Rosen sat down at the table as Giovanni came in and said something to the agent that she didn't catch. Rosen watched her a moment with a kind smile.

"How you feeling?" Rosen said.

"Like I'm in jail."

"You're free to leave. Did I not explain that to you?"

"I'm kidding. It's a huge step up from my apartment."

"Oh. That's good to hear. Do you have everything you need?"

"I thought I'd go grocery shopping today, if that's okay. Maybe we can have dinner here tonight."

"I'd like that." He looked at Giovanni. "Listen, we have a proposal. Giovanni was against it, but Kyle and I think it's a good way to resolve this case more quickly."

She looked from one of them to the other. Giovanni wouldn't look her in the eyes. "What is it?" she asked.

"We think that, if the story has piqued the Blood Dahlia's interest, there may be a good way to draw him out. If he knew where you were at a certain time of day, for example."

"You mean I'm bait?"

Rosen looked uncomfortable and glanced down at the table. "Yes."

"You want to use me as bait?"

"I wouldn't put it that way."

"How would you put it, Agent Rosen?"

Rosen leaned back in the chair and held her gaze this time. "It's up to you—no one will force you to do it. But we think if we put you in what he thinks is a vulnerable position, we can bring him out into the open. You'll be surrounded with agents and wired the entire time. At no point will we let him anywhere near you."

The coffee was now cold and bitter. She wondered if there was any sugar in the house and then chastised herself for thinking about something so trivial at this moment and only then realized she was obsessing. Pushing the coffee away from her, she met Rosen's eyes. "I'll do it."

Rosen nodded. Giovanni looked up at her but didn't say anything.

"Good," Rosen said. "We'll get everything set up, and hopefully this will be over tomorrow night. The sooner the better."

43

Wolfgram had never been one for nature's beauty. It was lost on him. But as he drove into Lancaster County, he was struck by how much open space there was.

The morning was cooler than the past few days—not enough that he could see his breath but enough that he had to wear a cheap jacket that looked expensive. He preferred, whenever possible, to dress well. People tended to be less suspicious of the well dressed.

He parked in front of the Kings' home. No use hiding anything. The space was simply too wide open to remain hidden. But the car was a rental under a fake name that he would dispose of after today, and he wore a blond wig that had hair down to his shoulders. Instead of a beard, he opted for thick glasses and a fake tattoo on his chest, the top of which poked out from his button-front shirt.

Wolfgram walked to the house Lott had described and knocked. It took a moment, but a woman in a plain blue dress that came down to her ankles answered. She appeared confused at first, then her expression hardened to one of distrust and annoyance.

"We don't have any business with the likes of you," she said.

"Funny, I was told much about the Amish sense of courtesy."

The woman suddenly grew embarrassed. Her face softened, but she didn't open the door any wider. "Who are you?"

"My name is Haden Caufield. I'm here to inspect your property. Is your husband home?"

"No, he ain't here."

Wolfgram smiled. "That's okay. I represent Rockport Developments, and several of your neighbors are looking into selling their property. I was hoping I could catch your husband today to have him show me around."

"We wouldn't be interested in something like that. And I ain't heard of any neighbors lookin' to sell. Now I'd appreciate it if you left."

She tried to shut the door, and Wolfgram stuck his foot between it and the frame. He smiled at her again, attempting to calm her. "Now, this property is quite valuable. Are you sure you won't reconsider? At least let me look around and make a proper offer to your husband."

"I'm asking you to please leave."

Wolfgram pulled out the pistol he had tucked in his waistband. He pointed it at her head. "I'm afraid I must insist."

The woman didn't move as he pushed the door open. It hit her and shoved her out of the way as he entered the home.

The first thing that struck him about an Amish home was the rugs. They were much thicker than most rugs he'd seen, and clearly handmade, with imperfections throughout. But they looked warm and soft.

Decorations didn't seem to be much of a concern, but Wolfgram didn't see any dust anywhere. Considering that they were in farm country, that was quite a feat.

He shut the door behind him. "Who else is here?"

"Just me and one of my daughters," she said, her eyes glued to the gun. "Please, just take what you want and leave."

"What I want is quite simple," he said, taking a seat on the couch, which was rigid, as if not meant for leisure. "Information."

"About what?"

Wolfgram held her gaze. The woman's hands were trembling. How odd that she had never had a gun pulled on her, he thought. He'd assumed that these country folk would always be in some sort of feud or another. "Sarah, your daughter." He looked over as another person walked in—a teenage girl. "Sit," he said to her.

"Mama, what's goin' on?"

"Sit down. Both of you. Now."

The women did as they were told. Wolfgram crossed his legs and waited a few moments. The gun was making them nervous, and when people were nervous, their memories tended to be affected. Wolfgram set the pistol on the couch cushion away from him.

"Tell me about her," he said.

"What do you want to know?" the mother asked.

"What was she like as a child?"

The mother swallowed before speaking. "What's this about, sir?"

"Oh, I'm 'sir' now? At the door I was an evil outsider you wanted to slam the door on. Now you show me courtesy? You see," he said, wagging a finger as though she were a child, "that's the problem with humanity. Force is the only thing people understand. Everything else seems to be in a different language. I attempted to be polite, and you could've shown me around, but instead, you brought yourself here." He sighed, looking from one to the other. "Doesn't bode well for us as a species. I'm afraid we are going to destroy ourselves."

The girl said, "My daddy will be home soon."

"Really? That would be grand. Because maybe a man could actually understand what I'm asking. Tell… me… about… your… daughter. Before I lose my temper."

The woman was silent a moment and said, "She was a shy child. Kept to herself. Other kids would try and play with her… but she couldn't play with them."

"Couldn't, or wouldn't?"

"Bit o' both, I guess."

"Why couldn't she play with the other children?"

The woman glanced at her daughter and then out the window. Clearly, they were actually expecting the husband to get home soon.

"She said that… that she could see what they were thinking and it frightened her. She knew what they wanted to do, what they really wanted to say. She didn't feel like she had friends because no one could hide their thoughts."

Wolfgram nodded. "How fascinating. What would that be like, if you knew the thoughts of all men and they couldn't lie to you?" Neither of the women replied, and he was glad—it had been a rhetorical question. "What else?"

"What else you wanna know?"

"What type of boys did she prefer to date?"

The mother shook her head. "She never dated boys. Same reason. But"—she looked tentatively at her daughter, as though she were revealing too much—"somethin' happened when she went through puberty."

"What?"

"She started havin' nightmares. She said there was dead people all around us, all the time. And they would talk to her. They wouldn't let her sleep. One time, one of her sisters locked Sarah in a barn as part of a game. Sarah started screaming and pounding on the doors. She said she was being attacked. No one believed her of course. But that night, when I was givin' her a bath, her back looked like… like it had been whipped. All red and cut."

Wolfgram was silent a moment. "She can see the dead?"

"Yes."

He didn't speak. The possibility was both exhilarating… and horrifying. Even to him. "Why did she leave here? It's my understanding Amish girls get married and stay close to their parents."

The mother looked down, unable to meet his eyes. Wolfgram instantly thought that they had done something they weren't proud of. He had to know.

"Please," he said, "tell me."

"We… we forced her out. At seventeen, we couldn't hide what she was no more. When some other folks in the community found out… she just wasn't welcome anymore. So we sent her on her way. Out into the world."

Wolfgram tilted his head slightly. "You kicked out your own daughter because your neighbors weren't happy?"

The mother swallowed. The girl wouldn't even look up. She was playing with her fingers, transfixed by them.

"You don't… You ain't a part of this community. You don't know what that's like. Sarah's of the devil."

Wolfgram, despite himself, laughed. "The devil? She has a marvelous gift that you dolts can't even begin to understand, and you throw her out on the streets to be eaten up by the world." He shook his head. "You disgust me."

The mother's lower lip quivered, but she didn't say anything for a long time. "Let my daughter go. Let my daughter go, and I'll tell you everything you wanna know about Sarah."

Wolfgram drew the hunting knife that was strapped to his ankle. He stood up with a groan. Only now was he feeling the tug of middle age in aching muscles and knees that cracked. The knife dangled from his fingers, and he tapped the edge against his leg.

"No," he said softly, "I think I've heard enough."

44

The last couple of days had been a blur. Sarah had spent most of her time at the safe house. Once, she'd gone out grocery shopping at a nearby Wild Oates, and one other time Giovanni took her out to a movie, which was awful, and they ended up teasing it throughout the film, cracking jokes about the star's acting and what he might be thinking in various situations. It was the most fun Sarah had had on a date as far back as she could remember.

After the movie, Rosen had been at the house, ready to go through what the plan was. Basically, an article had been planted in the Skid Row Gossip. Because that was where the story originated and it was cited by other news sources, it was likely the killer would begin perusing that website for information about himself, if he wasn't already. Rosen had told her that he had not had a serial murder case yet in which the subject had not followed themselves in the news. Something to do with their inferiority complexes, he assured her.

The plan was simple. Rosen had printed out an image where it would occur. The piece in Skid Row Gossip discussed Sarah's hobbies and listed one of them as Bikram yoga at Center Philly Yoga. The only class was on Thursday nights at eight.

The parking lot, Rosen told her, was probably where he would do it. It was dark and far enough away from the actual studio that someone might think they could do a quick grab in a van or SUV. The parking lot would be planted with agents in cars, and several vehicles would be covering both exits. Two snipers from the Hostage Rescue Team, the FBI's paramilitary unit, would be stationed on the roof of the studio and across the street on top of a small grocery store. She would be monitored with both audio and video, and a GPS tag would be placed on the inside of her thigh.

"More eyes will be on you than a model on a runway," Rosen told her.

Somehow, she didn't feel better.

The night before everything was going to happen, she sat on the front porch and sipped apple juice out of a bottle. Some children were playing hockey outside on the street, and the mother of one of the boys came out every few minutes to yell at him to come back inside. The boy would say he would be right there and then continue to play as though he hadn't heard her.

Sarah felt someone else come and sit next to her. Giovanni was quiet when he moved; his steps were light, and he carried himself as though he was constantly on alert.

"Can I have a sip?" he asked. She handed him the bottle, and he took a swig and handed it back. "You sure you're okay with this?"

"No. But Arnold seems to think it's the best way." She looked at him. "Do you?"

"I've been against it from the beginning."

"You're not really answering my question, though."

He watched the boys for a moment. "It might draw him out. But it's dangerous. He may just want to attack you, not kidnap you."

"Arnold said he won't get near me. As soon as they see him, they'll swarm in."

"We will. But it's still dangerous."

A long silence fell between them. Sarah watched the moon a bit and then turned her attention back to the boys. The mother came out again and yelled, and the boy again told her he would be there. "I can't handle this. This hiding. I want this to be over. What if they never find him? What if it takes years? Am I just supposed to look over my shoulder the rest of my life?"

He shook his head but wouldn't look at her. "I don't know."

"And what if—"

Giovanni took her face in his hands gently and kissed her. His lips were soft, and though she was surprised at first, she closed her eyes and kissed him back.

"Sorry," he said, pulling away. "I shouldn't have done that."

She grinned and put her hand on his. "No, you should have."

The next day was spent in preparation. Going over and over Sarah's actions. Though really all she had to do was walk out of the yoga studio after everyone else had left. Once she was at her car, she would pretend to be cleaning something out of the back. It would be well past 9:00 p.m. and dark. The FBI would fill the lot with cars beforehand so that she would be forced to park far away, toward the back of the lot in a dark corner.

A signal would be given. Rosen would just tell her, "Now," in her earpiece, and she was to immediately drop to the ground. They would take the suspect down at that point. If he didn't surrender, the snipers had instructions to fire if he threatened anyone.

"He'll never touch you," Rosen said. "He won't get within ten feet of you."

Sarah's nervous energy prevented her from doing almost anything else. She tried to go for a walk, with the agent watching her in tow of course, but was only allowed around the block. Rounding the block twice, she grew bored and went back inside.

Television was no help. The only books in the house were old encyclopedias and leather-bound editions of classics—just enough to fill bookshelves and help make the house look lived in.

She called Giovanni, but he was in the field and couldn't talk long. She thought about calling Jeannie but decided against it. Something told her that even though Sarah had tried to help her, just seeing or talking to her would remind Jeannie of what had happened. It would hurt her more than it helped.

So Sarah waited. Mostly, she sat on the front porch and watched the boys playing after school. Schooling among the Amish was a dreary affair, and she had never had friends like the ones the boys had—people to have fun with and rely on. As far back as she could remember, the only person she ever thought she could rely on was her sister, Star.

Though Star was much younger than Sarah, she had a maturity and sociability that Sarah had never had. All the boys paid attention to Star, whereas they left Sarah alone. Star had the blond hair and the face with perfect proportions. She was bubbling and happy nearly every moment. Sarah wondered if she had married yet. She wanted desperately to go back and visit but knew her father wouldn't allow it. Star had been the only one to stick up for Sarah when she was thrown out. For her troubles, Sarah had no doubt her father had given her a beating.

By the time evening came around, Sarah was starving and was relieved to see Giovanni pull up with a pizza and a six-pack of beer.

"You look bored," he said, walking up the front steps.

"I am bored."

He glanced back at the boys in the street. "This'll be over soon. I promise."

They ate on the front porch and talked about high school. Sarah knew nothing about what it was like but had seen television shows depicting it as the best times in people's lives.

"No," Giovanni said when she asked him about it, "it was definitely not the best time in anybody's life."

Darkness fell, and the boys had gone home, but Sarah didn't want to go inside. Sitting out here, talking to someone about trivial things, was something she desperately needed. And only now did she realize it.

Rosen drove up around six o'clock. He came up to the porch, his hands in his pockets and a worried expression on his face. "You ready?" he said.

Sarah took in a deep breath and got to her feet. "Yes."

45

Center Philly Yoga was little more than a run-down shack surrounded by trendy gift shops, a Mediterranean restaurant, and two coffee shops. When Sarah walked in, she was struck by the sheer smell of sweat and overpowering perfume.

As part of this whole thing, the FBI had bought her a yoga outfit, which she wore now. It was tight but comfortable, though she felt ridiculous in it. The plan was to make this as authentic as possible. She would have to do the Bikram yoga.

Her instructor was a young hippie-looking woman who seemed stoned. She was almost nude, only covered by the tiniest scrap of shorts and a sports bra. The room was so hot Sarah instantly felt as though she might pass out. Temperature was something she was acutely sensitive to.

Only lasting ten minutes, she knew that was her limit. She felt faint and dehydrated. She hadn't been told what to expect and didn't bring a water bottle. She left the class and toweled off but remained inside the studio.

When the class was over, she waited until the other people filed out. None of them had been told what was occurring, and even the instructor didn't say anything to her. She wondered how the government could do something like this without warning a business owner.

It didn't matter, though. Her mind was unfocused right now, and she was just jumping around from topic to topic. She had to stop it and focus. She needed to be aware of her surroundings. Her stomach was in knots, and she suddenly felt she might vomit. She sat down and inserted her earpiece. The GPS had been taped to her thigh by a female agent, and she could hardly feel it. The mic, a small black stick that was clipped to a strap on her black yoga outfit, was just as light and unnoticeable.

Once the earpiece was in, she said, "Arnold?"

"I'm here. You okay?"

"No, I'm not okay. I'm freaking out."

"You're fine. You wouldn't believe the manpower we have out here. There's still a few people from your class in the lot. I'll let you know when they're gone."

She leaned back in the seat, her arms on the armrests. The lighting in the studio was beginning to bother her, and then she thought of something. "Arnold?"

"Yeah."

"What if the owner asks me to leave? They're closing up."

"The owner knows what's going on. He's fine."

"Oh. Okay."

"Looks like the last of the class is driving off. You ready?"

"As I'll ever be," she said, standing up.

"I'll be right here. Just walk out casually... Okay, I got you. Pretend like you're distracted as you head to your car... You see that red one right there, there's an agent tucked into the backseat. Right across from you in the truck with the tinted windows are two of us. I'm across the street in that gray van."

She knew he was trying to put her mind at ease, but it was just making her more nervous. Despite what she'd been told, she couldn't help but look around. She had to. A quick glance around the lot, and she didn't see anything. No one waiting around with their lights off or anything.

"I don't see anyone," she said.

"Hang tight. We got a car on the street that just started and is pulling in."

A long silence followed as Sarah strolled to her car. Her heart was pounding. She wanted to open up the walls in her mind and see anything she could. Anything that would put her mind at ease about what was going to happen. But if the impressions rushed in too quickly, it would crumple her over in pain—something she couldn't risk right now.

"He's getting outta the car, Sarah. Keep walking."

Sarah realized that the hairs on the back of her neck stood up. And, if she listened intently enough, she could hear footsteps in the parking lot behind her.

"Is he behind me?" she whispered.

"Yes. Hang tight, just a little longer."

Sarah approached the car. She took out her keys and pretended to fumble with them. As she bent down to pick them up, she glanced over and saw a shadow approaching her. The man was in a jacket and had a cap on his head. He looked around, and their eyes met. He stopped in his tracks, and she didn't say anything.

"Now!" Rosen shouted into her ear.

She hit the ground just as the cacophony of shouting men and screaming tires filled the air. Several cars surrounded the man, and it sounded like an army swarmed over him. The man was tackled from two directions. His arms were twisted like rubber as the cuffs went on. He was searched for weapons and then lifted to his feet and slammed against the hood of a car.

He was shouting something. Something about checking his pockets for his identification.

Giovanni, wearing a T-shirt with the letters F.B.I. across the back and his badge dangling from his neck, sprinted over to Sarah and helped her off the ground. He stood between her and the hysterical man and held her, his arms wrapped tightly around her.

"You did great," he said softly. "You did great. It's over."

46

The FBI offices were the last place Sarah wanted to be. But she also knew she had to be here. She had to look the man in the eyes and… Well, she wasn't quite sure what looking him in the eyes would do. But she felt she had to do it to make sure this was the man who had killed those women so brutally.

Sarah sat in the hallway as Rosen and Giovanni interrogated the man. They were in there a long time, hours, and she spent most of the time wandering up and down the hallways. Down one long hallway were photos of special agents who had been killed in the line of duty. The photos were hung on plaques, and at the bottom were brief biographies of the men and women. She read a few. Almost all of them said "Beloved mother" or "Beloved father."

In a flash, she saw children standing next to grave sites. An expression on their faces of such utter loss and pain, they couldn't react with any emotion. So much agony coursed through them that their little minds had shut down.

She saw an entire fleet of children left directionless at the loss of a parent. A hole they would never be able to fill, though they would certainly try.

"Sarah?"

The name startled her for some reason, as though she had been in a trance, and she looked over to see Rosen standing in the hallway. Giovanni came out a moment later and shut the door behind him.

"What happened?" she said.

Giovanni looked distraught, his forehead creased. He put his hands in his pockets and leaned against the wall. Rosen looked at him and said, "What'd you think?"

"I think he's lying," Giovanni said.

"Me too."

Sarah looked from one man to the other as she walked toward them. "Lying about what?"

"He says he's a reporter that's been following you around since the story broke. Jerry Ridge, with the *Cardinal Post*. But he doesn't have any press credentials. His driver's license and credit card say he's Jerry Ridge from Philadelphia. So we're running him right now. We should know soon if he's telling the truth."

Sarah stopped between the two men. She looked at the door. "Can I see him?"

Rosen looked at Giovanni, who didn't say anything. "Sure. He's cuffed right now."

"I'll take her in," Giovanni said.

Giovanni opened the door and allowed her to enter. The room was carpeted in a dull gray carpet. A long table was there with an iron bar at the end. The man's wrist was handcuffed to the bar, and he was staring down at the table.

Suddenly, he looked up, their eyes met… And nothing happened.

Sarah took a step toward him, and Giovanni stopped her. She gently removed his hand and said, "It's okay."

The man was greasy and bald. He had a sweat ring around his collar, and his face was flushed from either exertion or alcohol. He didn't say anything, but his brow furrowed when he saw her sit across from him at the table.

Sarah swallowed. No use beating around the bush.

She reached out and grabbed his hand. The man, surprised, didn't remove it. And Sarah's head began to pound.

A cliff overlooking the ocean… A woman was there with this man, and she called him Jerry. They kissed as they watched the waves roll into shore. She said, "I love you," and he kissed her again and said, "I love you, too."

Sarah saw them screaming at each other next. Each looked maybe five or ten years older. They were in an apartment, and the woman was throwing dishes at him, and he ducked and tried to tackle her, though he never struck her. But he was hauled away by the police anyway.

Then they were in a courtroom with a child sitting at the stand testifying. The judge was asking her which parent she wanted to live with. The girl began to cry, and Jerry cried with her.

Sarah removed her hand and took a moment to catch her breath. "I'm sorry about your daughter. That she had to go through that."

The man didn't reply.

Sarah looked at Giovanni and said, "This isn't him."

She rose and walked out of the room without another word. Rosen was on his phone with a glum look on his face.

"Yeah… yeah I know," he said. "Yeah… okay, bye."

"What is it?" she asked. "What's wrong?"

He swallowed before speaking. Their eyes locked. Rosen cleared his throat and said, "I'm sorry, Sarah. Your mother and sister were attacked tonight. They didn't survive."

Sarah's eyes went wide and tears streamed down her cheeks. She turned and ran out of the building, Giovanni and Rosen both shouting from behind her.

47

Giovanni drove Sarah to Lancaster County. They hardly spoke at all. She wanted to tell him what she was feeling, what memories she was reliving right now, and what impact this would have on her. But she couldn't bring herself to talk. And her mind was tightly closed—the one thing she knew for certain right now was that she didn't want to see Star's death.

When they arrived and parked outside the home, the coroner's people were hauling the bagged bodies and a few sheriff's deputies were meandering around the property. Sarah sat and stared at the house for a long while. Long enough that Giovanni finally said, "You don't have to do this if you don't want to."

"No, I want to."

He looked at the home. "How long has it been since you've been back?"

She shook her head. "I haven't been back." She opened the door and stepped out, her eyes never leaving the house that she was born in. The house where she'd felt the greatest pain: her father withdrawing his love and telling her to leave.

Giovanni followed her inside, and the deputies didn't say anything. Even though she was just an assistant, she was one of them now, part of the brotherhood. They gave her the courtesy of silence without question.

The home hadn't changed. The furniture was the same, built to last a lifetime. The rugs, the curtains... even the dishes were the same ones she remembered from childhood. As she stepped across the living room to the two forensic techs bent over the living room rug, she felt tears on her cheeks again as she took in the two large bloodstains on it. One of the techs looked up at her, stared for a moment, and then turned back to what he was doing.

She felt Giovanni behind her.

"How did they die?" she asked the techs.

One of them, the one who had stared at her, said, "You're the sister, right?"

She nodded.

"They were... the same as the others."

Sarah's hands came up to her face and covered her mouth and nose. The tears wouldn't stop flowing. When she felt Giovanni's hand on her shoulder, she instinctively pulled away. "I need to get out of here," she gasped, turning around, and sprinting for the door.

Before she was even outside, she saw him: a bear of a man in dirty pants and suspenders, his hair permanently sculpted by the hat he wore from sunup to sundown. Her father.

"Daddy," she whispered.

He grimaced. "I thought," he said quietly, "that by throwing you out of here the devil would leave us alone. But we were cursed, weren't we? The day we had you was a curse."

"No," she said, shaking her head, sobbing, "no, Daddy, don't say that."

"You killed them… You killed them as surely as sticking the knife in them. You're a damned monster."

"No," her head slumped down. She didn't have the strength to lift it. Everything he said was true. She was a monster, and her mother and sister were dead because of her. Everything that had happened to their family was because of her.

She ran out of the house, past her father, and into the arms of darkness.

Sarah ran until she couldn't run anymore, until her heart was pounding and she tasted bile in her throat. The darkness here wasn't like in the city. There were no street lamps to light her way, no car headlights giving her a brief flash of the road ahead. There was nothing but the dark, and the trees and the fields.

Up ahead was a stream that ran right through the county and over into the next one. This was her place, where Sarah would come as a child and sit on the stones. She would dangle her feet in the ice-cold water and sometimes walk barefoot over the rocks that were slick with moss. The Amish frowned upon doctors, and people had to look for natural remedies. For foot injuries, Amish children would be brought to the stream and allowed to walk on the stones that would somehow take the swelling down and help with pain.

Sarah collapsed next to the stream, crying uncontrollably now. Every memory she had of her sister raced through her mind. The first day of school, staying up late talking about boys, holding hands as they raced through the fields and chased rabbits. Encasing the memories, as if it were some horrible lens that she could never remove, was blood. Every memory was now painted with the blood of her family, who were dead because of her.

She heard footsteps behind her and felt arms on her, lifting her off the ground and enveloping her. Though she couldn't see him, she knew Giovanni's scent, and she allowed herself to be held by him.

"It's okay," he whispered. "It's okay."

"They died because of me, Giovanni. They're dead because of me."

"Hey," he said sternly, lifting her head so their eyes locked, "you did not do this. This is not your fault."

"Yes it is... if I hadn't—if I hadn't been the way I am, they never would've died. They'd still be alive."

"Look at me, Sarah," he said calmly. "Sarah... look at me. This is not your fault. There are things in this world that we don't understand and that throw us around. This is one of those things. It was out of your hands. Blaming yourself doesn't help your family... It only helps *him*."

He said *him* with such venom that it shocked her out of her sobbing. And the only thought in her head was that he was still out there somewhere, watching, waiting, hunting. No one could stop him. He was too smart, too careful. Patience could win out over almost any other virtue. Sarah instinctively knew he didn't need to kill. He wanted to kill. And because of that, he could wait until the perfect moment.

That was when she realized something: they would never catch him.

"We need you," Giovanni said. "This guy.... We need you here. That thing inside you that's unexplainable... we have to accept it, just like we have to accept the horrible things that happen to us. Because we don't have a choice."

Sarah pulled away from him, forcing the sobs back; the tears slowed and then stopped. She wiped them away with the back of her hand. A decision had been made, though it wasn't conscious. It was deep in her mind, radiating out of her guts and telling her it was the only way.

She needed to open herself fully. To not hold anything back. To submit to whatever it was the universe had given her.

She closed her eyes a moment and then said, "I need to go to the morgue."

48

The morgue was just as awful to Sarah as the first time she'd been at one: fluorescent lighting, floors that made her shoes squeak, and a strong odor of cleaning supplies and what she thought was formaldehyde. A man in jeans and a T-shirt met them at the door. He had a turkey sandwich in one hand and a layer of mayonnaise caked on the sides of his mouth.

"You here for the two Amish women?" he said.

"Yes," Rosen said sternly. "Her mother and sister."

"Oh. Sorry. No disrespect."

"Please, just take us to them," Sarah said.

They followed the man down the hall and to a room. The room was lined with sinks and tools around her mother's and sister's bodies on two metal gurneys. Blue sheets covered both of them, but somehow Sarah knew which was which.

"I'd like to be alone, please," she said.

"Well, we ain't supposed to leave anyone alone with the bodies. Even law enforcement. You know we had this deputy once who—"

Rosen took out his cuffs. "You're gonna get the hell outta the room, or I'll arrest you for obstructing a federal investigation."

"Whoa, easy, man. I was just saying that's policy. Shit, no need to get all crazy."

The man left, and Rosen said, "Take all the time you need."

When she was alone, she took a slow walk around the room, touching the tools and listening to her shoes on the linoleum floor. Once she'd circled the room, she stood at the feet of the bodies and pulled down the sheets.

Her mother's and sister's bodies, yes, but neither had a face. Sarah didn't flinch. She'd known to expect this. She closed her eyes and opened her mind.

Any thought that came to her, she let take hold. Anything and everything her mind wished to throw at her, she allowed. She saw fires, raging infernos that burned entire buildings. A crimson sky with rain so putrid it would make people gag. She saw floods and tornadoes, wars and men dying. But she focused herself on what was in front of her, drew herself in, and then opened her eyes.

Her sister was sitting up. She was nude and breathing quickly. Sarah felt her eyes well up with tears again as she saw how frightened Star was.

"Sarah?" she said. "Where am I?"

Sarah held her hand. She felt the skin, the ridges of it, the fine detail. In some ways, it felt even more real than the hand of the living.

"I'm sorry, Star. I'm so sorry."

"Sorry for what? What's happened?" Sarah didn't respond, and Star shook her head. "No. No, please don't tell me that. Please tell me this is just a dream. That I'm asleep right now in Ma and Pa's house."

Sarah squeezed her hand. "Who did this to you, Star? Who came to the house?"

"Where—where am I? What's gonna happen to me, Sarah?"

"You'll find peace eventually, sweetheart." Sarah wanted to throw her arms around her sister and cry, but she resisted the urge. It would help neither of them. "I have to stop this man. Tell me what you saw."

"He… he came to the house askin' for you. Askin' all sorts of questions about what you were like as a child. And then he—he took out this knife, Sarah. He took out this knife, and I tried to run, but he stuck it in my chest and I couldn't breathe. And he made me watch while he took mama and…"

"It's okay. Shh, it's okay."

"I am… am I… am I dead, Sarah?"

Sarah looked down at the floor. "Yes."

Her sister sat quietly a long time, and Sarah held her hand. Neither spoke or moved. The only sound in the room was the soft hum of the fluorescent lighting.

"Do you know what happens now?" Star asked.

"No. Sometimes I can see you for a long time, and sometimes you cross over. I don't know how. It just happens."

"So you was tellin' the truth, weren't you? That you can talk to the dead?"

Sarah nodded.

"And no one believed you."

"Pa believed me. That's why he threw me out."

"And he wasn't the same, ever. He was always sad after that. Always hated himself for it. He thought about goin' out and findin' you, but people would talk him out of it. He never stopped loving you, Sarah."

Sarah wiped away her tears again and tried to appear strong for her sister's sake. "What else can you tell me about the man that did this?"

"I don't know nothin'. I don't know why he was there, and he never said his name."

Sarah nodded. "Okay. That's okay. You rest now, sweetheart. You get some good rest."

Sarah jolted awake. Her mother and sister lay lifeless on the metal gurneys. She realized her eyes had been closed the entire time, though she was holding her sister's hand.

The sheets felt cold in her hands as she pulled them back over the bodies. She bent down before pulling her sister's all the way and kissed her head. "I'm sorry, baby. Find peace now."

Sarah stayed with her sister for awhile before taking a deep breath and backing away. She was going to leave, and then a thought hit her. Not a thought really, a feeling. That she was going to have to do something she didn't imagine she would ever do.

She stopped at the counter and picked up a scalpel. She placed it in her back pocket, looked at her sister and mother one more time, and then left.

Rosen and Giovanni were waiting for her in the hallway. Sarah walked past them and toward the exit without saying a word. She didn't want to be in this building any longer.

Once outside, she put her hands on her knees and just breathed, letting the cool night air fill her lungs to capacity before slowly pushing it out again. She stood straight and looked at the men who were anxiously waiting for her to say something. "The first victim, Michelle Anand. I want to go to her grave."

Rosen nodded. "I'll take you there."

Mount Hope Cemetery was one of the largest cemeteries in Pennsylvania, with a little red chapel on the grounds and elaborate headstones as far as Sarah could see in this light. Rosen had called ahead and gotten one of the junior agents to pick up the groundskeeper and bring him here to pinpoint Michelle Anand's grave.

The groundskeeper was leaning against the fence when Rosen pulled up. He opened the gates for them, and they drove through, down to the red chapel, about in the middle of the cemetery. Rosen left the car on, soft chamber music coming through his speakers, as they waited for the groundskeeper.

When he arrived, they got out. "Thanks for coming out on short notice," Rosen said.

"Didn't sound like I had a choice."

"Not really."

The groundskeeper shrugged. "No biggie." He pulled something up on an iPad. "Which grave you need again?"

"Michelle Zullie Anand."

The man tapped a few times on the iPad and then said, "She's over here, not too far. We can walk."

As they followed the man, Giovanni held her hand. He didn't say anything or ask what she had seen at the morgue—which was good, because she was on the verge of breaking down and crying right there, and talking about seeing her sister that way would've pushed her over.

The grave had a large headstone with flowers by it. Sarah pulled away from Giovanni and stood in front of it. She bent down then, watched the grave a moment, and then thrust her hands into the dirt.

A small shock of electricity went through her, and she closed her eyes.

When she opened her eyes, Michelle Anand was sitting down against her headstone.

"I didn't think I would die like this," she said. "I thought I would grow old. With a husband."

Sarah was silent a moment. "Sometimes that just isn't in the cards."

Michelle nodded. "I don't know if you can stop him. He's too smart."

"I can stop him. But not without your help."

Michelle looked up at the stars and then down again at her grave. She ran her fingers over the dirt, a move that should've left traces in the ground, but nothing happened. "I saw my mother today," Michelle said. "I was screaming at her that I was right there. That I was all right and I was right there with her. But she couldn't hear me. How can you hear me?"

She shook her head. "I don't know."

"Will you do something for me? Will you tell my mother that I'm all right and that she doesn't need to be sad anymore?"

"I will. Michelle, who did this to you?"

"He called himself Professor Davies, but I know that wasn't his real name."

"Last time I saw you, you were wearing a Penn State sweatshirt. Is that where he's a professor?"

She nodded. "He has another girl picked out."

"I'll stop him before he gets her."

"The other girl is you."

Sarah was silent a long time and then stood up. The pain was intense, and she could feel her nose bleeding again. She simply wiped it away and said, "Not if I get him first."

49

As Wolfgram walked onto the university campus early in the morning, he was struck by just how antiquated Penn State really was. Some of the buildings were so run-down they looked like they could fall over any second. But there was grandeur to it, too—something about linking with the past that Wolfgram found pleasant.

His Introduction to Differential Equations class began at 7:30 a.m., and it was a timeslot he preferred. That early in the morning, mathematics was the last thing the students wanted to think about, but every once in a while, there would be a student who would be genuinely interested in the subject matter, even that early. Someone like himself, who found comfort and wonderment in numbers. Those were the students that Wolfgram taught for, and those were the students that he ended up wanting to be close to.

As he rounded a corner into the quad on his way to grab a cup of coffee from a cart set up in the student building, he saw something that made him stop in his tracks. He wasn't one to be startled, and so, other than stopping, he had no physical reaction to what he saw.

Sarah King and several men in black suits were speaking with someone whom Wolfgram recognized as the dean of undergraduate studies.

He jumped back and hid around the corner. Without a weapon, he was vulnerable. He leaned back around the corner and watched the dean speaking to them before leading them through the quad to the administration building.

Wolfgram had been fascinated with psychic phenomena as a curiosity. But now that he saw it, saw what it had brought on him, he thought Sarah King was an even bigger monster than he was. He looked around, unsure what to do for the first time that he could remember. Something akin to panic had taken hold.

He glanced back once more at Sarah and watched her walk into the building and disappear with the other men. Then he dropped his satchel with his notes and ran—he wouldn't be needing them anymore.

50

The morning had been spent at the Penn State campus. Sarah had led them to Professor Daniel Davies. He was an associate professor of mathematics, someone the dean of the college of science had informed her was well on his way to becoming one of the top mathematicians in the country.

"You sure this is him?" Rosen had asked.

When Sarah had seen his photo on the campus website, she knew it was him. She saw him again, nude and in a dark basement, a terrified girl chained to his wall. The image caused her pain, but she'd found that she could ignore it. "Yes, that's him."

"Well," the dean said, "he should be in class right now."

When they had gone to the classroom in the mathematics building, they found a group of students sitting and chatting or playing on their phones.

"He ran," Sarah said. "He saw us and ran."

Rosen glanced around the room. "Damn it."

He began shouting orders to the other agents. Sarah looked at the podium where this… *thing* taught every day, pretending to be human, to be relatable. She knew he shook hands with people and they felt his grip and they thought, in some way, they could relate to him, maybe even find their lives similar. But that was impossible. She knew that there was nothing behind his eyes.

She followed Giovanni off the campus grounds and back to the car. Once they were inside, he said, "I think it's best to take you back to the safe house."

She shook her head. "We have to find him. He's too smart not to have some backup plan. Maybe a house in South America or something. If he gets away, he won't stop. He'll just keep doing it somewhere else."

"What do you want to do?"

"I want to see his house."

The warrant was denied. Rosen hadn't wanted to apply for one, but Giovanni thought it was the best course rather than just knocking on his door and asking to come inside. But invading someone's home required probable cause, a standard that, they told Sarah, required a reasonable person to think that the subject of the warrant had committed the crime. And even then they were only allowed to search for evidence they listed in the warrant, unless evidence of criminal behavior was in plain sight. They would have to knock and ask his permission to enter.

When they arrived at the home address listed for Professor Davies, Sarah knew it was the place. She recognized it, but the house also emanated something—a darkness, a feeling that made her guts tighten up. She wasn't even sure that whatever she had, her sensitivity, was the cause. She had always believed that evil, true evil, was felt by everyone.

They stepped out of the car, and Sarah stood on the road a moment, just staring at the home. The neighborhood was as normal as one could expect, but the home had something to it. Maybe it was just because she knew the things that had occurred inside, but the home itself seemed sinister now.

As they walked to the front porch, Rosen stood next to the door as Giovanni stood in front. He stood far enough to the side that Sarah knew if someone shot through the door, they would miss him. Sarah stood off to the side, too. Giovanni looked at Rosen and then knocked.

A long silence followed. Giovanni pressed his ear to the door and then rang the doorbell. Another silence. He stepped away and looked into one of the windows.

"Don't think anybody's home," he said.

Sarah walked to the door. Rosen was scanning the street, and Giovanni was still peering through the front room window. She took out the scalpel, closed her eyes, and slid the blade across her left palm. The blade was so sharp that it hardly caused any pain, just a dull burning. Holding her hand above the doorknob and making a fist, several drops of blood fell over the knob and on the porch.

After placing the scalpel back in her pocket, she quickly took a step back and tucked her left hand under her arm, as though crossing them over her body because she was cold. Then she waited.

Giovanni had his hands on his hips, exposing his sidearm, something she'd seen him do a lot. He was comfortable around guns in a way most people weren't. He paced around a bit and then saw the blood on the doorknob. He walked over, bent down, and looked at it up close. Then he looked at the drops on the porch. His face turned to Sarah, and they held each other's gaze.

"Arnold," he said, not breaking eye contact with Sarah, "we've got blood."

"What?" Rosen came over and took his glasses out. He examined it more closely. "That's blood if I've ever seen it. Call it in."

Giovanni made a quick phone call as Rosen kept examining the blood. Once the call had been placed, Rosen took out his sidearm and held it low. "There might be a victim in there. We have to go in."

Giovanni removed his weapon and said, "They're on their way."

"You stay with Sarah."

"I'm not letting you go in there by yourself."

Rosen sighed, as though a child had frustrated him. "Fine. Sarah, wait in the car."

She nodded.

Giovanni took a position in front of the door, and Rosen swung around to the other side. Giovanni shouted, "FBI, open up!"

Simultaneously, he lifted his leg and kicked the door at the knob. It cracked opened about an inch. He kicked again, and it flew wide as Rosen rushed inside. Giovanni followed him, gun first, sweeping right and then left.

Sarah took a few steps down the porch and then turned around and stepped back to the front door. The interior of the home was immaculately clean. Not a speck of dust anywhere. She walked inside and heard Rosen and Giovanni searching the other rooms. But they wouldn't find anything up here. This was the surface appearance, the part of the home meant for other people to see. The real man lived downstairs.

Sarah found the stairs leading down and took them slowly. She listened for any sound, her mind open. Flashes came to her: the two children with masks and the screaming; she could see where the screaming was coming from. A nude woman had been before the two children, begging for her life. A grown man stood over her with a large knife and was cutting her, blood spraying over the children.

Sarah stopped at the bottom of the stairs. That scenario kept playing over and over in her head. Two children, masks, a dying woman. And a monster doing it to her.

The basement looked normal except for one thing: a door in a wall that didn't look like it should have been there. She walked to it and didn't do anything right away. But then, reaching up with her hand, she felt the smoothness of the doorknob, and everything rushed in.

All the blood, all the screams, all the pain. It came to her in one flash, all at once. The terrible wet noises and the women who pleaded for life. It hit her like a truck, and she instantly felt the tickle of blood flowing out of her nose as her eyes rolled up into her head, and she blacked out.

51

Wolfgram sat at a café with a hat and coat on. He was in the corner with his back facing the wall, his eyes glued to the door. How much did they know? Were any of his aliases safe? Did they know he had several passports under five different names? Were they at the airports?

Questions raced through his mind, and he couldn't slow them down. Panic gripped him and made his chest tighten. It was an unfamiliar feeling. Usually, he was calm under any circumstances. But he had made a mistake. He had been fascinated by Sarah King and allowed her to get close to him. He should have killed her the moment he'd found out about her.

"Did you need anything else, sir?"

The waitress was young, perhaps eighteen. Wolfgram had the strong urge to reach out and break her neck. But instead, he just shook his head.

"Okay, well, lemme know if you need anything."

She put the bill down on the table for the coffee and the slice of pie that he hadn't touched. Wolfgram stared at the check and then crumpled it up and tossed it on the ground.

A decision had to be made. Would he risk the airport or just go to the apartment he had rented in New Hampshire in case of something like this? The apartment was under an alias, a female alias no less, but he couldn't be sure what they knew and didn't know. If Sarah really was what everyone seemed to be believe she was… nowhere was safe.

The one chance he had was to be in a country that didn't extradite to the United States. Croatia was possibly the best option. He would have to risk the airports. Eventually, they would find him in New Hampshire. Maybe not soon, but someday. In the meantime, he would have to be looking over his shoulder, wondering if the footsteps he heard behind him were some federal agent who had come to drag him to an appointment with a needle.

He rose just as his phone rang. It was Dara. He was about to ignore the call when something hit him: they would be searching for a lone male. They weren't on the lookout for a family.

"Hello, Dara," he answered.

"Hey, hope I'm not bugging you."

"On the contrary. I was just going to call you. What are you doing this weekend?"

"Nothing much. Why?"

"I'd like to take you somewhere. And Jake if you're comfortable with him coming. I was thinking Mexico or the Bahamas."

Silence a moment. "Seriously?"

"I'm sorry, that was too fast. We've only been on a couple of dates. I just… I usually go on these trips alone, and I thought it'd be fun to have someone else along. I have the skymiles so it'd be my treat. But I'll just—"

"No, I'll come. That sounds like a lotta fun."

Wolfgram smiled. "It will be."

52

The lights glared so brightly that she thought she was staring at the sun. When Sarah woke, she brought her hand up to block the painful light when she heard a voice. Her ears seemed to be plugged up, and the only thing coming through was a muffled barking. Turning her head away from the illumination above her, she saw equipment and an oxygen tank. A paramedic was sitting on a metal bench to the side.

"Where am I?" she whispered.

The sounds still weren't coming through. The paramedic gave an answer, but she didn't know what it was.

Giovanni was sitting on the other side, and she grasped that she was in an ambulance. She had just enough strength to lift her head and see the blood on her shirt. Streams of the stuff coated her arms, dried and flaking off. She laid her head back and stared at the roof of the ambulance.

The lights shifted to darkness and then the fluorescence of the emergency room. Someone hovered around her—a nurse, she thought. The woman was asking questions, but Sarah couldn't hear any of them. And then she wasn't in the emergency room anymore.

She was back in the room with the screaming woman. Two children trembling before her. The man was cutting up the woman's face. But the woman was covered in so much blood, Sarah couldn't see her wounds.

Then the woman stopped screaming, stopped moving or breathing. The man still didn't stop stabbing her, not for a long while. But when he was done, he stood over the body, breathless, with sweat dripping down his face.

"Take off yer masks," he drawled.

The children did as they were told—two small boys with a sharp terror in their eyes.

Sarah snapped awake again. The white of the hospital room flooded her consciousness. She was in a room alone, a soft beeping coming from the machine that was hooked up to her arm and fingers.

Blinking a few times, she cleared her vision and tried to sit up but was too weak, no strength left in her.

Uncertain how long she lay there, it wasn't until Giovanni came in that she knew some time had passed. He pulled up a chair and sat next to her.

"How are you feeling?"

"Like I fell off a building. How long have I been at the hospital?"

Giovanni hesitated. "Two days."

"Two days? I was just brought in the ER."

"You were brought to the ER on a Tuesday. Today's Thursday."

She shook her head. "That's… not possible."

"Do you remember what happened?"

"I was down in the basement, and I touched the doorknob... and then I blacked out."

He nodded. "That's where we found you. You were on the floor, convulsing. We thought you'd been attacked." He glanced out to the hallway and then back. "You were in and out of consciousness, but you're fine. The doctors couldn't actually find anything wrong with you. They think maybe you had a seizure, but they're not sure."

"It wasn't a seizure," she whispered.

Giovanni leaned forward, his elbows on his knees and his fingers interlacing. "You won't believe what we found in the basement."

"A wall of masks. But they're not masks. They're faces that he's turned into masks."

"How did... Yeah. Yeah, forensics confirmed that saliva was found inside the faces of the victims. He was wearing them."

"I saw him, Giovanni. I saw him as a child. He wasn't born this way, he was made this way."

"How?"

She swallowed. "His father. Or who I think was his father. He would teach him and another boy. He would put masks on them and make them watch while he tortured women to death. But the other boy, he looked familiar, too. I think it was... Nathan Archer. Giovanni, I think they were brothers."

He shook his head. "No way. We ran his DNA from the saliva through FDDU. His name's Daniel Wolfgram. He grew up in Los Angeles and Cleveland. Nathan Archer grew up here."

"They were separated at some point. But they were together when they were young. I know it. I'm right about this, Giovanni. They were brothers."

He was silent a moment and then took out his phone and dialed a number. "Arnold, we need units over at Nathan Archer's house. I think he's related to Wolfgram. The mother might be hiding him… I know… I know, it's a hunch, but it's a good one. Okay… okay." He hung up and said, "If you're wrong about this—"

"I'm not."

"I know you believe that. But if you are, we're wasting time. Time that might let him slip out of the state or even the country."

She shook her head, fatigue overtaking her in a way that made her nearly fall asleep. "I'm not wrong." And then the fatigue washed over her, and she was asleep before Giovanni could respond.

53

Every FBI field office had a Special Weapons and Tactics operations squad. Their duties are the same across every state: take down dangerous and armed criminals, and storm barricaded buildings.

Rosen sat in his car as the SWAT team organized. Though he was a senior agent, the raid was out of his hands, and he had little else to do other than wait until they stormed into Melissa Archer's home and searched.

However the hell Giovanni had done it, he had been correct. Rosen had done the search himself. Daniel Wolfgram was the legitimate child of Melissa Archer. She was married once to a man named Clyde Wolfgram, before changing back to her maiden name of Archer.

Clyde Wolfgram was, briefly, a suspect in the original Black Dahlia murder, and in the Cleveland Torso Murders. He was cleared due to lack of evidence.

When they divorced, Daniel went with their father and Nathan went with their mother. However, Daniel was removed from his father's home due to neglect and put in the foster care system. The Department of Health and Human Services kept a file on each child put into the system, and Rosen had read Daniel's. Whatever abuse he had suffered at the hands of his father couldn't have compared with the abuse he suffered at the hands of a new foster father, Henry Buk, when he was around ten years old.

Buk was eventually arrested, and Daniel was back in the foster care system, for a while. Clyde Wolfgram later regained custody before losing it again.

Daniel ran away when he was seventeen, and Clyde died of a heart attack a short while later. Buk later disappeared under mysterious circumstances.

The SWAT team, looking like some special ops unit from the army, circled the home, and in a flash of movement that appeared chaotic but Rosen knew was drilled hundreds of times, they poured into the house.

He got out of the car and ambled up the lawn, waiting until the captain gave the all-clear sign. When the captain came out and signaled to Rosen, he scanned the neighborhood. Several people had come out to watch, and he looked at each of their faces. It was possible Wolfgram was still here, enjoying the spectacle.

When Rosen was convinced he wasn't watching, he brushed past the captain and went inside the home.

Melissa Archer sat on the couch, looking pale and fidgeting, but not surprised. Rosen guessed she knew this day had been coming for a long time. Rosen pulled up a chair in front of her and sat. Melissa glanced up at him and then down at the floor.

"Melissa, I want to help him. You saw what the SWAT team did. They're a weapon, not an investigation unit. If they're the ones who find him, he could get hurt. But I won't hurt him. I want him alive. I want him in court standing trial for what he's done. Do you understand what I'm saying? I want to save his life."

"He was always such a smart boy. Nathan was, too. Both of them. But Daniel was something else. He had… I don't know. I don't know what he had. But he got it from somewhere. His father was a surgeon. And his grandfather, my father, was a physicist. But the brains skipped me. I never could do well in school."

Rosen placed his hand gently on her knee. "Melissa, help me save your boy. Where is he?"

Her face bunched up, and she shook her head. "No, I can't help you. I don't know."

"Melissa, please. Let me save his life."

She was silent a long time. Her hands started trembling. "He… sometimes stays here. Upstairs. He has a room."

"Has he come to see you?"

She nodded. "He's leaving. That's all he said. That he's leaving, and he wanted to say goodbye."

Rosen nodded. He patted her knee and then rose. Wordlessly, he walked up the stairs to find Wolfgram's room. One of the SWAT members was right behind him, his finger off the trigger of his rifle and the barrel held low. Rosen glanced around a couple of rooms until he saw what he was looking for: a room with a bed and couch, a desk and chair.

He went to the desk. Rosen could picture Wolfgram sitting here, fantasizing about the women he had chained up in his basement, about their screams and their pleas for mercy.

On top of the desk was a sheet of paper with writing on it. Rosen slipped his glasses out of his pocket and put them on. He bent down over the paper. All it said was, BOOM.

Suddenly, Rosen became aware of the soft sound emanating from the closet. Almost like a…

"No," he gasped. Sprinting out of the room, he shouted, "Bomb! Everybody out now! Get—"

And then, there was a flare and nothing else.

54

Sarah didn't know how long she was in the hospital, but it must've been at least another day. She remembered waking up in the dark and seeing the moonlight coming through the only window in the room. She could hear the voices of the staff out in the hall, joking and laughing. She would sit up in the dark, and her head would start to throb as she saw two little boys in a basement with blood spattered over them.

In the morning, after getting what she guessed was only a couple of hours of sleep, Giovanni came to see her. Instantly, she knew something was wrong. He looked like he hadn't slept, and he was wearing the same clothes he'd had on yesterday.

"What happened?" she said.

He put his hands on his hips and paced the room, wiping at his nose with the back of his hand. "Arnold is…"

"What?"

"He's dead, Sarah."

She sat quietly a long time and watched as he walked to the window and looked down at the parking lot. Somehow, she knew. Already she knew. Without a vision or a flash of insight accompanied by pain. She already knew he was dead.

Giovanni spoke without looking to her. "The fucker had his mother's house rigged. Bomb squad said it was remote detonation. He was somewhere nearby watching and then… His own mother was in that house."

She let out a long breath. The sun was back out, and light was pouring through the windows, no clouds in the sky, and she thought she could hear birds in some of the trees. "I need to go back to his house."

"No way. We don't know what he has in there."

"Nothing. He couldn't bring himself to do anything to that house. There were too many fond memories."

Giovanni turned to her, and briefly, she saw a spark of anger.

"I'm sorry," she said. "If I hadn't said anything…"

"How did you see everything else but couldn't tell us there was a fucking bomb in the house?"

His voice had risen, and the anger had bubbled up to the surface. As quickly as it had come, it faded away. And he was calm again.

"I'm sorry, you don't deserve that. This wasn't your fault."

"You have a right to be angry."

Giovanni turned back to the window. "I can't believe he's gone. Just like that. I thought I left all this shit in the desert."

Sarah rose and then swung her feet around the bed. Planting her feet on the floor, she stood up and crossed to him, placing her hand on one of his shoulders and her head gently on the other. He leaned his head toward her, and they rested against each other. Two people who lacked the energy to keep going but somehow had to, Sarah thought.

"Take me to his house," she whispered.

He nodded. "Okay."

The home was what Sarah remembered, and the darkness was still there. Oozing out of it like pus from some wound. She sat in the car for a long while and stared at the home before getting out. Giovanni followed her but didn't say anything.

She could feel pain in him. A deep pain, but not because he was close to Rosen. The pain came from losing one of his own. It brought up memories he had buried deep inside himself. Later, she would help him. But right now, the house was calling to her, almost as though it could speak and was telling her to step inside.

The front door was unlocked, but there was police tape up. She ducked underneath. The living room was untouched. In a flash, she saw spray paint up on the walls, the word "bitch killer" scrawled in red across the white walls. But for now, the house had been left alone. The news of who the intelligent though aloof Professor Davies really was hadn't reached a wide audience yet.

Sarah stood in the middle of the living room… and felt nothing. As she had before. The soul of the house was in the basement.

She went there now, listening to the noises of an empty home. The creaks from the wood and the odd spurts of sound from appliances. The stairs now had dirty shoeprints from all the people who had gone in and out of the home. Soon, a padlock would be put on all the doors, and those who wanted to come in would break windows. The house would then be cleaned and sold to a couple who wouldn't find out who had lived here—not until after they'd already made their purchase.

At the bottom of the stairs, she turned to the door she had touched before blacking out last time. She hesitated only a moment before reaching out and touching the doorknob.

Agony went through her again, but only a short wave. It started in her head, rolled through her body, and dissipated through her feet into the ground.

She saw all of them, every single one. The weeping, the blood, and the suffering before their bodies finally gave out. He never killed them. They just died during the torture. Some died when he cut off their faces, others at the sheer shock of being brutally raped and mutilated, and any who survived all of that died when he finally sawed them in half and wrapped them in plastic to be dropped off at whatever site he'd chosen.

Sarah stepped inside the basement. Though Giovanni was behind her, she shut the door and he didn't protest. She was alone now.

Closing her eyes tightly, she let the thoughts take control, let all the horror and misery flow through her mind's eye like a film. When she opened her eyes, they were all here. All in the place of their death.

He'd had seven known victims, but there were easily over thirty girls here, all in various states of decay, all with blank expressions in their eyes, uncertain where they were or what was happening. None of them had found peace. They were stuck here, stuck to a monster who had linked them to himself.

And there was someone else here, too. Someone who hadn't died here. Sarah felt the presence behind her. Slowly, she turned and saw Nathan Archer standing next to the wall staring at her. A hole had been blown in his throat, and he was gray, the wound in his neck rotting. He took a step toward her, and she jumped back.

"Who are you?" he mumbled.

Sarah swallowed before speaking. "I'm searching for your brother, Nathan."

"He's not here."

"I know. Do you know where he is?"

Nathan took another step toward her, and Sarah took a step back. She glanced behind her to judge how far away the wall was, then she looked at the door and wondered how quickly she could get to it if she needed to.

"I know you," he said, "I know you."

"Nathan, where is Daniel?"

"Daniel," he said, his eyes drifting over the basement. "Daniel…"

"Yes, your brother, Daniel. Where is he?"

"It's not his fault."

"What isn't?"

He scanned the girls. "All of this. He made us do it."

"Your father?"

Nathan didn't say anything, just kept his eyes on a young woman in the corner. "He would make us watch, and we would wear their faces. He told us that was how they should be treated. That's how they wanted to be treated. If we were really his sons, we would do what he did. It's not Daniel's fault."

Hesitantly, Sarah took a step toward him. "Help me find him."

"He's leaving."

"Leaving where?"

"Far away. But not alone."

"Who's he leaving with?"

Slowly, he shook his head, revealing the sinew and bloody flesh of his neck.

"Is he leaving in a plane? Is he flying?"

"Yes. A plane. And he will kill whoever he is with... A woman. A woman and her child."

Sarah glanced around at the women in the basement. The faceless heads and severed torsos were too much. She had to look away, at the floor, at the walls, even at Nathan.

"I have to leave," she said, inching toward the door.

"I know you."

"I... helped find you. I spoke to one of your victims."

"What did she say?"

Sarah got to the door and opened it. "She said that she wanted me to kill you."

Opening the door, she saw Giovanni. When she looked back, the basement was empty.

"What happened?" he asked.

"We have to get to the airport. He's leaving today."

55

Sarah sat in the passenger seat as Giovanni took a curb too fast and nearly clipped a mailbox. Several police units, as well as some other agents, were already speeding to the airport, but Sarah needed to be there herself. She wanted to be there when Daniel Wolfgram was put into handcuffs.

The Philadelphia International Airport was the only major airport nearby. It was true Wolfgram could've tried to leave from another airport, but Sarah didn't think so. He had to have known his face was plastered everywhere and a drive to Boston or New York might've seemed too risky. But the fact was she didn't know. And, if she were in his shoes, she'd drive all the way to some rural airport like in Kansas or Wyoming and leave from there. But, if he were traveling with other people, it might seem suspicious to them if he wanted to leave from another state.

"I don't know if he's gonna be here," she said. "I just want to make sure you know that."

"This is all just a guess anyway. But it's a good place to start."

As they entered toward the first terminal, Sarah looked inside the airport from the car. Rubbing her head from a dull ache in the back of her skull, she said, "This isn't it."

"You sure? It's the closest airport."

"No, he's not here. I saw him. He was walking past a dinosaur fossil. Like a T-rex, but not quite."

"In the airport?"

"I think so. People had bags when they were walking past him."

"I don't know any airports that have dinosaur fossils. Lemme call the Bureau and get a clerk to run a search."

She shook her head and pulled out a phone. "You G-men need to think more practically." She ran a search for dinosaur fossils in airports on Google and came back with one name: Hartsfield-Jackson International Airport in Atlanta. "This is it," she said. "This is where he's going."

"That would make sense. It's the busiest airport in the country. Easy to slip through unnoticed."

Giovanni raced up a ramp and found parking near the terminal. He got out, and she followed as he placed a quick call. Sarah paced around the car, trying to drum up… something. Anything. A number on a flight ticket, a type of plane, anything. But nothing was coming to her.

"Okay, we're on the next flight to Atlanta. Leaves in forty-five minutes. You don't have to come for this, you know."

Sarah shook her head. "I need to be there."

Giovanni put his hands on his hips and looked at her. "Let's not keep Mr. Wolfgram waiting, then."

56

The flight was short, and no one else seemed bothered with it. But Sarah was gripping the armrests so hard her fingers were turning white. Giovanni noticed and said, "Have you never been on a plane before?"

She shook her head. He reached down and interlaced her fingers with his. It comforted her… a little. But she still had to close the blind on the window and pretend she was on a bus. Luckily, the flight was only a little over an hour.

When they landed, Giovanni rushed off the plane, holding on to her hand, weaving between the other passengers who were trying to recover their bags. The stewardess was about to say something when he flashed his badge. She wasn't quite sure what to say after that, so she just said, "Have a nice day."

The airport was massive. Trains zipped around, taking passengers between the different terminals. Crowds of people hovered around the entrances and exits, the baggage claims, and the ticket counters. Sarah had never been to a concert or sporting event, so this was the most people she had ever seen in one place. It gave her butterflies in her stomach and general uneasiness.

"That's the dinosaur," Giovanni said, pointing to a fossilized dinosaur that stood on its hind legs. "Do you know when he's supposed to be here?"

"No. I didn't see anything like that. He could've already left or not even thought to leave from here yet."

Giovanni scanned the crowds around them. "I'm going to have a look and see if I can find the other units here. Will you stay here and text me if you see him?"

"Sure."

"I'm serious, Sarah. You cannot do anything but text me. There are TSA people twenty feet away, so I don't think he's gonna do anything, but I don't want you acting like a hero."

"I won't. I promise."

He turned and walked off, leaving her staring at his back. She rubbed her bicep and then folded her arms, casually walking around the fossilized dinosaur as though she were just here on a stroll. Now that she was actually here, she realized this may not have been the best use of their time. When she saw this place, time wasn't something she detected. For all she knew, it could've been months or even years in the future.

As she came around the dinosaur, she glanced up into one of the shops and saw something that caught her attention. A white male in a fedora. It wasn't something that normally caught her attention, but the man was surrounded by what she thought were other people.

But they weren't.

The dead enclosed the man as though he drew them in like a black hole and they couldn't escape. At least forty people were packed into the shop. But when a person walked in and went to the candy bar section, he just slipped through the others like they weren't even there. Sarah recognized several of the apparitions around him... including Star, who was staring absently at the floor.

The dead were following Daniel Wolfgram around.

Sarah looked for Giovanni but didn't see him anywhere. She took out her phone and texted him, *HE'S HERE!*

Then she slipped the phone into her pocket. What Wolfgram appeared to her and what he appeared to others must've been vastly different. To her, he was a wound of dark energy. A tear in the normality of existence that blackened everything it touched. He didn't look human. But to others, he must've appeared perfectly normal, as though nothing were wrong with him at all.

Sarah began walking toward him. She wanted to look him in the face and make sure. She had to make sure that the person who killed her mother and her sister was really right there in front of her, that this wasn't in her head.

As she crossed to the shop, a crowd drifted by in front of her. She tried to keep her sights on Wolfgram, but she lost him for a moment. Instead of barreling through the crowd, she hurried around them. When she looked into the shop, Wolfgram was gone.

She looked in every direction. He wasn't here. She ran into the shop and searched the aisles. A few people were there, but Wolfgram, and her sister, were gone.

When she turned around to see if she could find Giovanni, she bumped into Wolfgram and felt the needle plunge into her belly. The pain took her breath away, and she couldn't even scream. Wolfgram leaned in close, close enough that she could smell his breath. But all she could do was let out little puffs of air. And she realized he punctured her lung.

"This syringe is filled with industrial bleach. Shot into your bloodstream, it will kill you in a matter of minutes. And there's nothing anyone can do to save you. All I have to do is depress the plunger. Do you understand? Just nod if you do."

Sarah, pain shooting through her, making her want to scream and vomit, blinked her eyes, lowering her head slightly.

"Good," he hissed. He leaned closer, smelling her, letting her hair run over his face. "You've cost me quite a bit of trouble. I should've killed you immediately. But I was curious to see if the phenomenon you claim is actually true. Even though you've found me, it's still hard to believe. So how about a little demonstration? Hm?" His tongue, warm and sticky, ran over her ear. "Show me something," he whispered.

Sarah closed her eyes and then opened them, calm washing over her, even though she could hardly breathe. She gazed into his eyes. "I know about your father. I know what he did to you and Nathan. No one deserves that, Daniel."

"Don't sympathize with me, you fucking cunt, because I will gut you."

"Okay, okay… there's something else, too."

Wolfgram seemed genuinely interested. He backed away half a foot, never breaking eye contact with her.

"I see," she gasped, "blood."

"Hmm, now that is intriguing. Is it your blood? Because, not to frighten you, but you will be vomiting blood after I push this down. Or, perhaps it's the blood of the woman and child whose throats I'm going to slit when we land on foreign soil?"

"No," she said, her voice little more than a whisper, "it's your blood."

Both of them were silent a moment, staring into each other's eyes. And Wolfgram knew what she had said was true because his eyes grew wider and they were filled with something they hadn't been a moment ago: fear.

Sarah jerked away, the needle pulling out of her just as Giovanni shouted, "Get down!"

She hit the floor as the shots rang out. Wolfgram raised the syringe to pummel into her as the first round tore into him. The impact knocked him off his feet, onto his back. Giovanni sprinted over as several officers ran to him to pin him down. One stepped on his wrist and pulled the syringe away as he gasped for breath, a gaping hole in his chest.

Sarah rose, holding her hand over the puncture wound. She watched as Daniel Wolfgram took his last breath, rage in his eyes as he stared at her. When he was gone, she was scared she would see him, have to talk to him. But he wasn't there. And the darkness she had felt was gone, too, as though it had sucked in on itself.

"Lemme see," Giovanni said, running over to her. He moved her hand away and was examining the puncture wound when she looked up and saw her sister.

Star smiled at her. She appeared youthful again, without the blood and wounds she had been covered in when Sarah saw her. Every wrinkle in her face had completely relaxed. All the tension and stress was gone, and she was, finally, at peace. And she waved goodbye.

Sarah blinked, and her sister was gone.

57

Sarah stepped off the towel and looked out at the ocean. Cape Cod during the summer was the most beautiful place she had ever seen. It was an interesting mixture of beach, town, and sand dunes. But today, the water was a shimmering green, and she thought she would never want to leave.

Before coming here, she had made a quick stop at Veronica Anand's home, Michelle's mother. Sarah had told her that Michelle wanted her to know that she was there, watching over her. Veronica had broken down in tears and held Sarah for a long time, as though she were holding Michelle.

Giovanni lay next to her in the sand, staring out at the water as he sipped a Heineken. The way his hair fell over his face, his sunglasses pushed up onto his forehead, he looked more like a beach bum than a special agent with the FBI.

"You know what Kyle told me?" he said. "He said that he'd like to test you some more."

She grinned. "I think I'm done being his lab rat for a while."

"I think he wants to verify your… well, abilities, I guess. But if he's not convinced yet, I don't think anything's going to convince him. He has an eye to bringing you on as an agent. You'd have to go through Quantico, but that's the fun part. You'd still have to apply, but I think Kyle would personally walk your application through. If you wanted it."

"Why would I possibly want that?"

"Because you have something that can help other people. People that might not have anyone else to help them." He took a sip of beer. "Or, we can start a one-eight-hundred number reading people's futures and retire. Up to you."

She laughed. "You want me telling people their love lives are going to improve or they're going to have a business opportunity presented to them? Things like that?"

"Well, you'd have to fake an accent and wear weird scarves and stuff. Not sure you could pull it off." He finished the beer and put the bottle down next to the cooler. "I'm serious, though. I think you'd be good at the Bureau."

She shook her head. "Maybe. I'll think about it." Exhaling, she lay back in the sand and let the warm sun soak into her body. "But not today."

AUTHOR'S REQUEST

If you enjoyed this book, please leave a review on Amazon at the link provided below. Good reviews not only encourage authors to write more, they improve our writing. Shakespeare rewrote sections of his plays based on audience reaction and modern authors should take a note from the Bard.

So please leave a review and know that I appreciate each and every one of you!

United States Store

United Kingdom Store

If you haven't left a review before, simply scroll down to the end of the reviews and find the "Write a customer review" button.

OTHER BOOKS BY VICTOR METHOS

Books in the Amazon United States Store

Books in the Amazon United Kingdom Store

Copyright 2014 Victor Methos

Kindle Edition

License Statement

This ebook is licensed for your personal enjoyment only. This ebook may not be re-sold or given away to other people. If you would like to share this book with another person, please purchase an additional copy for each recipient. If you're reading this book and did not purchase it, or it was not purchased for your use only, then please return to Amazon.com and purchase your own copy.

Please note that this is a work of fiction. Any similarity to persons, living or dead, is purely coincidental. All events in this work are purely from the imagination of the author and are not intended to signify, represent, or reenact any event in actual fact.

Printed in Great Britain
by Amazon